Published by Sandra Owens
Print ISBN- 978-0-9997864-4-4
E-Book ISBN- 13: 978-0-9997864-5-1

Edits by: Melody Guy and Ella Sheridan
Printed in the United States of America

Cover Design and Interior Format

All Autumn

Blue Ridge Valley

SANDRA OWENS

PRAISE FOR

SANDRA'S BOOKS

The Blue Ridge Valley series is Sandra Owens at her finest. Filled with Southern charm and a dash of humor, she had me churning through the pages. I laughed. I cried. This series has it all.
Heather Burch, bestselling author of ONE LAVENDER RIBBON

Take everything you love about a Sandra Owens novel—the dry humor, the hot alpha heroes—and transplant them into a quirky small town, and you have the Blue Ridge Valley Series. Charming, funny, and sexy.
Jenny Holiday, *USA Today* bestselling author

Snappy dialog, endearing characters, and a delightful plot . . . I loved, loved, loved Just Jenny!
Barbara Longley, #1 Bestselling author

Welcome to Blue Ridge Valley . . . A town you'll want to visit and never leave. You'll fall in love with the quirky residents who will make you laugh, and you'll cry tears for Jenny and Dylan—two hearts in need of healing—as they find forgiveness and love.
Miranda Liasson, Bestselling author of the Mirror Lake series

JUST JENNY, set in the picturesque Blue Ridge Valley, is just an all-around good time. It's got its share of colorful characters, juicy secrets, nosy neighbors, apple pie moonshine, and a romance that will touch your heart. Small town living at its best you

don't want to miss.
Tamra Baumann, Bestselling author

"If you are a fan of this author or enjoy romantic suspense or just love your heroes to be swoon-worthy, Jack of Hearts is highly recommended."
Harlequin Junkie Top Pick

"A heated romance is at the forefront of this novel, backed by a compelling story that will lure readers into Madison and Alex's world."
Publishers Weekly

"I love this new series! It's filled with ongoing suspense and tension, then sexy hot romance, and relatable people that you want to spend time with."
Reading in Pajamas.

ALSO BY SANDRA OWENS

This book is dedicated to you!
So if you're reading this,
you now know a book has been dedicated to you.

CHAPTER ONE

~ Autumn ~

TODAY WAS MY HUSBAND'S BIRTHDAY, and I planned to surprise him at his office. He'd once told me that he fantasized about bending me over his desk and having his way with me. I intended to make that come true, my birthday gift to him.

After a little playtime using his desk as a prop, I'd then talk him into taking the rest of the day off. His favorite cake, German chocolate, held center stage inside a glass-domed cake stand on the dining room table. Gaily wrapped presents surrounded a bottle of his favorite French wine. For dinner I'd made his favorite food, lasagna. All I had to do was slide it into the oven.

The table was set, candles ready to be lit, and I could already imagine how the flames would reflect off the crystal wine glasses. The interior designer in me ran a critical eye over everything, reassuring myself that all was perfect. Just before we sat down to eat, I'd turn on the Jacuzzi so it would be the right temperature when I led Brian out to the deck. My husband wasn't going to know what hit him, starting with my unexpected appearance in his office.

Sure, I'd gone a little crazy for his birthday, but we were newlyweds, and the glow hadn't worn off. Well, it had a little, and that was why I planned to put some spice back into our sex life.

We were truly blessed for a couple in their late twenties, both of us having great careers and the kind of income most people our age only dreamed of reaching someday. I would do everything in my power to see that we stayed blessed, including doing something as uncomfortable as walking out the door wearing nothing but a black raincoat and red stilettos.

I grabbed the bottle of champagne I had chilling in the fridge, and snapping up my purse and keys, I headed to Stratton Automotive, the car dealership Brian owned. I didn't love him because he gave me nice things, like a new Lexus, three-carat diamond engagement ring, a honeymoon in Hawaii, and a beautiful home.

All those things were great, but Brian was my soul mate. He made me laugh, listened when I talked, and usually respected my opinions. I'd love him even if he couldn't afford to give me more than a thin gold band and a small two-bedroom house. Hell, I'd live with him in a tent if it ever came to that. He was my world, my dream come true. Eventually there would be the happy laughter of children in our home, kids who would have a mother and father who doted on them. That was my promise to my future children.

Because we lived in Blue Ridge Valley, North Carolina, a small town surrounded by mountains, Brian had installed satellite radio in my car since it was impossible to keep stations in nearby Asheville from fading in and out. Brian was thoughtful like that. I turned the volume up, letting the station that played love songs all day get me in the mood for some loving.

How did I get so lucky? Of course, Brian was lucky to have me, too. How many wives showed up at their husband's office naked just so they could give him his fantasy? Not many, I bet. Well, I planned to do a lot of things like that so our marriage didn't go stale. It was important to keep a man happy and satisfied

This had been the best four months of my life. I loved every minute of my job as an interior designer, and the word had spread that I was good. Brian hadn't outright said that he was proud of me, but I didn't doubt that he was. I'd been busier than ever the past four years making Designs by Autumn successful, but I was firm about not allowing my career to interfere with my marriage. Brian was also good about not letting the dealership dominate his time. Sure, he had to work late once or twice a week to catch up on paperwork, but that was to be expected. He had a lot of responsibility on his shoulders.

I'd timed my arrival for Brian's lunchtime, knowing he closed himself up in his office for an hour of much needed quiet. Recharging his batteries, he called it. Well, today, he was definitely going to get them recharged. A little giggle escaped as I pulled into a parking space near the door. Boy was my husband going to be surprised.

"Autumn, what are you doing here?" Paul, Brian's sales manager, said as he rushed toward me.

"Just stopping in to say hi to Brian." I walked faster, hoping he'd lose interest in conversation. Although I'd normally stop to chat, I just couldn't, knowing I was naked under my raincoat. Not that Paul would even be able to guess such a thing, but he might wonder why I wore a buttoned-up raincoat when it wasn't raining.

His eyes flicked from me to the door. "Let me tell him you're here."

"No need." My hand on the doorknob, I glanced over my shoulder. What was with that panicked look on his face? "Do me a favor and make sure we're not interrupted."

"Shit," Paul said as I opened the door.

Well, that was a strange response. I stepped inside, closed the door behind me, and held up the champagne bottle. "Surpr..." My voice trailed off as I stared in horror at Brian and the woman he had bent over his desk.

"Surprise," I whispered.

"Autumn, what the hell are you doing here?" Brian said as he scrambled to stuff his penis back into his pants where it damn well belonged.

The woman kept her face turned from me, but I recognized that bleached blonde hair. Oh, did I ever. That was the thing about a small town. No one was a stranger. "Lina Kramer, get the hell out of here." I figured Lina heard the urge to murder in my voice because the bitch took off, trying to pull her panties up as she ran.

"Autumn," Brian said, holding up his hands as if asking for understanding.

Well, I'd show him understanding. I walked to the desk that I'd burn to ashes if I only had a blowtorch.

"I can explain, baby. Just listen, okay. She wouldn't give up, you know? I had a weak moment. It's never happened be—"

"Shut up, Brian." I slammed the champagne bottle down on the desk with all my strength, which was fed by the fury burning hot through my bloodstream. Shattered glass flew in all directions, the liquid drenching papers and folders, ruining them. I hoped they were important.

"Come on, baby. Let's talk this out."

I held out the neck of the bottle still clenched in my hand. "You say one more word, I swear to God, I'll stick this in your eye." He stepped away. Good, I had his attention. "I told you there was one thing I could never forgive." I didn't wait for an answer. "Considering what I just saw, apparently you didn't think I meant it. Well, I have news for you. We're done."

"I swear it didn't mean anything. It was just a stupid mistake."

"Yeah, it was stupid all right. Don't bother coming home."

At the door I paused and removed the ring I'd loved until a few minutes ago. Walking back to the desk, I set it in the middle of all the broken glass. I stared at it for a moment, my heart just as shattered as that champagne bottle. When the tears threatened to fall, I walked out, refusing to let Brian see me cry.

"Don't do this, Autumn."

I kept going. As I walked past the employees who'd gathered to witness my shame, I somehow managed to hold my chin up. I'd never been so humiliated in my life, and I didn't know which feeling to embrace. The embarrassment, the rage brewing inside me, or the ache in my chest that felt like someone had taken a sledgehammer to my heart?

CHAPTER TWO

~ Connor ~

I'D NEVER BEEN HAPPIER TO lose a customer. The Merricks had been the clients from hell. I bet I'd shown them more than a hundred houses over the past six months. Nothing had been right. The living room was too small. The living room was too big. Same for the bedrooms, bathrooms, and kitchens.

Then there was the land. The houses I'd shown them were either too high up in the mountains, too low, too close to the neighbors, or too secluded. They were too close to town, too far away. They cost too much—even though I'd never shown them a house above their stated budget—or the price was suspiciously low. That cheap, there must be something wrong with it.

Thirty minutes ago I'd stood in the middle of the living room of yet another house, listening to both of them complain about the paint colors.

"It's just fucking paint," I'd snapped. It was as if time had stopped, all three of us shocked into silence at my outburst.

Before I could apologize, Mr. Merrick said, "There is a lady present, Mr. Hunter. I don't think you're the right realtor for us."

There was a God. "Yes, I believe you're right. I'll email you the name of a realtor I think would be perfect for you." I faced Mrs. Merrick. "I sincerely apologize for my language."

She huffed, then marched out of the house, her husband giving me one last look of disgust as he followed her. "Good riddance," I muttered after the door banged closed behind them. I'd never lost my cool with a client before, but since it got them off my hands, I couldn't quite regret it. When I got back to the office, I'd send them Al Crane's contact information. He was always trying to steal other realtors' customers, and I'd gladly give him this couple on a silver platter. Al and the Merricks deserved each other.

Adam, my twin brother, and I owned Hunter Brothers Luxury Log Homes. He built them. I was a licensed realtor, selling our own properties, along with other houses in the area.

Driving home, I berated myself for letting the situation go so far downhill that I'd acted unprofessionally. I should have referred them to another realtor months ago. But they'd become something of a challenge, and I'd never backed down from a challenge. Live and learn, I guess. That was one mistake I'd never make again. From now on, if...

"The hell?" I yelled, yanking the steering wheel hard to the right. The car coming at me swerved back into its lane, but the driver overcorrected. I watched with growing horror in my rearview mirror as it disappeared off the side of the mountain. Making a U-turn, I sped back to where I'd seen the car go over.

When I reached the edge, I peered down, not even sure the car would still be visible. The roads around here were two lanes, often with steep drop-offs and heavy brush. There had been instances where drivers went over the side and no one was the wiser. Last month a woman had done just that, and three days passed before they found her, barely alive.

Luck had been on this driver's side. Not only had I seen the car go over, but there was only a ten-foot drop before the land flattened out, then dropped off again. The car's grill was embedded in a tree, which had stopped the vehicle from flying off the second drop-off. I slid down the side of the mountain, afraid of what I'd find when I reached the door.

I peered into the window. All I could tell was that the driver was a woman with long, honey-colored hair. The airbag looked like a huge blob of dough trying to devour her.

"Miss? Are you okay?" The airbag began to deflate, allowing me to see her face. "Autumn?" We'd been friends since grade school. My heart pounded with urgency as I pried open the door. "Autumn, are you okay?" She was crying, so that meant she was alive, thank God. "Talk to me, sweetheart. Tell me where it hurts."

She lifted her tearstained face. "Right here." She hit her chest with her fist.

"Your chest hurts?" Christ, did she have internal injuries? I needed to get rescue out here.

"No," she wailed. "My heart."

"You hurt your heart?" That was oddly specific.

"No, he…he did."

I glanced at the passenger seat, but there was no one there. Maybe she'd bumped her head, leaving her confused. I gently touched the bruise on her cheek from the airbag. It had probably saved her life, so a bruise was a small price to pay.

"Does that hurt?" Ignoring my question, she pushed the deflated airbag over the steering wheel. "Don't move," I said when she started to climb out. "You might be injured, your neck or something."

She rotated her head. "Nope, I'm fine." Tears filled her blue eyes again. "Except for my heart. That's irreparably broken."

"It'll make me feel a lot better if you'd stay still. I'll call for rescue to—" I think my eyes bugged out of their sockets when she flashed me as she swung her legs to the side of the seat. "Autumn, you're, ah, naked under that raincoat." And why was she wearing a raincoat on a sunny April day anyway, which, at the moment, was *not* strategically covering her below the waist? I glanced up, not seeing a cloud in the sky, and kept my gaze lifted, giving her time to cover herself.

"Yeah, well, you know what they say. The best laid plans and all that."

Whatever that meant. At least she'd stopped crying. There wasn't a man on earth who knew what to do with a crying woman. Actually, thinking about it, she'd gone from sobbing to pissed in mere minutes. I was more worried than ever that she'd hit her head.

"Are you decent?" I asked, still keeping my eyes averted.

She let out an annoyed sigh. "Yes, Connor, all my lady parts are covered. You don't have to worry about hurting your eyeballs again."

For sure, my eyeballs hadn't been hurt. Not even in the slightest. Like I said, Autumn and I were friends from way back. I'd never thought about the girl I used to climb trees with the way I was now. But hey, I'm a man. Flash us a picture of a woman's pretty pink lady parts and all bets are off. And Autumn's? Perfection.

She's your friend, douchebag. You will wipe that image out of your mind. Right. That's what I'd do. Besides, it was so not cool to get turned on when your married friend had just been in an accident and was traumatized.

"I wish you'd stay still and let me call for help," I said to her retreating back. Or not. When she stopped to study the steep hill she'd need to scale, I chased after her. "You'll never climb up that by yourself."

"You think so?" She eyed me as if I were a pesky nuisance. "I have so much rage inside me right now that I could probably fly to the top." She frowned as she studied the embankment.

I put my hand on her shoulder. "Autumn, what's going on?" At my touch she looked up at me, tears pooling in the eyes that were filled with anger only seconds ago. Oh, hell. She was crying again. Time to shut up. Whatever the deal was, it was none of my business.

Except she was my friend and obviously upset about something. What kind of friend would I be if I didn't try to find out what the problem was and do what I could to help?

"Here," I said, taking her hand. "I'll pull you up behind me." No way was I going to push her to the top because then I'd be looking up, seeing what I'd banished from my mind once already. Sorta. Okay, I was working on it. But getting a second look would permanently imprint it in my brain.

Autumn was pretty damn agile, thankfully, and we made it up the hill surprisingly easily. At the top we both stood at the edge, peering down at her car. I figured it was totaled, as the tree was implanted halfway into the engine. Did she have any idea how lucky she'd been? If not for that one, lonely tree on the plateau, she and the car would have tumbled thousands of feet to the bottom.

"Well," she said. "That was too close for comfort."

"No kidding." I was actually glad I hadn't known it was Autumn in the car when I'd watched it go over the drop-off. I'm not sure my heart could have handled that. "We need to call and report this."

"Would you just take me home? I'll send Brian an email telling him where he can come get the stupid car."

Uh-oh. Trouble in paradise? "I think that would be considered leaving the scene of an accident. Maybe you should stick around for the cops so you can explain what happened." I turned to face her. "Exactly what did happen?" She'd almost hit me head-on, for Christ's sake.

"I didn't see you, and then…" The blood drained from her cheeks. "Oh God, Connor. I could have killed you."

She launched herself at me, and suddenly there I was, standing on the side of the road with an armful of woman naked under her raincoat—yep, I hadn't forgotten—that I wasn't sure what to do with.

"I'm so sorry." She started crying again.

"Hush now." I patted her on the back. "Everything's going to be okay."

"No, it isn't." Pushing away, she marched to my car, slid into the passenger seat, and closed the door.

Okay. Now what? Other than wishing this day was over, I didn't have a clue what was going on with her or what I should do about it.

"I'll take you home, but we have to call this in first," I said after I got in the car.

She let out a weary sigh as she pushed her head back against the seat. "Fine. I'll call Jenn. She can send Dylan out here."

That was actually a good idea. Jenny Nance was not only Autumn's best friend, but Jenn's fiancé was our new police chief... Although he'd taken the job six months ago, so I guess he wasn't exactly new. Everyone just referred to him as the new chief and probably would for years.

"Crap. My phone's in my purse, which is still in the car."

"Use mine. I'll go get your stuff while you call Jenn." I put my thumb on the bottom of my cell to open the screen, then handed it to her. While she made the call, I retrieved her purse. When I returned, she was still talking to Jenn.

"I'm going to divorce the jackass, that's what I'm going to do. Listen, I'll call you tomorrow. We'll meet for lunch or something," she said.

Divorce? What the hell had happened? She hung up, then handed me the phone. "Is Dylan coming?"

"Yeah, she's calling him now."

"Autumn, why are you wearing a raincoat and nothing else?" I didn't mean to ask that, but the question was driving my mind nuts. And I should have kept my mouth shut. Her eyes filled with tears again.

"I was going to surprise Brian. It's his birthday, you know?"

No, I didn't know, but I wasn't so stupid I couldn't add

two and two. Something had happened to spoil her surprise, but what? Something so bad that she'd driven off the
side of a freaking mountain. There was only one thing I
could think of, and if my guess was right, as soon as I got
her home, I was going to find Brian and do him bodily
harm.

Jenn had told me a while back that she didn't trust Brian.
For one, according to Jenn, he had a tendency to check
out her butt when he thought no one was looking. "What
man about to get married checks out his girlfriend's best
friend's butt?" she'd once asked. I didn't have an answer,
but after she'd told me that, I'd taken to watching him. The
dude not only liked eyeing Jenn's butt but any other hot
woman's ass who happened to walk into his line of sight.

I liked Brian as a guy, but after that, I'd never liked him as
Autumn's future husband. Jenn had tried to talk to Autumn
about her concerns, but Autumn hadn't wanted to hear it.
Afraid she'd damage her relationship with her best friend
if she persisted, Jenn had shut up about Brian.

"What happened when you surprised him?" I hoped I
was wrong about my assumption.

"Ha! The surprise was on me." Her lips trembled. "I
caught him cheating on me, Connor. And the thing is, I
don't think it was the first time."

"Oh, honey, I'm sorry." When she started crying, I leaned
across the console and wrapped my arms around her, giving her my shoulder.

My twin, Adam, and I had been tight with Autumn, Jenn
and her twin Natalie—who'd died a few years ago—and
Savannah since grade school. At different times, Adam and
I had had fleeting crushes on one or the other of them
throughout high school. Only Adam and Savannah had
actually hooked up, though, and that hadn't gone so well.
Savannah had broken my brother's heart when she'd taken
off for New York to pursue her dream of becoming a
model. But that was a whole other story.

Right now my friend was hurting, and my protective instincts were out in full force. There was one more thing I needed to know. "Autumn, were you trying to kill yourself when you went over the mountain?" If she was, then Jenn, Adam, and I needed to set up around-the-clock guard duty so we could keep an eye on her. We'd lost Natalie, and I wasn't about to lose another from our group.

She reared back, looking at me as if I were crazy. "What? God, no. I was crying and my vision was blurry. I didn't see you until the last minute. I guess I jerked the wheel too hard. Believe me, I'm not about to kill myself over that jackass."

That was a relief. A silver Mustang pulled in front of us. "Here's Dylan."

"You go talk to him. I can't face him right now. Tell him I just want to go home."

"Sure." I got out of my car. "Hey, Chief. Got a little situation here," I said when I reached him.

"So I understand. Where's her car?"

Dylan Conrad was a cool dude, a big-city cop come to a small town, searching for peace. He'd found it with Jenn. They were getting married in May, and I couldn't be happier for Jenn. After suffering the crushing blow of losing her twin sister, she deserved some happiness in her life. I couldn't imagine my life without my twin in it.

"Down there," I said when we reached the edge of the drop-off.

Dylan whistled. "She was damn lucky."

"Yeah. Are you going to have to write an accident report? She's had a bad day and wants to go home."

"How'd you know her car was down there? You see her go over?"

"Watched it happen in my rearview mirror." I wasn't going to add to her problems by telling him she'd almost hit me head-on. "Scared the shit out of me. Just knew she'd gone down the mountain."

He glanced over at my car, where Autumn was sitting. "Jenny said she walked in on Brian with another woman. That makes me want to give him a piece of my mind."

"Tell me about it. Can we make this easy on her? She said she'd tell Brian where he could come get the car."

"I think I'd like to tell him in person. Get a feel for his intentions. If he wants to cause her trouble, maybe I can head him off."

"You're a good man, Chief." That was one reason I liked Dylan Conrad. He didn't see things only in black or white like a lot of cops. "I'm going to stay with Autumn for a while. Call me, let me know what he has to say."

"Will do. Jenny might stop by later. Autumn told her not to, that she'd talk to her tomorrow. Doubt Jenny will stay away, though. Not when her best friend just had her world turned upside down. If Brain's not still at the dealership, I'll track him down. He shows up after you get her home, let me know."

After he left, I returned to my car. "I can take you home now." I glanced over at Autumn. She was sound asleep, tearstains creating vertical lines on her cheeks, making me wish I were the one going to see Brian instead. He wouldn't like getting a visit from me.

"Let's get you home, sweetheart," I whispered.

CHAPTER THREE

~ *Autumn* ~

" AUTUMN, HONEY, WAKE UP. YOU'RE home."
Connor's voice was so tender as it penetrated my
consciousness that I started crying again. I didn't want to
cry over Brian anymore, but here I was, doing just that. It
made me angry. But I really wasn't crying for him, was I?
My heart was broken, so the tears were for me.

"Let's get you inside."

I nodded. What would I have done if Connor hadn't
come along? And he was being so sweet and protective. It
was almost too much, his thoughtfulness and gentle voice.
We'd been friends for what felt like forever, and I was more
used to his good-natured teasing. It would hurt Connor's
feelings, though, if I told him that was what I wanted from
him right now, not this treating me as if I were a helpless
female who needed taking care of. So I kept my mouth
shut.

When we reached my door, I fished the keys out of
my purse. Still in caretaker mode, he took them from me,
unlocking my door. I let out a tired sigh. Men really didn't
quite know what to do with a crying woman, I guess.

"Thanks for bringing me home. Thanks for everything,
Connor." Impulsively I gave him a hug. He wrapped
strong arms around me. Then, still being sweet, he kissed
the top of my head. I inhaled, his scent filling my lungs. He
smelled really good. Why hadn't I ever noticed that before?

"I'm just glad I was there, even though you scared ten
years off my life, girl. I think I'm going to need trauma
counseling now. I'll send you the bill."

I smiled against his chest. That was the Connor I knew and loved. The one who could make me smile on the worst day of my life.

"You can go now. I'm okay. Really," I said when Connor tried to follow me in.

"Of course you are, but I'm staying." He closed the door behind him, proving he had no intention of leaving.

Honestly I really wanted to be alone so I could wallow in my misery. "Connor, I know you have better things to do than hold my hand."

He tilted his head, his gaze shooting to the ceiling as if considering what better things he had to do. Then his eyes focused on me. "Nope, can't think of a thing that needs doing. What's for lunch?"

I sputtered a laugh. "You want me to feed you?"

"Well, yeah. We gotta eat, right?"

Oh, I was on to him now. That was his way of making sure I ate. "Connor Hunter, you're a real pain in the rear end. You know that?"

He grinned. "So I've been told."

Off he went to my kitchen, me following along like a puppy. I leaned on the island, watching him rummage in my fridge. The Hunter twins were identical, only their parents and a few close friends able to tell them apart. I was one of those. Black hair, blue eyes, and nice—really nice—bodies made for two very sexy men.

Women fell all over their feet attempting to get their attention. It was funny, but I'd never seen Connor or Adam as more than my friends, had never doodled their names in the margins of my notebooks. I guess it was because I'd been friends with them since I was a little girl in pigtails.

Jenny and Natalie had decided back in high school that they were going to marry the Hunter brothers. They'd thought it would be cool for twins to marry twins, but that fantasy hadn't lasted long. I think they came to the realization that it would be like marrying your brother, because that's what Connor and Adam were to us. Adopted brothers who'd beat up any boy who treated us wrong.

Only Savannah hadn't seen them that way, at least not Adam. They'd had a hot thing going during their senior year until Savannah graduated and took herself to New York City. I'm not sure Adam ever got over her.

"How about I make us an omelet?" Connor said, interrupting my trip down memory lane.

Accepting that he had no intention of leaving, I shrugged. "Sure." Not that I felt like eating, but I had to admit having him here did take my mind off my cheating husband. I dreaded going to bed. As soon as I closed my eyes, I was sure I'd replay the scene in his office, him with his pants down around his knees and Lina Kramer's lily-white ass sticking up in the air. Involuntarily I made a sound, causing Connor to turn around.

"What?"

"You ever date Lina Kramer?" I didn't think he had or I'm sure I would have heard. Blue Ridge Valley is a small town, and nothing stays a secret where everyone knows everyone's business. That was probably the main reason the Hunter brothers did their carousing in Asheville.

"Not my type. That's who it was?"

I nodded, not trusting my voice.

"Ouch."

"Yeah, ouch."

"Exactly what happened, Autumn?"

After I told him the scene I'd walked in on and how Brian's employees had gathered around to watch me leave, his blue eyes turned ice-cold. "Can I kill him for you?"

"Probably not a good idea, Rambo. I'd hate to see you behind bars."

"Pity." He went back to collecting stuff to make an omelet.

It would have hurt no matter who it was, but Brian had dated Lina Kramer before we started seeing each other.

He'd claimed there had been nothing between them but sex. "She's great in bed, but a bitch out of it," he'd once said. It hit me then that I'd closed my eyes and ears to what I should have seen as a red flag. A man shouldn't call a woman he'd been sleeping with a bitch.

I tried to remember if he'd ever told me I was great in bed, but he never had. "Do you think I'm sexy?"

"Huh?"

I laughed at Connor's deer-in-the-headlights expression as he stood frozen with a bowl in one hand and the fork he was whipping eggs with in the other. "You're dripping eggs on the floor."

"Right. I better clean that up before…" His eyebrows scrunched together. "Before whatever."

"It was a simple question, Connor. Yes, Autumn, I think you're sexy. No, Autumn, I don't think you're sexy."

"I don't think of you in that way at all."

"Oh." Well, that kind of hurt, although I'm not sure why. If he'd felt like a brother to me growing up, then it would work the same for him, right? And no brother thought of his sister like that. Ugh.

"Christ, Autumn, you're screwing with my mind." He let out a big sigh. "I just hurt your feelings, didn't I?" He gave the eggs a furious whip as if they'd thoroughly annoyed him.

Yes. "Of course not."

He set the bowl down. "Why don't you go put on something more comfortable than that"—he waved the fork at me, dripping eggs again—"trench coat while I finish cooking up some lunch."

How had I forgotten I was standing here practically naked? "Good idea."

As I passed the dining room, I glanced over, letting out a cry at seeing the cake and presents. I'd worked so hard to make this a perfect night for Brian, and with my rage burning hot all over again, I marched into the room.

I stared at the gifts I'd wrapped in foil paper with beautiful bows that I'd taken the time to make myself. "I'm such a fool," I whispered. With one sweep of my arm, I sent them flying across the room. The heavy present, the one with the monogramed car mats, hit the wall with a loud *thud*. The smallest box containing the TAG Heuer watch sat next to my foot. Brian would have loved that one. I kicked it away. It hit the sliding glass door, then bounced back, landing at my foot again.

"You can't come back," I yelled.

"Easy, sweetheart," Connor said, coming up behind me and wrapping his arms around my waist, pulling me against him.

Presents were scattered over the floor; the only thing still on the table was the cake in its glass dome, and that was only because I hadn't gotten to it yet. I squeezed my eyes shut, wishing like the devil that I wasn't crying because of my cheating husband.

Connor put his arm around my shoulders, leading me from the room. "Go change. I'll have lunch ready in a few. After that, we'll drink copious amounts of wine and eat gallons of ice cream." He angled his head, grinning down at me. "Isn't that what girls do when some schmuck breaks their heart?"

"That's a girl secret. You're not supposed to know about that."

"My lips are sealed." He put his hand on my back, pushing me down the hall.

I walked into my bedroom and came to an abrupt halt, staring at the bed. The one Brian and I had made love in. No way could I ever sleep on it again. Tonight I'd stay in the guest room, and tomorrow I'd go bed shopping.

My father had been a cheater—still was—and I'd seen how his behavior had destroyed my mother over the years. I'd made one promise to myself a long time ago. Never, ever would I stay with a cheater.

My trust in Brian had been shattered, and if I stayed with him, every time he walked out the door, the questions would come. Where was he going? Was he seeing Lina again or off to meet up with some other woman? The very same questions my mother had spent her marriage asking.

I was not going to be my mother.

Jenn had once tried to warn me about Brian, but I hadn't wanted to hear it. Not about the man who'd swept me off my feet two years ago. I'd been trying to get Designs by Autumn up and running. Since I didn't have money to spend on a decent car, I was driving an old clunker that had broken down on the way to one of my first client appointments.

I had been stranded on the side of the road, and Brian stopped. The next thing I knew he had my car towed to his dealership and I was on my way to my appointment in a brand-new Lexus he'd loaned me. We started dating, and I was sure I'd found the perfect man, one nothing like my father.

I'd told Jenn she was imagining things. Now I knew she wasn't. Oh, I knew there would be hard, sad days ahead of me. I wasn't done crying and definitely wasn't done feeling sorry for myself. After the scene I'd witnessed, I was entitled.

Oh God… What if Brian had given me some kind of sexual disease? If, as I suspected now, that hadn't been the first time he'd cheated since we'd started dating, who and how many had there been?

I was going to be sick. My legs gave out, and I crumbled into a heap on the floor. All right, tomorrow a new bed and get tested, I thought, wrapping my arms around my stomach and rocking my body.

I looked around the room, noting the things that were mine and those that were Brian's. There was no question in my mind I wanted a divorce. But after that, what did I want?

I made a good living as an interior designer, and although I could probably get some kind of settlement from Brian, I didn't want his money, even though he had plenty to spare. It would feel too much like I'd owe him if I took anything from him. But I did want the house.

Every corner had been decorated by me. I'd put my heart and soul into making our first home beautiful. As far as I was concerned, that gave me the right to keep it. Well, that and his cheating ways. He didn't get to poke his stick in another woman and expect nothing would change.

He'd put the deposit down, and too bad for him if he thought it wasn't fair that he didn't get at least half the house. Maybe I'd keep it, or maybe I'd sell it. I wasn't going to make that decision until I was thinking clearly again.

One thing I would do was go back to my maiden name. I'd be damned if I'd keep Stratton. Autumn Archer and the house. That was it. Brian was getting off easy.

"Autumn?"

"Yeah?" It sounded like Connor was in the hallway. I quickly pushed up before he could walk in and catch me wallowing on the floor.

"Lunch is ready."

"Be right there." It was kind of nice having Connor here, taking care of me.

CHAPTER FOUR

~ Connor ~

AUTUMN WALKED INTO THE KITCHEN wearing a pair of sweatpants, socks, a long-sleeve T-shirt with our high school logo, and her blonde hair up in a ponytail. I'd lied. I hadn't once thought of Autumn as anything but a friend until today. Now all I could think about was how sexy she was, even covered from neck to feet in her comfy clothes.

I was a bad man.

She slid onto a stool at the kitchen island. I'd been in her house before and had always liked it. Not as much as my log home, but she'd done a great job of decorating the place. She liked colors that matched her name, and there was a warmth and coziness about her home that made you want to settle in and stay awhile. I particularly liked her dark green leather sofa with the chaise on one end. It would be perfect for stretching out to watch a football game. Or nap. I should hire her to decorate my log house.

When I put a plate in front of her, she kept her eyes down, avoiding my gaze. I didn't like that I'd hurt her feelings, but she'd caught me off guard with her question. I'd wanted to say, *Hell yes! What I saw today was so sexy hot my eyeballs are still burning.* Maybe I could tone that down, give her what she seemed to need to hear.

I pulled a stool to the other side so I could face her. "Autumn." I waited for her to look at me. "I do think you're sexy."

"You don't have to say that." Her gaze went right back to her plate.

"You're right, I don't." I reached across the space between us, putting my hand over hers. "We've been friends for a long time. You know I don't say things I don't mean, not even if it was just to make you feel better. You are a very sexy woman. I've always known you were beautiful, but…" I hesitated, trying to think how to explain. "We're friends. Men try not to think of their female friends as sexy."

That got her attention. "Why?"

"Because then all we can think about is having sex with that sexy friend."

Her eyes widened. "Oh."

"Yeah, oh." And now that was going to be all I would think about. I really was a bad, bad man. We needed a change of subject, something to get my mind off the incredibly hot woman sitting across from me. When I got home where I could think straight, I'd figure out how to put that genie back in the bottle.

"Oh, almost forgot. Dylan called while you were changing. Brian told him it was no big deal what he'd done. Just a stupid mistake he'd made at a weak moment that didn't mean anything."

Her fork clattered when it hit her plate. "No big deal? No freaking big deal?" She drew air into her lungs.

"Yeah, the asshole. He was also not happy about the car. Dylan's with him now. They've called a tow truck out to pull it back up." I'd debated telling her what Brian had said but had decided she should hear it. If I thought the jerk really had made a stupid mistake as he claimed, and that he was genuinely sorry, I might have suggested she take her time to think about what she wanted. If saving her marriage was the answer, then I would have supported her fully. But I suspected she was right and this wasn't her husband's first so-called mistake.

Nor did I like him trying to blow it off as no big deal. That right there told me the only thing he was sorry about was getting caught. Men like Brian rarely learned their lesson. His next weak moment wouldn't be long in coming. I didn't want my friend married to the douchebag, so I hoped she meant it when she said she was done with him.

"There's one other thing. He told Dylan he wants to talk to you, that he can straighten everything out."

Her blue eyes turned glacier cold. "Like hell he can. He can talk to me through my lawyer."

"Dylan told him not to come here tonight, but he said don't be surprised if Brian shows up after they deal with the car."

She pushed away from the counter, taking off down the hall. Afraid I'd upset her again, I followed her. At first I didn't see her, but then a large suitcase on wheels rolled out of the closet, closely followed by another one. It was like some kind of freaky suitcase cartoon come to life.

"Are you moving out?" I asked when Autumn finally appeared.

"Nope. My lying, cheating, soon-to-be ex-husband's moving out." She tossed one of the suitcases onto the bed, unzipped it, then went to a chest of drawers.

"Need help?"

She stilled with an armload of shirts. "Do you think I'm being a bitch about this?"

I leaned against the doorframe. "Not even. I guess I'm just a little surprised by how fast you decided that your marriage was over."

"A long time ago I made a promise to myself not to ever become my mother."

Ah, that explained things. Autumn's father had never been able to keep his pants zipped. He'd get caught, her mother would kick him out, then he'd sweet-talk his way back home. Rinse. Repeat. Over the years her mother had gone from a smiling, happy woman to one of the most miserable people I knew. Autumn's parents were still on again and off again. It was wearying even to me, and I hadn't had to live it.

"Good for you," I said, going to a drawer and hauling out a handful of socks. We worked together until both suitcases were full, not bothering to pack anything neatly. Cheating Brian was going to need an iron.

She chewed on her bottom lip for a moment, then glanced over at me. "I'm going to ask you for a big favor."

By the tone of her voice, I figured I probably wasn't going to like it, but she was my friend and she was hurting and right now I'd do anything she asked. "Sure. What?"

"Brian's going to need to come in tomorrow and get the rest of his stuff. I'd like you to be here with me when that happens."

I was wrong. I very much wanted to be with her when the man showed up. "You bet. Why did we pack all this now?"

"So I can give them to Brian if he shows up tonight."

"Good thinking." I rolled one suitcase and she rolled the other one to the front door. She'd gone from sad and crying to mad and scheming. I liked her much better this way.

"I really appreciate everything you've done, Connor. I'm not sure..." She stared down at the floor. "I think I would have been lost without you here, but you've given me enough of your time."

Just go and slay me, Autumn. I think I was happier than her that I'd come along when I had so she hadn't been alone. "I'm not leaving you here by yourself. What if Brian shows up?"

She eyed the suitcases. "I could put them outside the door so he wouldn't have to come in."

"Since he has keys, I don't see how you can keep him out if he decides he wants to talk to you." A visible shudder passed through her at that. "Tomorrow I'll get our foreman here if you want the locks changed. In the meantime, just point me to your guest room."

"Um..." She scraped sock-clad toes across the wood floor. "I was going to sleep in there."

I almost asked why, but the answer popped into my head. She didn't want to sleep in the bed that belonged to her and Brian. Couldn't say I blamed her. "No problem. The couch will work just fine."

The sofa was long enough to accommodate me. I needed to call Adam, let him know what was going on. We were supposed to have a status meeting in the morning about the log home we were building for Dylan and Jenn, but I didn't want to talk to him in front of Autumn. She was already worried that she was taking up too much of my time.

"Give me a pillow and I'm good to go."

"Are you sure?"

"Absolutely." I was pretty sure I saw relief in her eyes that I was staying.

"Thank you."

"Stop thanking me, Autumn. That's what friends do, be there when you need them. Come here." I held out my arms. The girl needed a hug. When she walked into my embrace, I realized my mistake. She felt far too good snuggled up against me. Yep, I was seeing her as my sexy friend now. Before she realized the effect she was having on the part of me that had no business taking notice of her, I stepped away.

She gave me a puzzled look, and I couldn't blame her. I'd pushed her away a little roughly, but better her confused than knowing my male brain had reclassified her as *woman of interest in the vicinity*, which had immediately sent an alert down south to stand up and pay attention.

"What would you like to do for the rest of the afternoon?"

Her shoulders lifted in a shrug. "I guess we could watch a movie or something."

"Okay." We stilled at the sound of a car turning into the driveway. "You sure you don't want to talk to him?"

She shook her head. "Not now. I can't."

"Okay, go to the bedroom. I'll give him the suitcases. What time you want him to come get the rest of his stuff tomorrow?"

"Any time before noon. After that I have an appointment."

That worked for me as well. "I got this, Autumn. Go."

Since my car was parked in the middle of the driveway, blocking the garage door, Brian would have to come to the front. Curious if he'd give Autumn the courtesy of knocking, I waited. I rolled my eyes when I heard a key slide into the lock. What a jerk. Apparently he thought he could just waltz right in even after what he'd done.

I pulled the door open. "Oh, good. It's you." I pushed the two suitcases in front of him, blocking him from coming in. "Autumn was kind enough to pack up some stuff for you. I told her to just throw everything out on the lawn, but she's a nicer person than I am."

"What are you doing here, Adam?"

The dude never had been able to tell us apart, but I don't think he really tried that hard. By now he should know that I always wore an emerald stone earring and Adam a sapphire one. "I'm Connor. To answer your question, I'm taking care of my friend. The one whose heart you broke today." At his scowl I was tempted to slam the door in his face.

"Autumn shouldn't be discussing our private business."

"And Autumn's husband shouldn't have been screwing a woman who wasn't his wife, so I guess you're even. Oh, wait. I don't think she's close to being even with what you did. Take the suitcases and go. She said to tell you that you can come get the rest of your stuff tomorrow morning."

"I want to talk to her. We can straighten out this misunderstanding now."

"Seriously, dude? Misunderstanding? If that's how you see it, then you're a bigger idiot than I thought. You're not talking to her today, so go before I call the cops."

"Who the hell do you think you are, asshole? This is my house, and I'm coming in."

I was bigger and stronger than him, and he was pissing me off. Before I lost it and beat the crap out of him, I picked up one of the suitcases and used it to push him away from the door. "You try to come in and you won't like the consequences." I threw the suitcase out the door, then kicked the other one out.

After watching to make sure he left, I called my foreman. Although I'd planned to have him come over in the morning to change the locks, I decided that should happen immediately. I didn't trust Brian to stay away.

Next I called Adam, letting him know where I was and why. He was as angry on Autumn's behalf as I was.

"Want me to come over and stand guard with you?"

"No. Gary's coming now to put new locks in. I'll bunk on her couch, wait for Brian to show up tomorrow, then head home. I've got a showing tomorrow afternoon, but I won't make it to the office in the morning to go over the status of Dylan and Jenn's house."

"Not a problem. If anything changes, let me know."

"Will do." A few seconds after I hung up, a car pulled into the driveway. It was too soon for Gary to get here, and if it was Brian coming back, we were going to have some words.

I opened the door, prepared to meet him in the yard. Recognizing Dylan's Mustang—or was it Jenn's?—I relaxed.

"One of you needs to get a different car so I know who's here," I said as they both walked up. They had matching Mustangs, which Jenn thought was the cutest thing.

"I'm keeping mine," Jenn said, giving me a hug. "He can get a new car."

Dylan grinned at his girlfriend. "Not happening, Red."

Jenn peeked around me, trying to see inside the house. "How's our girl?"

"Not so good. Brian just left. He wanted to talk to her, but she wasn't ready, so I sent him away. Come on in."

"I'm so furious," Jenn said when we were inside. "I wish I'd been here so I could give him a piece of my mind. What a toad."

"That he is." I waved a hand toward the hallway. "She's in the guest bedroom. Why don't you go talk to her?" Dylan moved to the sofa after Jenn headed for Autumn. I plopped down in a chair. "I'm waiting for my foreman. He's headed over to change the locks."

"So she meant it when she said she was done with him?"

"Appears so. I hope she still feels that way tomorrow." I brought Dylan up to speed, telling him that Autumn had agreed to meet with Brian as long as I was here.

"Jenny and I can stay tonight if you need to get home."

"I'm good." She was under my protection now, and I took that job seriously. As for these new thoughts I was having about her, they'd go away soon enough and we'd get back to being just friends.

"I'm guessing he's going to cause trouble if she doesn't take him back," Dylan said.

"He can bring it on. I'll be ready for him." Unless she changed her mind and decided to forgive Brian, I planned to be her loyal sidekick for a while. If the man tried to mess with her, he was going to have me to deal with.

CHAPTER FIVE

~ *Autumn* ~

THE MINUTE JENN WALKED INTO the guest room, I started crying. I don't know why. I guess because along with Natalie and Savannah, she'd been my best friend for most of my life, and I trusted her without reservation. There was no one else I'd rather have with me now, unless Savannah was here to join in. As for Jenn's twin, Natalie had died shortly after we'd graduated high school, and I'm not sure any of us had gotten over that.

"Oh, hon," Jenn said, crawling onto the bed and pulling me into her arms.

That only made me cry harder. "Why didn't I listen to you?"

"Because you loved him and didn't want to hear it." She squeezed my hand. "You've always wanted a home filled with children who were happy and a man who loved you and only you. More than any of us, you wanted to get married. You wanted everything you didn't have growing up. You thought you'd found that with Brian."

"But you saw him for what he was."

"No, I only saw a man who appreciated women's butts. That probably applies to every straight, red-blooded male in the world. Because he was more blatant about looking, it did concern me, but it didn't alarm me to the point that I thought I needed to push the issue. Autumn, he was good to you."

"Yeah, he did love giving me presents." But I would have taken his fidelity over things any day.

"And it wasn't just that. Y'all had fun together."

"Are you saying I should give him a second chance? Because I just can't do that. I told him from the very beginning that if he ever cheated on me, I was gone."

"No, hon, not at all. If I'd grown up in your house, I would probably say the same thing. Honestly, I doubt I could stay with Dylan if I ever found out he cheated on me."

"Dylan would never do that."

"And in my heart I believe that, but there are no guarantees in life. Things can change." She brushed my hair away from my face. "If you have second thoughts in the coming days, don't let your stubbornness stop you from seeing if you can work things out with him."

Stupid tears were burning my eyes again. "I could never trust him after this."

"And that's a biggie. Listen, why don't you try to get some sleep? I'll be right here."

"I heard Dylan's voice out there. Go get your boyfriend and go home." I loved Jenn to death, but I just needed to be alone right now.

"We could send the guys home, then drink wine and eat cake in bed. I know you have at least one piece of Mary's cake hidden somewhere in this house."

I scoffed. "Like either one of them would leave us alone knowing Brian could come back."

"Yeah, I didn't think of that. Dylan and I could stay. Let Connor go home."

That probably would be the best thing to do, yet I wanted Conner here. Maybe it was because he'd rescued me, even after I'd almost killed him, but I felt safe with him.

"Go home, Jenn. I'm okay. Actually I just want to go to sleep." I yawned for emphasis. Not that I was going to sleep a wink, but if she knew that, she'd camp out on my bed all night.

After promising I'd call her even if I decided at three in the morning I wanted to talk, she finally gave me a kiss on my forehead, then scooted off the bed. "Love you," I called to her when she reached the door.

"Love you back, hon."

I might have a jerk face for a husband, but I had won the lottery with my friends. For the next twenty minutes I lay there, listening to the sound of their voices drift down the hall. Although I couldn't hear every word, I was picking up enough to know that Connor was telling them what had happened when I'd tried to surprise Brian. Good. I wouldn't have to tell the story again tomorrow when Jenn came over. Because she would.

"That bastard," Jenn exclaimed loud enough for me to hear that good and clear.

"Very true," I murmured. Not long after, I heard a new voice, one I didn't recognize. I got out of bed and eased over to the door, peeking around the corner. Jenn and Dylan were saying their good-byes to Connor while a guy wearing a tool belt stood off to the side. After Connor closed the door, the tool-belt guy went to work on the locks.

Having the Hunter brothers as friends was as good has having your very own Property Brothers. But where Drew and Jonathan were cute and adorable, Connor and Adam were downright hot. Before Connor caught me peeking, I left the bedroom door open and climbed back into the bed.

To keep the scene I'd walked in on in Brian's office from running through my head like a god-awful porno flick, I turned my mind to my appointment tomorrow afternoon. It was a big opportunity. I'd never done a commercial redo, and I'd been excited about the chance. Now I was having trouble finding any enthusiasm for the meeting I had with the property manager of the Blue Ridge Valley Country Club. But I was prepared, and I... Oh crap! All my samples were in my wrecked car. And how was I supposed to get there now that I didn't have transportation?

Without those samples I would come across as unprepared and unprofessional, and since I refused to look like a bumbling idiot, I had to get them tonight. Because I refused to talk to Brian, it would mean breaking into the fenced lot behind his dealership, where I'm sure the car had been towed, but it was my car and my samples. He'd never even know. All I had to do was get Connor on board.

What did one wear for breaking and entering?

☾

"No, absolutely not," Connor said when I told him my plan later that night. "And you look like a cat burglar's poor cousin."

I glanced down at myself. Okay, so I hadn't had much inventory in black to choose from. Where clothes were concerned, I liked colors. The black tights had holes in them—some Connor could see, some not—and should have been thrown away years ago.

The two-sizes-too-big, long-sleeved black T-shirt was Brian's. It almost reached my knees, hiding the hole in the tights at my crotch. Connor had seen more than enough of me there today.

Black rubber boots that I wore when working in the yard completed my ensemble. Oh, and the black knit cap that I'd tucked my blonde hair under. I'd considered putting some of Brian's black shoe polish on my cheeks to conceal their shine but thought that might be taking things a little far.

"You don't have to go with me. Just loan me your car." I almost laughed at the pure panic on his face. Connor and Adam were classic muscle-car nuts. Asking to borrow the whatever-special-year-it-was, whatever-make-it-was car sitting in my driveway was probably akin to asking him to give me one of his kidneys.

"I swear I won't drive it off the mountain." He turned green. Guess I shouldn't have reminded him of my little

accident. Right now he was probably visualizing his precious car with a tree sprouting out of the engine.

"No." He crossed his arms over his chest and glared
down at me.

"Please, Connor." I wasn't above using the weapons
at my disposal. The chance to land the country club job
meant that much to me. I'd never intended to call on an
old favor, but I didn't see that I had a choice. I regretted
what I was about to say before the words left my mouth.

"Remember when I didn't tell Adam you were the one
who spread the rumor that he didn't have a penis?"

"We were in high school, Autumn. The stupid years.
Besides, he knew I had a crush on Babs, but he still asked
her out. He deserved her thinking he was cockless."

I sputtered a laugh. "Is that even a word? Anyway, when
I told you I knew it was you who started the rumor, you
said, and I'll quote, 'I'll owe you big if you keep your big
mouth shut.'" I frowned. "And I did not have a big mouth,
by the way."

"Did, too."

When his gaze landed on my mouth, the weirdest thing
happened. I wanted to kiss him, like for a long time. Where
in all that was holy had that thought come from? I tore my
gaze away from his mouth—and yeah, while I was looking
at his, he was staring right back at mine—and said, "You
owe me, and now I'm collecting."

"Collecting what?"

"My favor." I spied his keys on the kitchen counter and
snatched them up.

"Come back here with those," he called after me.

I ran.

CHAPTER SIX

~ Connor ~

AUTUMN STRATTON—NO, BACK TO ARCHER now—had hoodwinked me. She'd locked herself in my '68 Camaro SS, just repainted its original matador red, and was threatening to take off. The woman had wrecked one car today. She sure as hell wasn't driving mine off on her harebrained scheme.

"Open the door, Autumn." I pulled on the handle.

"Not until you promise to take me to get my samples." She slid the key into the ignition. "Or, I'll just drive myself."

Exasperated with the woman, I gave in. "Fine. I will." I'd grown up with Autumn and knew firsthand how stubborn she could be. It was either give up or watch her drive away in a car that had more power than she'd know what to do with on these mountain roads.

"Thank you," she cheerfully said after unlocking the door, and then she slid over the console, landing in the passenger seat.

She gave me a smile, one that I'd never seen before. Sweet and shy, and with it my irritation evaporated. It was still a harebrained idea, but a harmless one. Or could be that my brain had short-circuited, stealing my good sense the minute I realized just how kissable Autumn's lips were. How had I not noticed that before? *Because she's your friend, douchebag.*

"If we get busted, you're paying my bail." I glanced over at her. "Just saying."

She rolled her eyes. "We're not getting busted. It's my car and my samples. I have every right to retrieve my stuff."

We settled into silence for a few miles, but I didn't like it. Autumn wasn't the silent type. "Are you going to be okay?" That was a stupid question to ask a woman who'd only hours ago caught her husband balls-deep in another woman. And the idiot hadn't even bothered to lock his office. I didn't doubt every employee in the dealership knew exactly how Brian spent some of his lunch hours.

"Maybe after I bleach my eyes so I can stop seeing . . ." She trailed off, shook her head, and turned her face to the window.

I had no idea what to say to a hurting woman, but what was there to say? Time heals all wounds? Maybe true but lame.

"Where would your car be?" I asked as we approached the dealership.

"Turn on the access road before the building. Go around the back, behind the service area."

When I came to the end of the access road, I stopped and stared at the fence that I estimated to be eight feet tall. "Um, Autumn? You have a key for that lock on the gate?"

"Nope." She got out of the car.

When Autumn was twelve years old, she'd decided she wanted to go to Dollywood in Pigeon Forge, Tennessee. Why? So she could ride the Tennessee Tornado roller coaster. The reason? Because she'd never ridden a roller coaster and was determined to correct that wrong.

Her father refused to take her, but did that stop her? Not even. She convinced Jenn, Natalie, and Savannah that they should hitchhike to Pigeon Forge. The other girls wanted to ask one of their parents to take them, but Autumn was pissed at her dad—what else was new?—and had made up her mind that she'd show him.

Exactly what she thought she was proving by hitchhiking to Tennessee, I'm not sure, but that was what she'd said. "I'll show him." Autumn could and can talk just about anyone into anything—witness me sitting here about to break into a fenced-in area with a big NO TRESPASSING sign. The first person to come along had been Hamburger Harry, our infamous moonshiner. He called Jenn and Natalie's father, who was our mayor at the time, and the Great Dollywood Caper ended before it even began.

The point was, when Autumn makes up her mind, either get out of her way or throw in the towel and join her. I sighed as I got out of the car.

I stopped next to her. "What's the plan here?"

She tilted her head, staring at the top of the fence. "I'm going to climb it."

Like that was going to happen. "No, I'll do it." When she smiled at me as if I were her hero, I had the stray thought that I'd like to wake up in the mornings to that smile. That kind of thinking had to stop.

"Here's my spare key. In case the car's locked."

"There's not a vicious junkyard dog hiding under those cars, waiting to chew my leg off, is there?"

"For goodness' sake, Connor." She snatched the key out of my hand and was halfway up the fence before I could stop her.

Autumn had always been able to climb like a monkey, but I wanted to be her hero on a day that heroes in her life had been sorely lacking. Before she managed to get out of reach, I grabbed her by the waist and lifted her off the fence, putting her feet back on the ground. Taking the key, I scaled the fence.

Her car was right in front, the doors unlocked. Tree branches were still caught in the engine, and the way the front was split in half almost to the windshield reminded me how close she'd come to being seriously hurt or worse. I didn't want to think of a world without Autumn in it.

A few minutes later I tossed her sample case over the fence and then made my way to the other side. As soon as I jumped down the last few feet, Autumn threw herself at me.

"You're the best friend ever," she said, wrapping her arms around me, giving me a hug.

Since recently becoming aware that my childhood friend had grown up without me paying attention, the last place she should be was in my arms.

"Well, isn't this cozy?"

We both froze long enough to widen our eyes at each other. Then I swear I saw flames ignite in her pupils. I dropped the arms I had wrapped around her back, stepping away as if I'd done something to be guilty of when all I'd been doing was hugging my friend. Okay, there might have been some lecherous thoughts going on when she was pressed against me, but Brian didn't know that. Truthfully I wished I didn't know that myself.

Autumn put her hands on her hips, glaring at her husband. "What the hell are you doing here, Brian?"

"Because I own the ground you're standing on?" He lifted the flashlight he held, shining it into Autumn's eyes. "Breaking and entering isn't a laughing matter." Then I got the flashlight treatment. "Don't think you're walking away from this either." He pointed the flashlight at the top of a pole. "See that camera up there? I've got all the evidence on tape. The police are on the way as we speak."

Ass. "All she did was get her samples out of her car. She didn't steal anything."

"Don't care. And it's not her car." He stepped in front of me, blocking my view of Autumn. "Autumn, you need to stop your silliness. You're my wife, and—"

"Which I plan to correct as fast as possible. Stop being a stupid jerk, Brian."

I stepped around him but decided this was her battle. For the moment. If he touched her or said much more, then I'd be all in.

She narrowed her eyes. "Wait a minute, what do you mean, it's not my car? You gave it to me."

"No, I loaned it to you. It's a demo." He tried to put his

hand on her arm, but she yanked it away. "You're overre-
acting to everything, Autumn. So I made a little mistake.
Nothing we can't get past."

The fire I'd seen in her eyes burned brighter. "Not my
car? A *little* mistake? You son of a bitch."

"What about you and him?" He jabbed a thumb my way.
"You were wrapped around him like white on rice."

I'd known Autumn a long time. In about three seconds
she was going to explode. I stepped behind her, and just as
she went for Brian, I grabbed her waist with both hands,
holding her back.

That was how Tommy Evans, one of Blue Ridge Valley's
cops, found us.

CHAPTER SEVEN

~ Autumn ~

"I'M SO SORRY, CONNOR." I stared at the cell across from mine, where Connor was housed. "I can't believe Brian had us arrested for breaking and entering."

Stretched out on a cot that his feet hung over, he lifted his head enough to see me. "You know the words to 'Jail-house Rock'?" He winked, then went back to napping.

Of course I did. I was a classic movie junkie, and he knew that. He was trying to make me think this was no big deal. But it was. He must hate me.

The Blue Ridge Valley Police Department had three jail cells. I was in one, Connor in one, and the Emery brothers, Dick and Ted, occupied the third cell, their second home. Dylan should put a plaque with their names on it over the door.

Oh God, I was a criminal with a record now. How mortifying! And my toad-faced husband, The Cheater, had confiscated my samples. My car that wasn't really my car was totaled, I was in jail, and I'd dragged Connor into my mess. Why was he so calm about this?

"Connor?"

He lifted onto his elbows. "Yeah?"

"Do you hate me?"

Did he just snort?

He lifted his head again. "I could never hate you. Now hush so I can finish my nap."

Throughout the years I'd known Connor—ever since first grade—he'd always protected me, no matter what she-nanigans I'd gotten up to. And I'd probably been up to more shenanigans than I had a right to. I plopped down onto the cot in my cell. How had I not seen that Connor has always been my personal hero?

"Well, well, what do we have here? You two got a Bonnie and Clyde thing going on?"

At hearing Dylan's voice, I jumped up and pressed my nose between the bars. Dylan stood exactly halfway between my cell and Connor's, way too amused considering the laughter dancing in his eyes and the smirk on his face.

Connor lifted a hand in a lazy wave, then went back to napping.

What was wrong with those two? This wasn't funny. Connor and I were in jail, for goodness' sake.

"Don't I get one phone call?" I was almost positive that was one of my rights.

Dylan nodded, and I was pretty sure I saw his lips twitch. "You do. Who do you want to call?"

Well, I hadn't thought about that, so I didn't have an answer.

The Emery brothers started banging tin cups against the bars. Why didn't I have a tin cup? Dylan pivoted, giving Dick and Ted a look that had them scurrying back to their cots.

"I want to call Jenn," I said. Was it weird to call the fiancée of the man whose jail cell you were being held in?

Dylan chuckled. "I already called her. She's here to bail you out."

"What about Connor?"

"What about him?"

"None of this was his fault. You need to let him go."

Dylan turned his back on me and moved to Connor's cell. "You want your phone call now?"

Was Dylan whispering something to Connor?

"Nope," Connor said after a delay in answering the question. "This is the most peace I've had all day. I'll call my brother after I finish my nap."

"Hey, guys, what's going on?" I needed a tin cup to bang on the bars.

"Not a thing," Dylan said. He unlocked my cell door. "You're free to go."

"You need to let Connor go, too." I walked over to his cell. "I'll bail you out." He let out a snore, a very fake one. "Fine. Stay here and rot, for all I care." But I did care. He'd stayed by my side since I'd almost killed him this morning . . . yesterday morning? And what had I done for him? Besides almost killing him? Landed him in jail, that's what. Some friend I was.

"You could bail us out," Ted, or maybe Dick, said. I never could keep them straight.

"Maybe next time." I followed Dylan down the hall to his office.

Jenn jumped up from the chair she was sitting in. "Are you okay?" She pulled me into a tight hug.

"Yeah." And much to my embarrassment, I burst into tears. Again. I was tired of crying, but the wounds were still raw.

What kind of husband cheated on you, and then had the gall to charge you with breaking and entering when you refused to laugh off his *little* mistake? The rotten kind, just like my father. Not only had he been a rotten husband—still was, actually, since my mother kept taking him back—he hadn't been the greatest dad in the world, either.

My judgment in the opposite sex can't be trusted. That's it. You're done with men. Do you hear me, Autumn? Done. I wished I were Catholic so I could go be a nun, unless there were rules against joining a convent if you've already had sex. I'd have to google that later.

Jenn caressed my back. "Let's get you out of here, sweetie."

"I'm all for that."

"Jenny's going to take you to our apartment for the rest of the night," Dylan said. "Oh, and I have your samples."

"Really?" I lifted my teary face from Jenn's shoulders. "How'd you manage that?"

He shrugged. "I have my ways."

"You're a good man, Dylan Conrad." And he was. Blue Ridge Valley had lucked out when he'd decided to quit his job as a vice detective in Chicago to come to our little town as police chief. Although after learning his story, I didn't blame him for wanting to come to a place where he could find peace. And he'd found it in both the valley and Jenn.

Jenn tugged the knit cap from my head. "I don't think you need this anymore, since your cat burglar days are officially over."

I snorted. "Yeah, I think I'll keep my day job. I pretty much suck at cat burglaring."

"Go on, get out of here, you two." Dylan put his hand on Jenn's butt, giving her a push.

"Copping a feel, there, Chief?" she said, then squeezed his butt, copping her own feel.

That was what I wanted, what I thought I'd had with Brian. To be totally in love and loved that way back, to know that there was no other woman in the world for him but me.

Not only did I suck at being a cat burglar, but obviously at choosing who to fall in love with.

CHAPTER EIGHT

~ Connor ~

"WHAT'S UP?" I ASKED AFTER taking a seat in Dylan's office. When he'd mouthed *stay behind* to me before he freed Autumn, I knew he wanted to talk to me privately.

"I called your brother to bail you out. You want to wait for him before I bring you up to speed? He should be here any minute."

"Where's that hooligan who claims he's my brother?" Adam leaned in the doorway, a smirk on his face.

"That would be me. Come in. Pretty sure Dylan's about to lay some heavy shit on me."

Adam and I were identical twins, and the only way most people who knew us could tell us apart was by the color of the small earrings we each wore in one ear. I suppose we could wear our hair differently, but we both liked the same style, longer than a military cut, but not over our ears or touching our collars.

"I filled Adam in on why you were arrested when I called him, so we'll just get to the meat of the problem. I didn't include Autumn in this conversation because of some of the things Brian said that I don't think she needs to hear right now." Dylan leaned back in his chair. "Brian's being a real dick. He's insisting on charging you both with breaking and entering unless Autumn takes him back. If she refuses, she'll still be charged, but he'll drop them on you if you sign a statement that you'll never talk to her or go near her again."

"That's bullshit," Adam and I said together. Autumn had

been my friend years before Brian had ever come on the scene, and I wasn't giving her up for a man who was turning out to be a real prick.

"Figured that's what you'd say. Apparently he sees you as a threat. Even if you signed a ridiculous statement like that, I don't see how he can enforce it. But he's going to cause you as much trouble as he can if you don't step out of the picture, so take that as a warning."

"Whatever. I'm not signing anything of the sort, so he can bring it on. He obviously didn't care enough about Autumn to keep his pants zipped. Why's he so determined to keep her?"

"I guess in his mind he loves her, but he doesn't see why what he did was such a big deal." Dylan's lips curled in disgust. "He said, bumping shoulders with me as if we were best buds, 'It's different for men, right? A little pussy on the side doesn't mean anything.' I wanted to knock him into next week."

"What a shithead," Adam and I said together. It was a good thing Brian hadn't said that to me. Forget next week. I would have knocked him into the next millennium.

"You two do know it's spooky when you do that," Dylan said. "Say the same thing at the same time."

"It's a twin thing," Adam and I said as one, getting a laugh from our new police chief. Adam glanced at me. "What's the plan, baby brother?"

From the time we'd learned Adam was older by two minutes, he'd loved rubbing that little fact in by calling me *baby brother*.

"Well, *old* man, the plan is that Brian can go fuck himself. At the moment that's all I got." It wasn't, but that was my business. Hearing Dylan confirm what an ass I'd already begun to think Brian was, I decided I'd glue myself to Autumn's side for a while and do what I could to see her happy again. I did love seeing her smile.

C

"What didn't you tell Dylan?" Adam asked after we got back to my place.

I handed him a beer, then stretched out on my distressed brown leather couch. One problem with having a twin who could read your mind was that, well, he could read your mind. Not always a good thing.

"What time is it?"

"Two in the morning," he said without looking at his watch.

"I should be dead on my feet, but I want to go build a cabin or something."

Adam raised a black brow identical to mine. "I'm the builder. You just sell them. Stop ignoring my question. What's going on between you and Autumn?"

I rested my elbows on my knees, staring down at the floor. "I don't know. I saw her pretty pink girlie parts this morning, and I haven't been able to think straight since." *Shut your mouth, Connor.*

"Whoa, back up. All Dylan said was that you rescued her when she wrecked her car. He didn't say a damn word about you seeing things you shouldn't have."

"Because he doesn't know that part and neither should you. My mouth got ahead of my brain."

I leaned my head back and closed my eyes. Adam and I didn't have secrets from each other. Never had. But for the first time that I could remember, I didn't want to share what was going on in my mind.

Not that I knew exactly what was going on in that gray matter. There was a jumble of things up there. Of seeing something I shouldn't have, of Autumn being a friend, of me in the blink of an eye wanting that friend under me—or over me—and of me being a douchebag for even thinking of her that way when she was both my friend and hurting.

"I'm not going to talk to you about anything I saw."

I stood, then walked away from my brother's concerned face.

"Connor?"

At the hallway of my log home, I paused. "Yeah?" I said, not looking back.

"You need to think real hard before you cross a line with Autumn that you can't uncross."

Like I didn't know that. I went to my bedroom, closing the door behind me. Adam didn't need me to show him the way out.

❦

Autumn giggled. "That tickles."

I leaned on the wall next to Dylan's kitchen the next morning, sipping a cup of coffee as Autumn rolled around on the floor with eleven rambunctious Labrador puppies doing their best to lick her from head to toe. Daisy, their mother, looked on with what appeared to be amusement in her big brown doggy eyes.

"Autumn manage to get some sleep?" I asked Jenn. Dylan had already left for work when I'd arrived to pick up Autumn. She was supposed to meet Brian at their house this morning, and we'd need to leave soon if we were going to beat him there.

Jenn nodded. "A few hours." She pulled me into the kitchen. "Are you going to tell her what Brian's demanding from you?"

"I don't want to, but she'll hear it one way or another. Probably from Brian." Autumn had enough on her plate. I didn't want her to worry about me, but she would.

"Probably. Well, you better get going. Dylan said to call him if there's any trouble."

"I will."

"Thanks for picking me up, but Jenn could have run me home," Autumn said as we walked to the car. "By now you're probably thinking I'm a real pain in the butt."

"Nah, haven't once thought that. You look better than the last time I saw you." The jeans and white turtleneck sweater were tighter on her than what she usually wore. And speaking of butts, hers was pretty damn sexy in those jeans.

"Jenn loaned me some clothes."

Ah, that explained it. Autumn was curvier than Jenn and a bit more endowed in the chest. I was looking forward more than I should to spending the day with her. After she finished with Brian, I was taking her to lunch and then to her appointment at the country club.

When that was done, I was driving her to Asheville to rent a car until she could make other arrangements. I hadn't told her that I'd rescheduled a showing I had this afternoon so I could spend day with her. She'd only feel even more guilty about monopolizing my time than she already was.

I put my hand on her lower back, liking it there, as we walked the last few steps to my car. And as I opened the door for her, getting another one of her special smiles, my heart took a little bounce. I wished it wouldn't do that.

Brian's arrival ended up being anticlimactic. Autumn decided she had no desire to see him and went for a walk, leaving me to deal with him.

"Where's Autumn?" were his first words when I opened the door.

"Beats me. She said you can come in and get your stuff. I'm tasked with making sure that's all you take."

The glare he sent me could have burned me where I stood if I'd been a weaker man, but I was Autumn's protector today, the only fire wall between my friend and him, and I refused to cower.

"You don't seem to understand that I can destroy you, and in doing so, destroy your brother right along with you."

"I'm quaking in my boots," I mocked. "Threaten us all

you want, but two against one, meaning me and Adam if you're too dense to get that, doesn't seem like a fair fight. You might also want to consider that if you decide to mess with us, you'll be taking on the whole town. We were born here. You weren't."

"Asshole," he said, then pushed past me.

"Dirtbag," I muttered. I followed him into what had once been his bedroom with Autumn, watched everything he took, and then followed him back to the front door.

"You haven't heard the last of me," he said as he not so accidently bumped into me, pushing me against the door as he walked out.

Although I wanted to smash his face in, I didn't for Autumn's sake. "Bring it on, dude," I said loud enough for him to hear.

His father had arrived in Blue Ridge Valley fifteen years ago, opening his car dealership after some murky dealings with his Charlotte, North Carolina, location that no one had been able to get to the bottom of.

Fifteen years was still considered a newcomer by our residents, and Brian had attended private school in Asheville, so he wasn't close to being one of us. He could make all the threats he wanted, but my town would always have the backs of their family. Because that was what a small town was. Family.

CHAPTER NINE

~ Autumn ~

"SHE'S WHAT?"

"You heard me," Jenn said a week after I'd been freed from jail. "Log on to Facebook. She's live streaming it right now."

"Hold on." I set my phone down, then flipped open my laptop, brought up the *Life in the Valley* page, and stared at it in horror. Mary Ballard, owner of Mary's Bread Company, stood in front of Brian's dealership, holding a sign that said NO DONUTS FOR CHEATERS. Her hair was purple today, but tomorrow it might be chartreuse. Or pink or green.

Mary was the best doughnut and pastry baker in all the Blue Ridge Mountains. I suppose if you were going to punish someone, depriving them of her baked goods was high on the list, and Brian did love her chocolate-iced doughnuts.

Standing with her was Hamburger Harry, our infamous moonshiner, and Melba Waters, the owner of Melba's Pancake House. Harry's sign said NO MOONSHINE FOR CHEATERS, and Melba's naturally said NO PANCAKES FOR CHEATERS.

I turned on the sound to hear them chanting, "Brian Stratton is a cheater," over and over. Crazy people. I closed my laptop.

"Unbelievable," I said, coming back on the line. "It's both funny and embarrassing."

Jenn chuckled. "Well, it's not like what he did is a secret anymore. He's the one who should be embarrassed."

Yeah, the big disadvantage of small-town living. Everyone knew your business almost before you did. "Can you get Dylan to talk to them, make them stop?"

"He's already headed that way. Brian called, wanting them arrested."

"Will he do that?" How many people was I going to have to feel guilty over for getting them jailed?

"No. He's just going to send them on their way."

That was a relief. After hanging up, I grabbed my purse and keys to go to my mother's for lunch. I didn't bother changing out of my yoga pants and favorite oversize T-shirt. In her depressed cycle Mom wouldn't look any better than me. Dad had been kicked out again, and it would be the same thing I'd heard countless times before. How miserable she was, what a bastard he was, a detailed report on his newest squeeze. And then at the end, how much she missed him and wanted him back. I dreaded the visit, but she was my mother.

She only lived ten minutes from me, and as I drove over in the used SUV that I'd bought yesterday, I wished that Connor was with me. She was always on her best behavior when there was a man around. Sometimes she was even flirty, and I often wondered if she was practicing for when she took my father back, because she always did. But who knew what went on in her mind? Not me.

Since walking in on Lina and Brian, it had been seven days of crying jags, feeling sorry for myself, and then being angry that I'd fallen for Brian's charm. Except when I was with Connor, I'd forget that I was supposed to be miserable.

I didn't know how he managed to cheer me up, but he did. And he'd been there for me every day. Jenn would have been, too, if I'd let her, but she's got Dylan now, and they're planning their wedding. She doesn't need my mess dumped on her.

The good news—I had a new bed, and a call from my

doctor this morning that my test results were all negative. Brian could count his blessings for that because if he'd passed anything on to me, I would have made his sorry life miserable.

Mom's car was in her driveway, which was odd because she always parked in the garage except when Dad was home. Had she forgiven him already? That would be a new record, since she'd kicked him out again only yesterday. If he was here, I wasn't staying. The two of them in the same room were toxic.

Before I reached the front door, it opened, my mom stepping out to meet me. When she was alone, miserable because of my dad's latest cheat, she lived in her robe, no makeup, and her blonde hair limp. Today she was, as she liked to say, "all dolled up." That meant my father was inside. I was tempted to turn on my heels and get back in my car. She must have sensed I was on the verge of bolting, because she grabbed my hand.

"I guess Dad's home?"

"Why would you think that? I told you on the phone last night that he'd moved out."

Okay, I'd apparently stepped into an alternate universe. "Well, you look nice." And she was smiling. Very weird.

"Thank you, honey. Come in. Lunch is ready."

And she was cheerful or was pretending to be. Her smile seemed forced though, and there was an edge to her voice, which put me on alert. Something was up. I dropped my purse on the foyer table and then followed her into the kitchen.

"Oh no." I came to a dead stop at seeing Brian leaning against the counter. "What are you doing here?" And it was a dirty trick to hide his car in Mom's garage.

When I turned to leave, my mom grabbed my arm. "He just wants to talk to you."

"If you would answer my calls, maybe answer the damn door"—he glared at me as if I were the one who was a slimy worm—"which you had no right to change the locks to, since my name is also on the mortgage, then I wouldn't have to pull a sneak attack." His expression softened, and I trusted that even less. "I screwed up, babe, but you love me, so stop this foolish drama trip you're on. You've made your point."

"Foolish drama trip?" And yes, I was shouting like a deranged person. All I needed were about six dozen cats and I could be classified as certifiably crazy.

I walked up to him and poked him in the chest. "This is the last thing I'll ever say to you. From this moment on you only communicate with me through my lawyer." As for still loving him, it might not happen overnight, but I was working on putting an end to that.

With his chestnut-colored hair and golden brown eyes, Brian was a good-looking guy. I think I fell in love with his dimples and easy smile first. There had been a few times this past week that I'd had some doubts, that maybe I was being unreasonable. But they hadn't lasted long. Mostly because of how he'd cheated on me. In his freaking office where every one of his employees—people I personally knew—had to be aware of what was happening. That told me he didn't have any respect for me.

Then there was the fact that he'd never really apologized. He made a mistake. He was weak. It was Lina Kramer's fault. All of that was an excuse for his behavior, and I think the only thing he was sorry for was getting caught.

Where was the man I'd fallen in love with? The one with the sweet dimpled smile and honest eyes? The man standing in my mother's kitchen wasn't him. How had I been so blind to his faults? In my heart I knew the answer. Because I'd wanted my dream of a loving, stable home to come true so badly that I'd refused to see the warning signs, but I saw everything clearly now. There was no difference between Brian and my father.

"Please, just listen to what he has to say, Autumn."

"There's nothing he can say that I want to hear." You would think, considering what my mother had dealt with for most of her marriage, that she'd be helping me toss Brian out the door. She was, after all, a master at showing my father the door.

She tugged on my arm. "Sit down, honey, and let's have a civil lunch and conversation."

I looked from my mother to Brian—who wore an air of confidence that he'd get pesky little me back in line—and decided love was off the table for me. That particular emotion wasn't all it was cracked up to be. If there was any proof of that, it was my mom and dad's relationship. From now on it was going to be all fun and games. Without saying another word, I collected my purse. If Mom wanted to have a nice visit with The Cheater, she was welcome to him.

"Autumn, just hear him out. That's all I'm asking," my mother said as she followed me outside.

I turned and faced her. "Why? So he can sweet-talk his way back into my good graces like Dad does with you? I can't do it. You of all people should understand that. In fact, if you cared a lick about my happiness, you'd be telling me to run from him as far and as fast as I can." I looked into her eyes and saw that she didn't get it, that she never would.

"Men can't help themselves, Autumn. It's just the way they're built. Brian's always been good to you, and you're the one he loves."

"So that makes him cheating on me excusable? Maybe that kind of thinking is good enough for you, but it sure as hell isn't for me." I left before she could say more.

As a mother she should be doing everything in her power to ensure that her daughter didn't repeat her mistakes. That she didn't see that hurt more than anything Brian could do to me.

Back home, I buried myself in the plans for the remodel

of the country club. I was done feeling sorry for myself, and I was done being sad over the breakup of my marriage. If nothing else, the little lunch episode had made me see the light. A new and improved Autumn Archer had been born.

C

Connor had called before I left for the lunch that never happened, telling me he wanted to stop by this evening, that he had a surprise for me. All Connor had seen of me this past week was a crazy woman. One minute angry and defiant, and in the next, a weepy, depressed mess who favored her oldest pair of yoga pants and ratty T-shirts.

The new Autumn shaved her legs for the first time in seven days, put on makeup, and dumped the poor-pitiful-me clothes in favor of skinny jeans and a pale blue sweater. She also decided to make Connor's favorite meal, a big fat cheeseburger and fries.

He'd been so good to me this past week, and I didn't know how I'd have managed without him. The doorbell rang, and with it, my heart did a little bounce.

CHAPTER TEN

~ Connor ~

"HEY . . ." MY voice trailed off as the door opened fully, revealing a very different Autumn from what I was used to seeing the past week. "Um, you look nice." Real nice, and I particularly liked that blue sweater. And not because it hugged her breasts. Nope, I wasn't even looking there. Mostly.

"Hey back." She stepped aside to let me come in just as Beauregard gave an excited bark. I think he recognized her voice from the times she'd played with him. Her eyes widened, and then she leaned forward, peeking around the doorframe. "You borrow one of Jenn and Dylan's puppies to come for a visit?"

Not exactly. I picked up the carrier. "Do you know which one this is?"

She took the carrier out of my hand, and as soon as I closed the door behind me, she let the puppy out. Dylan had rescued Daisy from the streets, not learning until later that she was pregnant. Daisy was a full-blooded black Labrador. Her vet guessed that the puppies' father was a German shepherd mix.

"It's Beauregard," she exclaimed as the puppy pranced around her feet, yipping for attention. "Hey, Beau. How's my best guy?" She picked him up, letting him lick her chin.

Jenn had told me that Beau was Autumn's favorite of the bunch. I'd had some doubts about my plan driving over, but seeing the two of them together, maybe Autumn would be happy that Beauregard was now hers.

Beau was the closest in color to his mother, almost black,

but with a reddish tint and longer fur than Daisy. He'd been named Beauregard after the bull Dylan had found and returned to its owner, and that was a story the town's residents still talked about.

I followed the two of them into the living room—Autumn giggling and Beau doing his best to clean her neck with his tongue—and settled on the sofa. Autumn sat at the opposite end with Beau on her lap.

It was great seeing her laughing and looking like the Autumn I'd known before Brian broke her heart. What had changed between yesterday and tonight? For all my effort not to, and for all the talks I'd given myself over the past week, I was still thinking dirty thoughts of her.

But I didn't do girlfriends. Not after seeing how broken Adam had been after Savannah left. I would never let a woman rip my heart out like that. And even if Autumn was interested in having a little fun, she was still married. I didn't touch married women, even separated ones. I dated a lot, but I didn't play in my backyard, another reason Autumn was off-limits.

Dating local women when you lived in a small town tended to get messy, especially if the relationship ended badly. The whole damn town thought they were entitled to put their nosy noses into your business, and when they took sides, no good could come of it. Although I had nothing to compare them to, Blue Ridge Valley being the only place I'd lived, it wouldn't surprise me if someone did a study that proved our denizens were the number one nosiest residents on the planet.

After giving the puppy a few minutes to calm down, I said, "What's new?" The question was an invitation for Autumn to clue me in to the change in her since I'd seen her last night when I'd dropped by with a pizza. I'd taken to doing that each evening, knowing that if I didn't come by, some kind of food in hand, and sit with her, she wouldn't eat.

After she told me about Brian showing up at lunch and her mother begging her to listen to him, I pushed my ass deeper into her sofa to keep from storming out the door. First I'd find Brian. I was normally an easygoing guy, but I'd like to see him missing a few front teeth, courtesy of my fists. As for her mother, I wanted to give that woman a tongue lashing. Considering all that Melinda Archer had lived through since marrying Ray, you'd think the woman would love her daughter enough to not want to see Autumn repeat her mistakes.

"So I had this epiphany," Autumn said, bringing my attention back to her. "I'm not meant for love or marriage. My parents made sure of that, considering they suck at being role models for a happy marriage. Because of them, I have lousy judgment in men, witness Brian. But since I like sex, I'm only going to have affairs from now on." She gave me an entirely pleased-with-herself grin.

I about swallowed my tongue while somehow managing not to stick my hand in the air, eagerly waving it to volunteer for sex with Autumn. "You don't mean that," I said, wincing at how angry my voice sounded at the thought of any man touching her.

"Oh, but I do. I've been trying to think of who should be my first, but what are my choices here? Hamburger Harry is way too old and Dylan's taken, but maybe Tommy Evans? A cop in uniform is kind of sexy, and he's single." She scrunched her eyebrows together. "Probably not a good idea to troll for guys around here. Everyone would know about it within minutes if I spent the night with Tommy." She smiled brightly at me. "I should go to Asheville for the weekend, see what cute guys they have."

Like hell that was going to happen without me being there to watch over her. Thinking of some dude's hands on her made me want to break something. This entire conversation was pissing me off. "Beau is yours," I said, as much to surprise her as to get her off the subject of Asheville's cute guys.

She glanced down at the puppy, now asleep on her lap, then looked at me. "What do you mean?"

When I'd thought of asking Jenn if she and Dylan would be willing to give up one of Daisy's puppies, the idea had been to cheer Autumn up. Somehow she'd found her cheer without my help.

"I mean that he now belongs to you if you want him. You work from home unless you have an appointment, and he'll be good company. As he grows older, he'll make a great guard dog. If you don't, Jenn said to send him back home."

Her eyes lit up, and she lifted the puppy in the air. "Did you hear that, Beau? You're mine now." Beauregard yawned.

"I have a bunch of stuff for him in my car. Food, leash, bed, his favorite treats. I'll go get them."

When I stood, she set Beau on the sofa, then jumped up and gave me a hug. I closed my eyes and swallowed a groan while managing not to bury my nose in her hair and breathing in her cinnamon and apple scent.

Down, boy.

She was going to feel what was happening below my belt in about five seconds. "I'll just go get that stuff." When I reached my car, I put my hands on the roof and dipped my head, giving myself a firm talking-to. Everything about Autumn suddenly fascinated me, and I was seeing a woman who'd been a friend since first grade in a whole new light.

My timing sucked. Why couldn't I have had this revelation before Brian came into the picture? All she needed from me now was to be her friend. Not to mention that if Jenn got a hint of what was going on in my head, she'd castrate me for the things I'd like to do with Autumn.

I slapped my hand on the car's roof. Orphaned at the age of nineteen, Adam and I had made something of ourselves by sheer willpower and determination. Those were both strengths I would call on to get my act together. Loaded down with puppy supplies, I headed back inside, satisfied I'd gotten my head back where it belonged.

☾

"I can't believe Dylan and Jenn were willing to give up one of their puppies," Autumn said as we ambled along behind Beau.

"Only because it was you." We'd grilled hamburgers, each had two glasses of wine, and I think we were both feeling pretty mellow. Autumn was still in her happy place, and I hoped she meant it when she'd said that she was done being sad. I didn't hope she meant it when she'd said she was going to go trolling in Asheville.

It was a clear spring night, only a little chilly. The dog was stretched out to the end of his leash, darting from one interesting smell to another. I breathed in the fresh mountain air as I lifted my head to see the stars.

"Quick, make a wish," I said as a falling star shot across the sky.

She tilted her face up. "Oh, cool. Okay, I made mine. What'd you wish?"

I bumped shoulders with her. "If I tell you, it won't come true." Without even thinking about it, I'd wished that someday I'd get to kiss her.

"Then I'm not telling you either." She slipped her arm around mine.

Now that I'd thought it, wished it, kissing Autumn was in my mind like a drug I had to have. To knock the image of my mouth on Autumn's out of my head, I said, "Are you nervous about our upcoming trial?"

She exhaled a long breath. "A little. I can't believe Brian refuses to drop the breaking and entering charges."

"I'm guessing he's hoping that will be your incentive to take him back." I still hadn't told her the offer he'd made to me.

She gave a very unladylike snort. "Not going to happen."

Which meant we would have to keep our court date next week. That was going to be interesting.

"Think we'll be found guilty and have to go to jail? I don't look real good in orange."

I grinned down at her. "I choose to believe our attorney." We'd hired Jed McConnell, one of two lawyers in Blue Ridge Valley, to represent both of us. He was young, aggressive, and smart. He swore that, if we were found guilty, the most we'd get was community service. Of course, if we were found guilty, that would mean we'd both have a record. Brian was proving to be a real pain in the ass.

"Do you still love him, Autumn?" That question had come out of my mouth from nowhere. Probably because as hard as I'd tried to stop thinking of kissing Autumn, I'd failed.

"I don't know. I don't want to."

It wasn't the answer I wanted to hear.

CHAPTER ELEVEN

~ *Autumn* ~

THE COURTROOM WAS PACKED. THERE was nothing the citizens of Blue Ridge Valley loved more than a delicious scandal, and because of Brian they were sure getting one. Dylan, Jenn, and Adam were front and center, there to support Connor and me.

On one side of them were Hamburger Harry and his ninety-something-year-old mother, Granny, dressed as always in her old-fashioned flowered dress, covering her from her chin to her feet, which were encased in well-worn, lace-up black half boots.

Hamburger should feel right at home considering he'd come in front of Judge Padgett more times than anyone could remember. So far Judge Padgett hadn't been able to put a stop to Hamburger's moonshining activities, which was a relief to those who were lucky enough to get one of his mason jars. Jenn's favorite was his apple pie flavor. Mine was the peach pie.

On the opposite side of Jenn, Dylan, and Adam were our mayor, Jim John Jenkins, and his wife, Dorie. Next to Dorie was Mary, and today her hair was pink, her eyeshadow pink, and her multiple earrings also pink. Her dress was lemon yellow. Mary was in her sixties and had more energy than I could ever hope for.

The only people missing seemed to be my parents. My mother was mortified by her daughter, embarrassed that I was the talk of Blue Ridge Valley. Shouldn't she be angry with Brian about that instead of me? As for my dad, he was too wrapped up in his new squeeze to much care about what was going on with me.

I glanced at Connor, who was sitting next to me, getting a wink and a warm smile from him. He didn't look at all concerned, which helped calm me. Our attorney had wanted to ask for separate trials, but Connor and I had refused. If we went down, we were going to do it together.

The buzz of voices all of a sudden quieted, and then the whispers started. "Cheater," Mary hissed before I could turn to see what was happening.

Brian had come in. I decided it was a good time to make some notes. The only thing I could think of was a grocery list, so keeping my eyes downcast, I wrote *eggs*. I'd made it to number four on my list, *wine (lots of wine),* when from under my lashes I saw a brown belt I recognized. Why was Brian standing in front of me? Was that allowed in court? Wasn't it like intimidating a witness or something?

"Autumn?"

I put my hand over my list so he couldn't see it and wrote *cabbage, cabbage, cabbage and more cabbage.* Brian hated cabbage, couldn't stand the smell of it cooked, so cabbage wasn't allowed in the house. I was going to make cabbage soup and anything else I could think of with cabbage in it.

"Autumn, I'm speaking to you."

Next to me Connor growled. Before he decided to tackle Brian and take him to the floor, I figured I'd better acknowledge The Cheater's presence.

I took my time lifting my head. "Oh, were you?" It gave me a little thrill that, as I met his gaze, there wasn't the slightest hitch in my breathing when I looked into his flecky gold-brown eyes. Score one for me.

He scowled at Connor, then leaned down, putting his face close to mine. "This is your last chance to stop this. Tell me I can come home, and I'll drop the charges." He glanced at Connor. "I'll even drop them on him."

"Want to hear a secret?" I closed the gap between us, almost laughing when he smiled, as if he really believed he was about to be invited home. It had grown eerily silent, as if everyone behind me was straining to hear us. To make it easy on them, I raised my voice to say, "I'd rather go to jail than live with you."

"Ya tell him, girlie," Granny yelled loud enough for those even in the back to hear, following it with the pounding of her cane on the floor.

I glanced over my shoulder, grinning at her.

"Tha jail ain't sucha bad place," Hamburger said. "Might wanna bring your own piller, though. Ones they got now be hard as a rock." Well, he'd know, considering how much time he spent there. He glared at Dylan as if Dylan should immediately do something about the jail's pillows.

"You people are ridiculous," Brian said. "Don't say I didn't give you a chance, Autumn." He stomped over to the prosecutor's table.

"Wouldn't think of it," I muttered. I patted Connor's arm. "I'm proud of you for not punching his lights out."

"It was a close call, believe me."

What Brian didn't know was that Connor and Adam had done a little investigating by way of taking Lina out for a drink. Between two gorgeous guys giving her attention, along with the drinks they plied her with, she'd gotten rather chatty. Turned out that she had a lot of dirt on The Cheater, like the names of three more women he'd been with since we got engaged a year ago. At this point it wouldn't surprise me if there were even more.

That had gone a long way in hardening my heart against him. I'd almost had to bite off my tongue a few minutes ago to keep from telling him I was on to him. But—and no one knew this, not even Connor—I'd slipped over to Asheville after learning about Brian's cheating heart and met with a divorce attorney. She'd told me to keep that information to myself for now, that it was best Brian didn't know that I knew. It was going to be our ace in the hole.

Jed McConnell, our attorney, and Macon Prescott, the

prosecutor, walked out, taking their seats at their respective tables. Jed slid a note over to Connor and me.

Celebratory drinks later?

Connor took the note, writing, You buying?

Jed snorted. "Trust me, you are. Client drinks are a billing item," he said, talking out of the corner of his mouth.

Although I liked their confidence in the outcome of the trial, I didn't understand how they could joke at a time like this. In a few hours I could be wearing god-awful orange.

"Hear ye, hear ye. Court is now in session," Herman, the court bailiff for as long as anyone could remember, said in a booming voice.

I sat up straighter when Judge Padgett entered from a door off to the side. Maybe in his sixties, he was about five feet tall with a full head of pure white hair. I'd never been in his courtroom before, but I'd heard stories about him.

One rumor was that he'd gone to the Big City—what locals called New York—after graduating high school, hoping to make it big as a comedian. When that failed, he'd made his father happy by following in the older man's footsteps and going to law school.

His nickname around town was The Funny Little Judge, but he was known to be fair. He fluffed out his robe, then sat in his chair high above us. When he banged his gavel, I almost jumped out of my skin.

Connor put a hand on my knee under the table. "Everything's going to be okay, Autumn," he whispered.

Alert brown eyes narrowed onto Connor. "Unless you want to share with the court what you're whispering into her ear, Connor Hunter, you will be quiet unless told to speak."

"Yes, sir," Connor said.

Seriously? Not even a minute into the trial that could ruin my life, we were already being reprimanded? Then the judge winked at me. I had no idea how to interpret that.

Judge Padgett surveyed his courtroom, his gaze stopping on someone behind me. "Glad to see you in the peanut gallery for a change instead of at the defense table, Hamburger."

"Not half 'in glad as me, Judge," Hamburger said, causing a ripple of laughter, including from the judge.

Judge Padgett's gaze landed back on Connor and me. "Seems like you two are the entertainment of the day."

Oh joy. I didn't want to be anyone's entertainment.

"Last time I had a courtroom packed this full was back in '82 when Ruben Crane sued his own self for letting himself get drunk, which resulted in his falling from the bar stool, flattening his nose." Judge Padgett's eyes scanned the courtroom. "Y'all remember that?"

A chorus of, "Yes, Your Honor," sounded behind me, and I think that was Granny cackling and slapping her knee.

"Well, let's get this show on the road." He banged on his gavel again, but I was ready for it this time. Connor and I had talked it over with our attorney and had decided to forgo a jury trial. In this town that could have turned into a three-ring circus, and Jed trusted Judge Padgett to do the right thing.

After opening statements, Brian was called to the stand and sworn in. "Your Honor," Macon Prescott said. "Before I question Mr. Stratton, I would like to show the court the video taken from Mr. Stratton's dealership's security camera on the night in question."

Connor and I had seen it in our attorney's office after it was entered as evidence. It hadn't seemed so bad then, but now, watching it along with practically the entire town of Blue Ridge Valley, it was embarrassing. Connor had been right. I did look like a cat burglar's poor cousin, and I looked guilty as hell. I picked up my pen and, at the bottom of my grocery list, added, *Buy a jailhouse ~~pitter~~ pillow.*

Honestly I could barely stand to look at Brian as he sat on the witness stand, a smug expression on his face. I was beginning to wonder what I'd ever seen in him. But that was good, right? It meant I was over him.

"What's that Mr. Hunter just tossed over the fence?" Judge Padgett asked, drawing my attention back to what was going on.

"My wife's sample case," Brian answered.

"Objection," I said, the word shooting out of my mouth before I could stop it. Judge Padgett looked at me; Connor looked at me; our attorney looked at me, as well as the prosecutor and Brian. Most likely the entire audience behind me was staring a hole through the back of my head.

If I had one wish in my life—just one—I'd use it right now and have the floor open up and swallow me whole.

"And what are you objecting to?" Judge Padgett said.

"Um ..."

"Stand up, young lady."

Oh God, I wasn't sure my legs would hold me up. I stood, putting my hands on the table for support. "My ... ah, my objection is to him calling me his wife. Could you make him stop doing that?"

CHAPTER TWELVE

~ Connor ~

"WELL, SHE IS MY WIFE, so I don't see why I can't say she is," Brian said.

"Then you shouldn't have cheated on her," Mary said. A chorus of agreements rumbled through the room.

Judge Padgett banged his gavel. "Order in the court! Order in the court!"

I tuned out the noise, focusing my attention on Autumn as she sank into her seat. "Well, that was fun."

She giggled. "Tell me I didn't do that."

"Nope, you did it, all right."

"Next time you want to make an objection," Jed whispered, "might be best to let me do it."

"That's my first and last time doing that," Autumn assured him.

Judge Padgett banged his gavel again, getting a quiet courtroom. He turned in his seat to face Brian. "Mr. Stratton, the court orders you not to refer to Mrs. Stratton as your wife from here on out."

"Can I object to that, Judge?" Brian said.

I rolled my eyes. What an idiot.

"No, you cannot." He nodded at Macon Prescott. "You may continue."

Macon glanced over at our table, and I was pretty sure his heart wasn't in this case. Adam and I had built him a log house, and I'd gotten to know him. He was one of the good guys.

He walked to the witness box, standing to the side, giving everyone a clear view of Brian. "Mr. Stratton, did Mr.

Hunter or Mrs. Stratton steal anything that belonged to you?"

"Well, no, but they—"

"Did they damage any property?"

Brian's eyes narrowed. "What's your point?"

"Please answer the question, Mr. Stratton."

"No, but—"

"Would you have given Mrs. Stratton her sample case if she'd asked you for it?"

Silence.

"Mr. Stratton?"

"Why should I have when she kicked me out?"

"She kicked you out 'cause you're a cheater," Mary said, and not in a quiet voice.

"Cain't abide cheaters," Granny hollered. She was half-deaf and tended to yell. "Nary a one of my six husbands cheated."

"Paula Sue's pa used to look at Mirna Lawson's boobies," Hamburger said.

Granny snorted. "Cain't blame a man for looking when a hussy shows off her ankles and her titties 'bout fall out the top of her dress." This was, of course, shouted, and giggles and laughter filled the room.

Paula Sue was Hamburger's half-sister, long dead now, along with Granny's six husbands. I had no idea who Mirna Lawson was. I glanced over my shoulder. Dylan was pinching the bridge of his nose, his eyes squeezed shut and his lips quivering. My twin was mimicking him. Next to Dylan, Jenn had her face buried against Dylan's arm, her shoulders shaking.

Autumn was doing a head-desk thing, her shoulders also shaking. Jed was as rigid as a stone, staring straight ahead. I got the impression that if he moved an inch, he would lose it.

Judge Padgett was in the middle of a coughing fit with tears rolling down his cheeks. Macon Prescott, still standing near the witness box, seemed to be attempting to bite off his thumb. The bailiff was bent over, slapping his knee as laughter poured out of him.

Any Blue Ridge Valley resident not here today would hear about the proceedings within minutes of court being adjourned. That was how small towns worked. Every single person missing this trial, when repeating the story, would swear they were sitting in the courtroom and were telling the tale firsthand.

I absolutely loved my town. Brian seemed to be the only one not amused. He sat in the witness box, scowling, his attention fixed on Autumn. I wanted to poke out his eyes just for looking at her.

❦

"To the best attorney in the world," Autumn said, raising her champagne glass.

I raised mine, clinking it against Jed's. "Hear, hear." We were celebrating in the lounge at Fusions with Jed, Adam, Dylan, and Jenn. Fusions was the only other restaurant in town besides Vincennes with a decent lounge. It was our go-to place for a beer because Jenn worked at Vincennes, so hanging out there felt like going back to work for her.

"Can't say I did much," Jed said. "In fact, I'd say Macon won the case for you. After he finished questioning Brian, the smartest thing I could do was rest my case."

That was true, and it had confirmed my suspicion that Macon didn't think much of Brian's insistence on charging us with breaking and entering. Still, I gave Jed credit for recognizing that.

As for Judge Padgett, he was a cunning old coot. Without leaving the bench to think it over, he found us guilty of trespassing, a misdemeanor offense, then said to Brian, "You happy now, Mr. Stratton?"

"No, I am not," Brian said.

At that, the judge immediately reversed his own decision, finding us not guilty of anything, saying, "Well, if you're not going to be happy with my decision, might as well go all out." Then he shook his finger at Brian. "You brought this turn of events onto yourself, Mr. Stratton, and now you're wasting my time and the court's with this foolishness."

I had no idea if it was legal for Judge Padgett to reverse his own decision like that, but I wasn't about to question it. As for Brian, I got a death glare as he stormed out of the courtroom. I somehow managed not to give him the finger.

"I thought I was going to die when Granny started talking about titties," Jenn said.

"You and everyone else in the courtroom." I grinned at Autumn. "We're notorious now."

"Oh, yay. Always wanted to be a legend."

"How's Beauregard?" Dylan asked.

Autumn's eyes lit up. "He's so adorable. I'll bring him to visit his mama and brothers and sisters."

I watched her as she talked dogs with Dylan and Jenn, and as I'd often done since the day I'd rescued her, I wondered why it had taken me so long to see how special she was. It bugged me that my attraction to her had begun with her flashing her lady parts, but like it or not, that had been the catalyst in seeing her in a whole new light. Trust me, I wasn't sorry for that. Not at all. Still, I'd like to be able to say I was attracted to her before she flashed me.

Feeling my twin's eyes on me, I glanced at Adam, who was drilling a hole right through my head, plucking out the secrets I'd been trying to hide, like this new thing I had for Autumn.

He didn't look happy.

"I need to head out," Jed said. "I'll take care of the tab."

"Let me get ours." Dylan pulled out his wallet.

Jed shook his head. "This one's on me. You can get it next time."

"Thanks, man." Dylan pushed his chair back. "Jenn and I are going to take off, too."

"You need a ride home?" Adam asked Autumn.

The hell? "I'll run her home." My brother wasn't trying to make a play for Autumn, but he was trying to keep me away from her. Or more accurately, trying to protect her from me.

He gave me a we'll-talk-later look. "Take care, Autumn," he said, squeezing her shoulder, then walked out with Dylan and Jenn.

"And then there were two." I poured the last of the champagne from the bottle our waiter had left on the table into our glasses. "Happy you're not going to be wearing orange for the next six months or whatever?"

"You have no idea." She drained her champagne glass. "I need to get home and let Beau out. He's been in his crate all afternoon."

I stood and held out my arm. "Your chariot awaits, my lady."

É

"I went to Asheville a few days ago and talked to a divorce attorney," Autumn said.

"Oh?" I perked up at hearing that. "What did he say?" After returning from Fusions, we were taking Beau for a walk. I enjoyed these evening strolls with Autumn. Sometimes we talked and other times we walked in comfortable silence.

"She. That I can be divorced in forty-five days if Brian doesn't contest it."

"That's fast." It was great, too.

"Yeah, well, that's the good news. The bad is that in North Carolina you have to live apart for a year before you can file. We're on day thirteen, so only three hundred and fifty-two days to go, and then I'll file."

"That sucks." I wanted her to be back to Autumn Archer

right now.

She nodded. "What I said."

Autumn wrapped her arm around mine, something she liked to do when we walked. It was a beautiful mountain night. She was a pretty woman, but in the moonlight she was breathtaking. We'd been spending a lot of time together, and my interest in her was growing. She was supposed to be off-limits, but I was having a hard time keeping her in that category.

It seemed that she didn't think of me as anything more than a friend, except . . . except every once in a while I'd catch her looking at me in a way she never had before. As if she liked what she was seeing.

Beau found a bush that apparently had the most wonderful smells and was sniffing it from top to bottom. Autumn leaned against a nearby tree, letting him have his fun.

I stood a few feet in front of her, my hands stuffed into the pockets of my jeans. I was dying inside to touch her, to spread my fingers over her cheek, and with my thumb under her chin, lift her face as I slowly lowered my mouth to hers. What would she taste like? Apples and cinnamon, I guessed. Like fall, all the scents and tastes of my favorite season.

"Why are you looking at me like that?" she whispered.

"I want to kiss you." I hadn't meant to say that.

I was forming an apology in my head when she said, "I wouldn't say no."

She should, and I should tell her that, but I didn't. Instead, like a man entranced by a sorceress, I closed the distance between us, and as I had imagined, I splayed my fingers over her cheek and slid my thumb under her chin, lifting her face.

"Autumn," I said and then lowered my mouth to hers. Just a small kiss, I told my brain. My brain went deaf the second my lips touched hers.

I moved my hands to her hips and pulled her against me,

aligning our bodies, then angled my head, deepening the kiss. Our tongues met, caressed, tasted. Autumn moaned, and a bolt of lust shot through me, the power of it so great that I vaguely wondered if a storm had moved in and, somewhere close by, lightning had struck. I'd kissed my fair share of women, but none had almost brought me to my knees, not like this. I was on fire for this woman.

Somewhere in the back of my mind warning bells were going off, but I didn't want to hear them. I let go of her hips and slid my hands under her shirt, flattening the palm of one hand over her lower back, while the other hand found a breast.

When I dipped my finger inside her bra and brushed it across her nipple, she moaned again. It was the most erotic sound I'd ever heard in my life. Her skin was warm and silky, her lips were soft, her mouth delicious. The hand not holding the leash was just as busy as mine, exploring under my shirt.

I kissed my way across her cheek and then down to her neck, to the soft spot under her ear. Before the night was over, I was going to taste her from head to— A car turned the corner, its headlights lighting us up.

We both froze as it passed, the driver honking the horn. Beau barked back. Christ, I'd been so far gone that I'd been ready to make love to her next to a public street. I stepped back.

"Connor?" Her eyes searched mine.

"I'm sorry." She was still a married woman. What if a week, or even a month from now, she decided she still wanted Brian after all? Although she was adamant she was done with him, there was always the chance it could happen. I was not going to be her shame. Since I obviously couldn't be trusted around her, I wouldn't allow myself to be alone with her again as long as she was still married.

I should have let Adam take her home.

CHAPTER THIRTEEN

~ Jenn and Dylan's Wedding ~

"YOU LOOK BEAUTIFUL, AUTUMN," JENN said when I slipped into her hotel room.

I rolled my eyes. "Stop stealing my compliments. Only the bride is allowed to be beautiful on her wedding day. And my God, you're insanely beautiful."

And she was. Her auburn hair was pulled back from her face by a crystal-studded headband and then fell in a cascade down her back. I'd been with her when she picked out her gown, but I'd forgotten how gorgeous it was.

The strapless fall of white silk, close fitted down to her waist, and then a swirl of soft-as-a-cloud material below, was exquisite in its simplicity. Diamond stud earrings and the heart-shaped necklace Dylan had given her were her only jewelry. Strappy white heels completed the perfection of a bride about to marry the love of her life.

Her smile was brilliant. "I never expected to be this happy again. Not after Natalie died. Do you think she's looking down on us?"

"I know she is." We hugged, our love for and memories of her twin sister never forgotten. I'm not sure another person on the planet, except for Savannah, could understand the tears we both tried to vanquish thinking of Natalie missing Jenn's wedding day. And thinking of Savannah, I pulled away, needing to tell Jenn something she wasn't going to like.

"I just ran into Jackson. He said he and Savannah are leaving right after your wedding." I hadn't liked Savannah's agent boyfriend any more than Jenn had on first meeting him.

At the rehearsal dinner he'd never left her alone. At one point, frustrated that we hadn't gotten any time alone with Savannah, we'd tried to pull her away. "We just want some girl time with our best friend," I'd said when he put an arm around her waist, holding her in place.

"Savannah doesn't like leaving my side," he'd replied. "Do you, doll baby?"

Doll baby? Seriously? I'd wanted to stick a fork in his eyes. I'd glanced at Jenn, seeing the same worry on her face. When I tried to capture Savannah's attention to let her know Jenn and I would tackle her ass of a boyfriend to the ground if that was what she wanted, her gaze was glued to the floor. What was so damn interesting about a damn floor?

"No, I don't like leaving you, Jackson," she'd said, sounding like a freaking robot.

Then we'd tried to get her to have lunch with us the following day, and he'd nixed that, too. After the rehearsal dinner we hadn't seen her. They weren't even staying in the valley. Jackson had booked them a room in Asheville. I guess we should feel lucky that she had even shown up.

"I hate him," Jenn said.

"I do, too, but today is for you. We'll worry about her tomorrow." I stepped back and ran my gaze over her. "Dylan should worry about embarrassing himself when he drools at the sight of you walking down the aisle." That put a smile back on her face.

The door opened, and Savannah slipped in. She rushed to us, then pulled us into a hug. "You look so beautiful, Jenn. Please be happy."

"I am and I will be." Jenn glanced toward the door. "Where's Jackson?"

"Mary cornered him, so I was able to sneak away. She's asking a thousand questions about what it takes to be a model."

Jenn and I laughed, and then my amusement faded. "You shouldn't have to sneak away to see your friends, especially on one of their wedding days."

Savannah turned pleading eyes on me. "You don't understand. Please, don't hate me."

"We could never hate you," Jenn said. "We're just so worried about you, and you won't explain anything to us."

"There's nothing to explain. But I couldn't let today go by without telling you both that I love you and miss you so much. I have to go before he comes looking for me." Then she glanced at me. "I'll meet you at the door to the church."

"Nothing to explain, my ass." I said after she was gone. At my wedding she'd at least dressed with us, but apparently even that wasn't allowed now.

"She's starting to scare me."

I glanced at Jenn. "Me, too. But today is your happy day. Don't let her take that away from you, okay?"

"You're right. No sad pandas allowed at weddings, especially when the bride is marrying the most amazing man in the world."

"He is that." He really was, and I was a little envious. I'd thought the same thing on my wedding day. The difference was that Dylan was the real deal. He'd even followed Jenn to Greece just to tell her he loved her. That had been the most romantic thing ever.

"I don't care if you are on your honeymoon. I want to see pictures in my e-mail of Italy and the villa y'all rented as soon as you get there."

She smirked. "You might have to wait a day or two. I'm guessing I'll be a little too"—she made air quotes—"*busy* to take pictures right away."

"Well, since it is your honeymoon . . ." I waggled my eyebrows, causing her to giggle.

A knock sounded on the door, and I went to see who would show up next. It was her parents. Her mom and dad were the coolest people in the world, and I'd often envied her, wishing they were mine. Growing up I spent more time at Jenn's house than my own. Her parents treated us like the kids we were, never putting us in the middle of their problems. Not once had they expected Jenn to choose between them, and I envied her for that.

"Dylan asked me to give this to you," her mom said, handing Jenn a small, square box. I'd intended to leave, allowing Jenn and her parents a private moment, but giving in to curiosity as to what Dylan's wedding gift was, I stayed.

Jenn opened the box, and her smile was as beautiful as everything else about her was on this day. With love shining in her eyes she held up heart-shaped dangling earrings that matched the emerald heart necklace he'd given her when he'd tracked her down in Greece.

"You're one lucky dog, Jenn," I said to her with a smile, and then I slipped out of the room.

She'd hit a billion-dollar lottery in Dylan Conrad. As I walked out of the hotel, heading to the wedding chapel to wait to walk down the aisle ahead of her as her maid of honor, I tried not to envy her.

My jumbled thoughts were on my own wedding and how my dreams had been crushed by my cheating husband. I no longer missed Brian, but I did miss Connor.

Savannah leaned against me when I stopped next to her, but she didn't say anything. Even here where we gathered to walk down the aisle ahead of Jenn, she wasn't free of Jackson. He stood not more than four feet away, his attention on her. Was he worried she'd say or do something he wouldn't like? I slipped my hand down and squeezed hers, getting a squeeze back. She was breaking my heart, but I didn't know how to help her.

I glanced down the aisle. Dylan stood, hands clasped in front of him, his gaze intent on the entrance where I stood. He smiled, and then his eyes moved past me, waiting for his first sight of his bride.

Connor and Adam stood next to him, and I tried not to admire how handsome they were in their black tuxes. But my eyes insisted on seeing nothing but Connor. Since that night we'd kissed a month ago, he'd made himself scarce, and I wished I knew why.

Was our kiss so terrible that he couldn't bear to be around me anymore?

❦

She was so beautiful that I couldn't take my eyes off her. Autumn, not the bride. Although Jenn was beautiful, too. But it was Autumn I couldn't stop looking at. She wore a strapless pale blue, knee-length dress that was a perfect match to her eyes. Her blonde hair was swept up in a fancy do, with tendrils curling around her face and down the back of her neck. My mouth watered just looking at her.

My head was so full of Autumn that I barely heard the words of the minister as he performed the ceremony. Her gaze hadn't once strayed to me. I hadn't even gotten a brief smile as a longtime friend. I wanted to take her by the hand, drag her out of here, and explain why I'd been avoiding her. Would she understand that she was too much of a temptation? That if I got anywhere near her, I'd end up doing more than kissing her?

Until her divorce was final, though, she was strictly hands off. Until Brian was completely out of the picture, I'd stay away. I didn't sleep with married women, even ones separated from their husbands.

I tore my gaze away from her, shifting my attention to Savannah. She was different from the Savannah I'd known in high school, more confident and polished. No surprise since she was now a famous model. She wore a dress identical to Autumn's except it was a darker blue. Her hair was swept up in a style similar to Autumn's.

With her raven-black hair, unusual but beautiful gray

eyes, and creamy skin, she was striking. It wasn't a surprise that she graced the covers of magazines. But I'd noticed a few things at the rehearsal dinner. She'd been unusually quiet and distant—not like the Savannah who once easily laughed—and she had an aura of sadness about her.

I looked at Adam to gauge his reaction to seeing the woman he'd once loved, maybe still did. His gaze was downcast, as if the floor was the most fascinating thing he'd ever seen.

As for Savannah, I'd caught her darting glances at him and thought I'd seen longing in her eyes. Or maybe it was only regret for hurting him when she'd broken up with him that I was seeing. Whichever it was, I would never forgive her for almost destroying him.

"I pronounce you husband and wife. You may kiss the bride."

At the minister's words, I tuned back in to the ceremony. Dylan put his hands on Jenn's cheeks, stared down at her and said, "I love you, Jenny Girl." Then he kissed her.

Reminded of kissing Autumn, I glanced at her to find her looking at me. As soon as our gazes collided, she turned away, shifting her attention to the bride and groom. Had that been hurt I'd seen in her eyes? I almost rolled mine. This wedding was messing with my brain. I was attributing all kinds of emotions to people's eyes.

I'd briefly considered explaining to Autumn why I was keeping my distance but, in the end, had decided it wouldn't be a good idea. Getting her divorce finalized was more than enough for her to deal with right now. It wouldn't be cool to add to her problems with a confession that I lusted after her. It could possibly ruin our friendship. So I'd keep my mouth shut and bide my time until she was Autumn Archer again.

Later, at the reception, I managed to stay on the opposite side of the room from Autumn, figuring that if I was in her general vicinity, I'd end up dancing with her, and then I'd forget I was supposed to be keeping my distance. In fact, I'd been here long enough to pay my respects, so I decided to slip away.

As I walked down the hallway of the country club, headed for the exit, I passed a door that had been left ajar, and hearing my brother's voice. I peeked in, surprised to see Adam and Savannah standing close together, having a quiet conversation. I couldn't hear what they were saying, and Adam's back was to me. When he put his hand on her arm, she flinched.

I gritted my teeth. Why was he even talking to the woman who'd broken his heart? Footsteps sounded, and I glanced down the hall to see Savannah's boyfriend walking toward me. Before he could discover Adam and Savannah together, I headed his way.

"Jackson, you look lost." There was something about the man I didn't like. For one thing he never let Savannah out of his sight. I'd come to the conclusion that he was a controlling bastard.

"I'm looking for Savannah. You see her around?"

"Ah, yeah, not five minutes ago. She was out on the patio. Said she wanted a little fresh air. Come on. I'll show you where the patio is."

Back in the main room, I pointed to the French doors on the other side of the dance floor. "She was out there."

As soon as he walked away, I took out my phone and texted Adam.

Jackson's looking for S

He didn't answer, but a few minutes later Savannah appeared. "I told him you were out on the patio," I said as I walked past her, not waiting for a response as I went in search of my brother.

I caught up with him in the parking lot. "Leaving?"

"Yeah." He clicked the remote on his car.

"You okay?"

"I'm fine."

He wasn't. I could read him like a book. "I'm out of here, too. Want to go get a beer?"

He paused with his hand on the door handle. "Not tonight."

I stood in the parking lot of the country club and watched his car as he drove away. From the day we'd popped out of our mother's womb, Adam and I had shared our thoughts, our dreams, our problems. Until Savannah. He'd refused to tell me what she said when she broke up with him, and he wasn't sharing what was going on in his head now. As far as I was concerned, she couldn't return to New York soon enough.

We were a pair, Adam and I, apparently both wanting women we couldn't have.

CHAPTER FOURTEEN

~ Connor ~

ONE YEAR AND FIFTY-TWO DAYS *after the kiss.* It had felt like a lifetime. Since the night we'd kissed, I'd avoided Autumn as much as a man can avoid a woman in a small town. It hadn't been easy to stay away from her. I still saw her during that time, but never alone.

As for vowing to protect Autumn, I'd done that from afar. No one knew I'd paid a little visit to Brian a few days after I'd kissed her. My warning that I was keeping an eye on him and that he'd better leave her alone seemed to have worked.

It was something of a surprise that a year had passed, and my desire for her hadn't cooled off. I'd even gone to Asheville, to a few clubs on occasion, thinking I'd hook up and would get her out of my system. But my heart hadn't been in it, and I'd done nothing more than buy drinks for a few girls and dance a little.

Then I'd come home alone.

But Autumn's divorce had been final yesterday, so game on. As that day neared, I'd given a lot of thought to what I wanted from her. Answer? I didn't know. All I did know was that she was the only woman I wanted in my bed.

Adam was the one who'd wanted to be in love, and look what that had gotten him. A broken heart. Watching how Savannah had almost destroyed him had taught me one thing. Never allow a woman to have that kind of power over you.

Autumn had said men were good for one thing, that as far as she was concerned, they existed for her personal enjoyment. "End of story," she'd said.

I hadn't heard any doubt in her voice that she meant that, and as far as I was concerned, she could enjoy me to her heart's content. It was the perfect setup. Because of Brian, she was as soured on love as I was. We were friends, liked each other, understood each other, and most importantly we had chemistry. At least I hoped all these things were still true. Maybe she thought I wasn't such a good friend after avoiding her all this time.

The chemistry was there, for sure. Throughout the past year, whenever we were in the same room, something was there between us, something sizzling on the back burner.

She was having a divorce party at her house tonight, and my time avoiding her was over.

❧

The party had been going on for two hours, and I'd stayed back, prowling through Autumn's house like a hungry wolf with his eyes on the prize. The prize Gary Smith, the country club's property manager, was trying to steal from me. The man had been following her around all night like a lovesick puppy.

She'd finished the remodel on the country club, and the results were spectacular. The mayor's wife had been so impressed that she hired Autumn to redo their house. As soon as Adam had finished Dylan and Jenn's log home, they'd asked Autumn to decorate it. She'd reached a point where she now had a waiting list and not just folks from Blue Ridge Valley. People in surrounding towns had heard about her and were hiring her or trying to.

It was a chilly late spring night on her back deck where she had a fire pit burning. Some of her guests were roasting marshmallows for s'mores, while others were drinking mulled wine or beer. Everyone was loose and happy. Well, everyone but me. Gary leaned his mouth close to Autumn's ear and whispered something that made her laugh.

"They'd make pretty babies," Mary said, sidling up next to me, interrupting the plan I was developing in my mind on how to get away with killing Gary Smith.

I grunted.

She smirked up at me. "Thought that was how the wind blew. You need to get your head out of your butt, Connor Hunter, and claim that girl before some other dude does."

"*Dude?*"

"Exactly. Like that one hovering over her right now. Never trust a man with beady eyes." She tottered off on glittery purple heels.

I shook my head, smiling at her retreating back. Tonight her hair was rainbow colored: blue, purple, green, and pink. A gay couple had recently moved into the valley, which had stirred some talk. Mary was rainbow themed—from her head to her feet—to support our LGBT community, all two of them.

I studied Gary Smith's eyes. Yep, they were beady all right and, at the moment, staring down Autumn's tank top. When he slung an arm around her shoulder, I decided it was time to separate my girl from the invading weasel. As I took a step toward her, Brian staggered around the corner of the house.

"Get your hands off my wife," he yelled, his words slurred.

Gary raised his arms, backing away from Autumn. "Hands are off." Still holding them up, he waved his fingers. "See."

What a douchebag. I stepped next to Autumn. "You need to leave, Brian," I said, keeping my voice low, trying not to attract more attention than Autumn and Brian were already getting. Autumn had a large crowd here tonight, and by the pink traveling up her neck and on her cheeks, she was embarrassed.

Brian sneered. "You gonna make me?"

"No, but I am," Dylan said, moving in front of Autumn.

"I just want to talk to my wife." He swayed, doing a shuffle to keep from falling on his ass.

"Well I don't want to talk to you." Autumn scowled. "And as of yesterday I'm not your wife."

"You're as drunk as a skunk that got into Hamburger's stash," Dylan said. "Tell me you didn't drive here."

Adam appeared next to me. "His car's out front, Chief. How about you drive him home? I'll follow and bring you back."

"Better yet, how about he spends a night in a jail cell contemplating the reasons why he shouldn't be driving a car in his condition," Dylan said.

As efficiently as a team of SEALs on a mission, Adam and Dylan flanked Brian and had him out of here before most of Autumn's guests knew he'd crashed her party. Enough had seen and heard, though, and the story would spread. But no one would blame Autumn for Brian's idiocy. Honestly I got why he'd shown up in that condition. He was now officially divorced from an amazing woman. Losing Autumn would definitely have a man thinking it was a good idea to drown his sorrows in drink.

"You okay?" I asked her.

She scoffed. "Other than embarrassed, yeah, I'm fine. I just want him to leave me alone. Is that too much to ask?"

"Nope." This was the closest I'd been to her since the night we'd kissed, the first time I'd caught her cinnamon-and-apples scent in a little over a year. I'd missed everything about her, from her scent to the way her blue eyes lit up when she was happy. I wanted to be the one to put that light back in her eyes.

"Wow, what a jerk," Jenn said, coming up to Autumn and giving her a hug. "You okay, hon?"

"Yeah, but I'm ready for everyone to go home."

"I'll take care of it. Why don't you go inside?" Jenn glanced at me.

Getting the message, I nodded. "I'll stay with her." I picked up her hand and slipped her arm around mine.

I leaned over, breathing her in. She smelled tongue-licking delicious. What was it about her that had me even dreaming about her? I'd never dreamed about a woman before. It was disturbing.

"Hey, babe. Not cool of your ex showing up like that," Gary said, blocking our path to the French doors. He held up a beer. "Brought you a brew."

Autumn shook her head. "No thanks."

"Come on, party's just getting started."

I pushed his bottle-holding hand away from her face. "She said no." *Jackass.* "Party's over. Go home."

"But—"

I bumped him out of the way with my shoulder. We entered her house, and I pulled her to a stop. "Tell me you don't have the hots for him."

CHAPTER FIFTEEN

~ Autumn ~

"SO WHAT IF I DO?" Connor hadn't come within twenty feet of me since the night he'd kissed me. Even a year later I could still feel his lips on mine if I closed my eyes. It made me angry that I'd done that a lot since then, mostly late at night when I couldn't sleep.

Brian had been a total pain the first month, and then he'd miraculously disappeared. Strange that. I did suspect that the late-night breathing-in-my-ears phone calls were from him, so I blocked his number. The only reason he'd finally agreed to sign the divorce papers was because I'd threatened to have my attorney subpoena the women he'd slept with after we'd gotten engaged and after we'd married.

On the nights when I needed to forget about Brian and his betrayal, I'd hug a pillow, close my eyes, and remember a kiss that had shaken me to my core.

After rocking my world, Connor had acted as if it had never happened. Had, in fact, hardly been around. That had hurt. So his asking me now if I had the hots for Gary Smith infuriated me. Gary was an okay guy, but he wasn't the man I wanted to kiss.

Connor narrowed his eyes. "So what if you do? He's a player, Autumn."

"You mean like you?"

He didn't respond. We'd been friends forever, and I knew Connor didn't do serious. Women came and went in his life, and the thing that fascinated me was that they all still liked him when their time with him was up. Ever since the night he'd kissed me, I'd wanted my turn. A fling that would lead nowhere. I was done with love, especially since I no longer trusted my judgment in men. You couldn't depend on them to stay faithful. Brian and my father were proof of that. No, *you scratch my itch, I'll scratch yours* was my new thing going forward.

"Why'd you ignore me?"

His eyebrows furrowed as he peered down at me. "Does it look like I'm ignoring you?"

"I meant all of last year. You avoided me. I want to know why." I hadn't intended to ask him that question, but now that it was out, I was glad.

He pulled us to a stop and then faced me. "I knew if I got near you that I'd kiss you again. And more. Much more."

"Oh."

"Until yesterday you were still married. Now you're not."

"Oh," I said again, apparently reduced to that one word.

"Yeah, *oh*. It's a new day, and you're no longer off-limits." He put his hand on my neck, guiding me down the hall, apparently done with this conversation.

"I need to say goodbye to everyone," I said, craning my head to look behind me.

"Jenn's taking care of that." He pushed me into the bedroom, then backed me up against the wall. "Got any plans for tomorrow?"

His face was close enough to feel his warm breath on my cheek, making it hard to think.

"Easy question, Autumn. Yes or no?"

I shook my head. "Just clean up the house from tonight, then work on a proposal I'm making next week."

"Let's go hiking."

"Really?" Out of our group, Connor and I were the only ones who loved to hike.

"Yeah, really. Sleep in. I'll pick up some lunch to eat on the trail and then swing by to get you around eleven."

I hadn't been hiking since getting serious with Brian, and I grinned with excitement. Brian hated woods and trails and working up a good sweat. Once, after I got engaged, Connor and I had talked of spending a day hiking, and Brian had gotten all pissy about me spending a day in the mountains with Connor. Wasn't proper for his fiancée to be off in the woods with another man, he'd claimed. Never mind that Connor had been my friend since first grade and there had never been anything between us.

Well, until that kiss, anyway.

Maybe Brian had recognized something in Connor that I'd missed, but I didn't think so. More like Brian had a guilty conscience and was afraid I might screw around on him like he'd been doing on me.

I looked up to find Connor staring down at me. The heat in his gaze, the way his blue eyes darkened even as I watched, ignited a low fire in my stomach. And as we stood there, my gaze held prisoner by his, the fire burned hotter.

Conner lowered his face until it was a breath away from mine. "Yes or no?" he said.

I didn't have to ask what the question was. It was no longer about hiking. "Yes," I whispered.

For a year I'd wondered if I'd imagined how good it felt to be kissed by Connor, if I'd exaggerated in my mind the thrill that had coursed through me when his mouth had touched mine. I hadn't. He tasted like the beer he'd been drinking earlier, malty and tangy. His lips were soft yet firm, and they were hot, as if he were burning with the same fever I was.

"Let me in," he said, his words vibrating against my mouth.

When I obeyed, he slipped his tongue in, sliding it around mine. He reached for my hands, pulling them up and around his neck. Then he grunted a sound that seemed like approval when I scraped my fingernails across his skin.

He put his hands on my hips, holding me still while he plundered my mouth. With just a kiss Connor possessed me in a way that Brian never had.

It was thrilling, and it was scary. Before I could think too hard, he lifted his head and stared at me as if trying to solve a puzzle. I didn't know what to say, but even if I did, I was too breathless to speak.

"So, hiking?"

Not capable of forming words, I nodded.

"See you tomorrow." He swiped his thumb across my damp bottom lip and then walked out, closing the door behind him.

"Wow," I whispered, bringing my fingers to my tingling lips. I slid down the wall, and when my bottom hit the floor, I brought my legs up, burying my face against my knees. Just wow.

Although I'd missed the touch of a man, I hadn't messed around since leaving Brian. I'd talked big about taking off for a night in Asheville and having some fun, but I hadn't followed through. Until my divorce was finalized, I was a legally married woman, and I wasn't Brian. I wouldn't break my vows. But now I was free, and I knew just the man I wanted to scratch my itch with.

Connor was actually the perfect choice. Because we were longtime friends, he would care about my feelings and respect my wishes. And based on the two times he'd kissed me, I was pretty sure he was going to be one hell of an itch scratcher.

⟪

"Beau's coming with us," I said the next morning when Connor arrived.

"Great." Connor bent over to rub my dog's ears. "Good morning, Beauregard."

I'd never noticed before what a nice ass Connor had. Very nice. Dressed pretty much the same as me, he wore a

T-shirt, lightweight jacket, hiking boots, and cargo shorts. I managed—just barely—to resist the urge to pat his butt.

After a few excited barks of welcome and licks to Connor's knees, Beau flopped over on his back for a belly rub. As Connor's long fingers glided over Beau's tummy, I found myself envying my dog. And just like Beau, if Connor were stroking me like that, my eyes would probably be rolled up in my head and my tongue hanging out.

"I don't remember if I thanked you, but Beau was the best present ever." I loved that dog like nobody's business. I'm not sure what I would have done without him this past year.

Connor glanced up, giving me a smile that curled my toes. "You're welcome." His gaze returned to my dog. "Ready to go for a ride, Beauregard?"

Beau barked as he scrambled to his feet and raced for the door. We loaded him and my backpack into Connor's Jeep. It was a gorgeous day, and he had the canvas top and the side doors off. It had been our tradition when going hiking to tune the radio to a country station—because those were the best songs to sing along with—and turn up the volume. Connor hadn't forgotten that, and I smiled at him. He smiled back, making my stomach fluttery.

Between the music we had blaring and the wind, it was impossible to talk. Like we had in the past, we sang along with the songs at the top of our lungs. Neither one of us could carry a tune, but we'd never cared about that. Whenever we hit a high note, Beau would howl, singing right along with us. And each time he did that, Connor and I would look at each other and laugh.

Something warm and contented settled in my soul, something I'd been missing lately. The past year had been hard, and I needed a day like this. One straight out of a country song—the warm sun on my face, a hot-as-hell man I was having fantasies about, and my dog. It didn't get better than that.

I hadn't asked where we were going, but as we turned onto Highway 64, heading toward Cashiers, I knew he was going to Silver Run Falls, one of my favorite hikes. I smiled, realizing Connor hadn't forgotten that. The bottom of the falls was an easy hike with a calm, cold pool to swim in. Getting to the upper falls was a steep and hard hike, and we always enjoyed a refreshing swim in the pool when we came back down.

Connor parked the Jeep, and we hefted our backpacks. "Ready for some fun, Beauregard?" He hooked Beau's leash onto his collar.

Beau jumped out of the Jeep, barking his excitement. We easily reached the bottom falls, and Connor let Beau wade into the water. It wasn't summer yet, and there were only a few tourists taking selfies in front of the falls. When the weather turned hot and school was out, the pool would be crowded with kids.

Like most Labradors my dog loved water and was happily splashing and playing. "A dog's life," Connor said, a smile on his face as he watched Beau.

"Yeah, it's a tough one," I answered, watching Connor. The first time I'd met him and Adam, they both had been missing their two front teeth. I could even remember the cowlicks that caused their black hair to stick straight up. It was kind of funny to find myself attracted to a man I'd known as a boy who liked to throw spit wads at me because he knew it would make me giggle.

His front teeth had grown in, his cowlick had been tamed, and instead of getting spit wads from the boy, I was getting toe-curling kisses from the man. Who would've thought it? He glanced at me, caught me staring at him, and winked. Well, just melt me into a puddle at his feet.

Before I tackled Connor to the ground and had my way with him, I elbowed him in the ribs, getting an, "Oof."

"Last one up is a rotten egg." I took off, leaving him to get Beau out of the water.

"Not fair," he called after me.

I laughed, feeling freer than I had in a long time.

CHAPTER SIXTEEN

~ Connor ~

"COME ON, BEAU, MY MAN. We can't let a girl beat us to the top." The dog looked up at me as if to say, *But, dude, water.* Dumb dog. I tugged on his leash, and he grudgingly trotted up to me. He came to a halt at my feet and then shook his body hard, spraying me with icy water.

"Not cool, Beauregard," I muttered. He grinned back at me.

I headed up the mountain behind Autumn. Actually, being behind her wasn't such a bad thing after all. It allowed me a spectacular view of her ass and her legs as she climbed ahead of me. Who knew the skinny, gap-toothed girl I'd known for what seemed like forever would grow up to make me want to grab ahold of her ankles and drop her right here on the trail and kiss her senseless, among other things? She'd worn braces in the tenth grade that had vanished the little gap between her front teeth, and that was too bad. I'd liked that little imperfection.

The trail up grew steeper and more slippery as we neared the top, and I concentrated on not tumbling down and cracking my head open. Beau had no problem climbing up, and although it might mean turning in my man card, I let him pull me up with him. Autumn, meanwhile, was scampering ahead like a freaking monkey.

BB—Before Brian—we used to go hiking two or three times a month, Autumn and me. I'd stopped going when Autumn wouldn't come with me because Brian objected. I'd missed it and her. I just hadn't realized how much until now.

We reached the top, and at least Autumn was breathing as hard as me, so I didn't feel like a total wuss. But it was the light in her eyes and the big grin on her face that drew me to her.

"Having fun?"

She nodded. "I've missed this."

"I was just thinking the same thing."

"Yeah?"

"Yeah." We were alone at the top of Silver Run Falls, so I took advantage of that to kiss her. I could become addicted to kissing Autumn. She let out a sigh when our tongues met, and that little sound went straight to my groin. But we were on a trail where anyone could walk up, so before I did what I wanted and took her right here under a blue sky, I pulled away.

I looked around us. "I'd forgotten how beautiful it was up here."

"Huh?"

"The falls. Beautiful." Her eyes were dilated and dazed, a look I liked on her.

She blinked as if coming out of a trance, and then scanned the surrounding landscape. "It is." Her gaze landed back on me. "Why do you keep kissing me?"

Okay, wasn't expecting that question. "Because—"

"Help. Oh God, please help," someone yelled, sending Beau into a barking frenzy.

He strained at the end of his leash, and when he tried to take off, I let him go, jogging along behind him. I could hear Autumn's footsteps following us. Beau raced around the back of the waterfall along a narrow path.

Whoever was calling for help was a woman, and she'd apparently heard Beau barking. She kept calling out, and I yelled back to her. "We're coming!" As her voice grew louder, and not sure what we'd find, I slowed, pulling Beau back.

"Easy, boy." I glanced at Autumn. "Get your phone out, see if we have service."

"He understands the command 'heel,'" she said as she reached into a pocket on her cargo shorts.

"Heel, Beau." Sure enough, he positioned himself at my side. He kept his ears up, though, and his body was on full alert.

"I've got service," Autumn said.

That was good. "Okay, keep your phone out." Adam and I were both trained in rescue and often participated in finding lost tourists or rescuing someone who'd fallen at one of the many falls in our area. The woman screamed again.

"We're coming. Are you hurt?" I hollered back.

"Bear!"

That was all she said, but my blood ran cold. A black bear was the last thing I wanted to tangle with. We came around a large rock, and I stopped, holding tight to Beau's leash. A woman was in a small tree, hanging on for dear life as a bear pushed on the trunk. The tree was swaying, the woman looking like she was barely hanging on. And she was bleeding heavily from her arm and leg.

"Oh my God," Autumn said, peeking around my arm. "He's going to bring down the tree."

If the woman didn't fall first. She had to be getting weak from losing that much blood. "Call Adam. Tell him to get rescue up here." While she got my brother on the phone, I glanced around, stilling when I saw two bear cubs. Hell, the worst thing to mess with was a mother bear protecting her cubs.

Beau whined, then, apparently forgetting the command to heel, ran to the end of his leash. "No, boy. You don't want to go over there." I had a knife on me, but that wouldn't do much good against a pissed-off bear.

"He's putting out the call," Autumn said, slipping her phone back into her pocket.

Somehow I had to get the bear away from the tree, and the only way I knew to do that was to get its attention on me. "Autumn, I want you to take Beau and go down the mountain."

"What are you going to do?"

"Get that mama bear focused on something besides the woman."

"Meaning you?" Autumn grabbed my arm. "No, that's too dangerous." She eyed Beau, straining at the end his leash. Before I realized what she was going to do, she went to him and unhooked the leash from his collar. The dog took off, alternating growls with barks, heading straight for the bear.

"Why'd you do that?" He was going to get hurt.

"He's too smart to let a bear catch him."

I hoped she was right. She loved that dog, and it would kill her to lose him. At hearing the racket Beau was making, the bear swung her big head around. Without a sound—contrary to bears roaring or growling in movies, they actually made very little noise—she dropped to all fours.

Beau darted in, his teeth snapping at the bear's rear end. The bear turned to face Beau and swiped a paw at the dog. Beau backpedaled, the bear's claws just missing his face. Autumn yelped as she grabbed my hand. I didn't doubt her heart was beating as fast as mine. Beau backed up, then stopped. When the bear headed for him, he backed up again, then stopped as if waiting for the bear to follow him.

The dance between the dog and the bear continued until they both disappeared into the woods. As soon as the two cubs cautiously followed their mother and were out of sight, I pulled my KA-BAR knife out of the holster at my waist, wanting a weapon in my hands should the bear return.

"Stay here." I dropped my backpack to the ground.

"But—"

"I mean it, Autumn. Stay damn here." I kissed her. Hard. Maybe it was the adrenaline running through me that sent me into Neanderthal mode, but the thought of her putting herself in jeopardy if the bear decided to come back . . . Hell no.

When I reached the tree, before I could decide how to rescue the woman, she let go and fell into my arms. As soon as I realized she was coming down, I dropped the knife. Thankfully she was small, but I still fell onto my back from her weight, ending up with her sprawled on top of me.

"Are you okay?" When she didn't answer, I eased out from under her. She'd passed out, but I wasn't comfortable staying here. Beau was barking not too far away, and if the bear came back, we'd be in trouble. Her wounds needed to be treated, but the first priority was to get her to a safer place. I grabbed my knife, sticking it back into its holster, then picked up the woman.

"What do you want me to do?" Autumn asked as soon as I reached her.

"Take my pack. I'm going to carry her to the other side of the falls."

We got the woman back to the edge of the trail down the mountain. There was no way I could carry her down without slipping and hurting us both. We'd have to wait for the rescue team to arrive. Autumn and I both always carried first-aid supplies in our backpacks, and we got to work, doing our best to stop the bleeding.

The woman looked to be in her mid- to late twenties. All she wore were shorts and a T-shirt. If she had a pack, she'd dropped it somewhere, but I guessed that she didn't. Like too many people, especially tourists, she'd come out here alone and unprepared. At least I hoped she'd been alone and there wasn't another person out there, hurt or worse.

"It's probably going to be another thirty minutes or so

before anyone gets here." After putting a pad on one of the wounds, I wrapped gauze around it.

Autumn tore off some more for me. "Those wounds are really deep."

I nodded. "Bear claws are nasty business." Although the woman had deep gashes in her legs and arms, I couldn't see any bite marks. Somehow she'd managed to get away from the bear long enough to get in the tree. She was damn lucky we'd come along when we had because she wouldn't have held on much longer.

Autumn hadn't taken the first-aid classes that I had, but she didn't shy away from helping me. "That's all we can do for her for now." The wounds were bandaged, and it seemed like she'd stopped bleeding.

"She looks familiar," Autumn said, then tilted her head. "I hear sirens. I wish Beau would come back."

"As long as he's barking, he's okay."

"I'd call him, but I'm afraid the bear would follow him here. He's the hero of the day, though."

"Amen to that." The day hadn't gone as expected. I'd hoped about now that we'd be swimming in the bottom pool. Autumn had a bathing suit on under her shorts and shirt, and I wanted to know if it was a bikini.

"Where am I?" the woman said, her voice weak.

"You're going to be okay." Autumn brushed damp hair away from the woman's face. "Is anyone else with you?"

"No. Alone."

"What's your name?" Autumn asked.

"My . . . Taren Blanton." Then she passed out again.

Autumn glanced up at me with wide eyes. "I knew she looked familiar. Senator Blanton's sister."

The senator on *People Magazine's* latest Sexiest Men Alive list. What the hell was his sister doing traipsing around in the woods by herself?

CHAPTER SEVENTEEN

~ Autumn ~

AFTER ADAM AND THE RESCUE team arrived and got Taren Blanton down the mountain, I called for Beau. Within minutes he came bounding to me. My knees buckled at seeing him safe, and I let out a relieved breath as I hugged him. "My hero."

He licked my face, making me laugh.

"Crazy dog," Connor muttered. "You're supposed to be afraid of bears, Beauregard."

Connor's gaze traveled over me, his mouth turning down in a frown. I looked down at myself. We were both covered in blood from our necks to our hiking boots.

"Time for a bath," he said, grabbing my hand. We half slid, half ran down the trail. At the bottom we tossed off our backpacks before tumbling into the water without stopping. Beau dived in with us, loving whatever this new game was.

I came up sputtering. "Oh God, it's cold." I glanced around us. The people who'd been at the bottom of the falls earlier had left, and we were alone.

"Nah, it's like bathwater," Connor said, his chattering teeth and blue lips putting a lie to his claim. "Come here. I'll warm you up." He pulled me to him.

His tongue invaded my mouth, and I whimpered. At least I think that needy sound came from me. I leaned into him, pressing my breasts against a chest that was as solid as a rock wall. His hands slid into my hair, his fingers tangling in the wet strands.

When I wrapped my legs around his waist, he lifted his

head and stared down at me. A connection like I'd never felt before zinged between us, invisible sparks dancing all around us. It seemed as if the world had disappeared and it was just Connor and me.

And Beau.

My silly dog wanted in on the kisses. He paddle-splashed around us, gleefully barking and licking water droplets off our faces. Connor and I looked at each other, then burst into laughter. It was probably a good thing Beau interrupted us. Another few minutes and we would have been frolicking naked in a public place. I wasn't sure where this thing between us was headed, much less what Connor wanted from me . . . Well, besides sex.

That was pretty obvious by the erection pressed against my stomach. If he wanted more than a bit of fun between the sheets, however, he'd picked the wrong girl. I was solidly cured of wanting the little house with a white picket fence that came with a husband. Husbands couldn't be trusted. At least where the Archer women were concerned.

"You're shivering," Connor said. "Let's get you out of here." Back on dry land, he dug a hoodie out of his backpack, handing it to me.

"What about you?"

He smiled. I'd grown up with the man, had seen him smile thousands, maybe millions of times, but all of a sudden my heart bounced in response to that smile. What in the world was wrong with me that I was imagining connections and sparks happening between us, along with a heart that was acting twitchy?

☾

Connor dropped me off at home to shower and change. Because I couldn't stop worrying about Taren Blanton, he was going to pick me up later so we could go to the hospital and check on her. Our little hospital didn't have a trauma center, and in a phone call with Adam we learned that she'd lost a lot of blood, so they'd transported her to Mission Hospital in Asheville.

I love Asheville, which Connor knew, and he'd said that after we paid Taren a visit—hopefully they'd let us see her—we'd have dinner at one of the downtown sidewalk restaurants.

"What should I wear?" I asked Beau. He tilted his head as if attempting to translate my words into doggie talk. "No opinion, huh?"

Was this a date? Connor hadn't said, *I'd like to take you out.* But it kind of felt like one, and I wanted to look nice for him. Okay, I wanted him to look at me and drool. Yet, we were paying a hospital visit, so my sexy red dress was out. Since spring nights tended to be chilly in the mountains, I decided on a dark blue turtleneck sweater dress, a silver medallion belt, and black ankle boots with four-inch heels and lace around the top.

My only jewelry was dangling silver earrings and a ruby ring I'd bought with the money my father had given me for Christmas to buy something "pretty" for myself. He was always generous with money on my birthdays and Christmases, but I'd just as soon have a poinsettia if he'd been the one to pick it out. Sadly that was wishing for more than he knew how to give his only daughter.

I pushed thoughts of my father away before I let them depress me, because he'd disappointed me for as far back as I could remember. Or maybe I was the one who disappointed him. Anyway, I wasn't going to let him ruin my night with Connor.

As for Conner, it still felt a little weird to be having erotic thoughts about a man I'd known since he was a boy whose tree house Jenn, Natalie, Savannah, and I had stormed, determined to find out what he and Adam did up there. And now that boy was looking at me with hunger in his eyes. I was hungry for him, too.

The doorbell chimed, sending Beau scrambling down

the hall, barking a greeting aimed at whoever was on the other side, because surely they were here to see him.

"It's just Connor, silly dog." Apparently Beau had learned Connor's name, as he went into turbo excitement mode.

Couldn't say I blamed him. My excitement mode revved up a notch or two, right along with Beau's. And when I opened the door, my breath swished out of me. Not that I'd never seen Connor dressed up. I had; at my wedding and Jenn's, at a funeral or two, or at community events. But that was BTK, because everything to do with him now seemed to fall into two categories: *before the kiss* and after.

BTK I would have thought, *Connor looks nice tonight.* Now my girlie parts were screaming, *Gimme, gimme, gimme!* Charcoal-gray pants, a thin black, silver-buckled belt, a light gray shirt—rolled up at the sleeves—a silver watch, and my favorite thing, his one emerald earring, all added up to a man who could give a girl erotic dreams. I was very much afraid I was going to start drooling the way Beau did at the sight of a new chew stick.

Before I could say anything, Beau barked, demanding attention. Connor bent over, scratching Beau behind his ears. "And how is Beauregard tonight?"

While his attention was on Beau, I let my eyes feast on Connor, on his black hair, not quite touching his collar, and the full lips that were curved up, the smile reaching his eyes, as man and dog greeted each other as if they hadn't seen each other only two hours earlier. My gaze was caught by the way Connor's muscles bunched under his shirt and the way his long fingers stroked Beau's fur. I wanted to snatch his hand away and put those fingers on me.

And seriously? I was jealous of my dog?

CHAPTER EIGHTEEN

~ *Connor* ~

THE ONLY REASON I WAS fussing over the dog was to give me a few minutes to get my feet back on solid ground before I decided to throw Autumn over my shoulder in a fireman's carry and haul her straight to her bedroom.

Good God, that dress clung to her every curve, and those little black boots with the heels put all kinds of naughty thoughts in my head, like her stripped of everything but the boots, for a start.

Once I was sure I could talk without sounding strangled, I straightened. "You look nice." *Dumbass.* You'd think I'd never paid a girl a compliment before. "Beautiful. Hot. Sexy. Delicious," I rushed to say when the light faded from her eyes at my lame praise. "Take your pick of any of those."

She smiled, kind of shyly, which was strange because I'd never known Autumn to be shy about anything. Had it really mattered that much how I saw her? We were still standing in her foyer, and it seemed as if this was an awkward first date with a girl I had a crush on. I hadn't experienced this kind of ineptness since high school when I was trying to impress Kyla Hamlin, head cheerleader and the lead in all my teenage wet dreams.

"You pick one."

"Huh?" Oh, right. The compliments. "I can't. Pick just one, I mean."

What the hell was wrong with me? I've always been at ease around Autumn, but something had changed. It had to be the boots.

I glanced at Beau, who was sitting on his haunches, his big brown eyes peering up at me with what seemed like disappointment, and I imagined him saying, *You need to up your game, dude. You're really letting us guys down here.* Totally weird getting encouragement from a dog—even if it was in my imagination—but I wasn't about to let Beauregard down.

"I can't pick one because you're all those things, Autumn." I trailed my knuckles over the smooth skin of her cheek. "But if I did have to choose only one of those words, it would be 'delicious' because I want my mouth all over you." Her breaths quickened right along with mine. My gaze roamed over her, stopping on her feet. "It's those boots. In my mind I'm seeing you digging the heels into my back. I should point out that they're the only thing you're wearing when that happens."

My friend since first grade whimpered. "Connor," she said, or rather, rasped, and how the hell did I even know *rasp* was a word before hearing that sound coming from her lips?

I had two choices here. Forget we had plans and talk her into staying home, which I was positive I could do considering the way she was looking at me, or stomp down on that idea and take her out. She'd wanted to visit Taren Blanton and so did I, but more than that I wanted to take Autumn to dinner in Asheville. It had been an afterthought, just something to do, but her eyes had lit up when I'd suggested it, and now I was determined to follow through.

But damn, that rasp. I wanted to hear it again, specifically when she was screaming my name. The sooner we made our hospital stop and then dinner, the sooner we could get back so I could make that happen.

"Let's go."

She raised her brows at the command that came out harsher than I'd intended, but when a man is hot for a particular woman, he'll barrel through obstacles in his way like a jackhammer tearing through asphalt. And to the best of my memory I'd never been hotter for a woman than I was for Autumn Archer.

☾

"I understand Taren Blanton's in room 323," I said to the nurse manning the desk on the third floor. "Is she receiving visitors?"

"Who's asking?"

A man in an expensive suit stepped up to us, and I immediately recognized the face I'd seen numerous times on the news.

Autumn held out her hand. "Senator Blanton, I'm Autumn Archer, and this is Connor Hunter."

"The couple who rescued Taren." He wrapped his hand around Autumn's, and I managed to stifle a growl when he didn't let go. "You have my gratitude, Miss Archer."

"Autumn," she said. Rasped? My growl was getting harder to contain. She tugged her hand away. "Connor and my dog were the real heroes, Senator."

"I'm Lucas," he said to Autumn before offering his hand to me. "You have my gratitude, Mr. Hunter."

"We're just glad we were there to hear her call for help." Our handshake only lasted a few seconds, the acceptable length for a man shake. Maybe I was being rude not offering him the use of my first name, but I was feeling annoyed and a bit territorial where Autumn was concerned.

Even being a man, I could concede that Lucas Blanton was what women referred to as man candy. He was no slouch in the clothing department either. At a minimum he must've spent a thousand bucks on the Armani suit, and I wasn't sure which designer the dress shirt was from but it was easily another couple of hundred dollars. All subdued but still shouting money.

The senator owned a cattle ranch on the outskirts of Asheville, along with several businesses throughout the state of North Carolina. From all accounts he worked hard for our state, he was connected, he dressed well, had the looks that turned women's heads, and had come to his sister's side within a few hours of her rescue, but I didn't like him. Mostly because he'd held Autumn's hand too long.

So eff him. I appreciated her more than he ever could or would. "Can we visit Taren? We'd like to see for ourselves that she's okay." I put my hand on Autumn's back, a possessive claim that every man on the planet understood. His gaze traveled from my arm to my eyes. Understanding shone in his, that Autumn was mine, but underneath that acknowledgment was a challenge.

He wanted Autumn.

I might not have as much money—even as successful as Adam and I were—as Lucas Blanton, have as much power, or spend insane amounts on my clothes, but I wasn't about to stand by and let him go after my girl. If Autumn realized a male war was brewing over her, she'd slap us both silly. I knew that, but I doubted the senator did.

"Can we see her?" I asked again, keeping my hand on Autumn's lower spine. And yeah, she was leaning back against my palm. Definitely a good sign.

"I don't know," Blanton said to Autumn as if she'd been the one to ask the question. "I just got here. Walked out of a meeting in Raleigh and flew up in my Lear the minute I was notified." His gaze still on Autumn, he said, "Don't leave."

"We'll be right here," I said, reminding him of my existence. Damn it, I was letting the senator get to me. I dropped my hand from Autumn's back. "Nice guy," I muttered, watching her watch Blanton walk away.

"Seems so."

Seems so? How was I supposed to interpret that? *Seems so* as in he was the hottest thing she'd ever seen, or *seems so* as in he literally was just a nice guy?

CHAPTER NINETEEN

~ Autumn ~

THERE WAS SOMETHING GOING ON with Connor. I wasn't sure what, but he'd gone all squirrelly on me. His fingers had been making circles on my back, and then they'd gone away. Then there was the tension in his voice. The conversation between him and Lucas had sounded strained. I'd known Connor long enough to pick up on his nuances, and he was not his easygoing self right now.

"I was impressed that Lucas walked out of a meeting the moment he heard about his sister. Shows he really cares for her."

"The senator is just an all-around impressive guy, hm?"

It took a second, but then it hit me. Connor was jealous. Was he afraid I'd go for a man like Lucas Blanton? Granted, Lucas was extremely good-looking. His amber-colored eyes were the most intriguing thing about him. They were beautiful and full of intelligence. I supposed he had to be smart to be a senator.

But he didn't make my heart flutter the way Connor did. I did like thinking Connor was jealous. That knowledge gave me a little thrill. Although it was tempting to test my theory when Lucas returned, I didn't play games like that.

I trailed my finger down the buttons of Connor's shirt. "I suppose, but I have to say, he's not nearly as impressive as you."

"Yeah?"

"Well, in my humble opinion, anyway." That got a bone-melting Connor smile.

"Yours is the only one that counts."

"I'm sorry, but Taren's sleeping," Lucas said, walking up to us. "They have her pretty drugged up."

"But she's going to be okay?" I slipped my arm around Connor's.

"I think so. I'm still waiting to talk to the doctor to learn how much damage the bear did."

"Will you tell her we stopped by?"

"Of course." Lucas glanced at our linked arms, then lifted his eyes to me. "Again, thank you both. I hate to think what would have happened to her if the two of you hadn't been there."

"What was she doing out there by herself?" Connor asked.

"That's going to be one of my first questions when she's awake." He stared down at the floor for a second, as if considering his next words. "You've probably heard that Taren's husband and baby girl were recently killed in a car crash."

I had. It had been all over the local news a few months ago. "Yes, and I can't imagine how hard that must be for her."

"She . . . she's been very depressed, which is understandable. Our family has been fussing over her, trying to take care of her. Maybe she just needed some time alone and decided to go for a hike. She's always loved the mountains."

"I've always found peace in the mountains," Connor said. "If there's anything we can do, please ask."

"Actually, there is. I'd like you both to come back and see her when she's a little better. I think she'd want to thank you."

"We'll do that," I promised. We took our leave, and when we walked out of the hospital, it was to a torrential rain.

Connor and I came to an abrupt halt under the overhang. "Stay here. I'll go get the car," he said.

"Guess dinner on the sidewalk in Asheville is out."

He laughed. "You think?" Then his laugh faded as he

brushed a thumb over my bottom lip. "I know how much you love doing that. Take a rain check on another night?"

A shiver of pleasure streamed through me at his touch. "You bet. How about we go back to the valley and have dinner at Vincennes?"

"Sounds good."

℃

When we walked into Vincennes, arguably the best restaurant in the valley, the place was packed. Jenn saw us and came over. She'd started as the bartender, but Angelo, Vincennes's owner, had recently promoted her to manager. These days he pretty much stayed in the kitchen where he was happiest and let Jenn run the restaurant. Smartest thing he ever did.

"Mary and her new squeeze are leaving. Go grab their seats," Jenn said.

Connor glanced over at the bar. "Who's her flavor of the month?"

"Gerald Ferguson from over in Waynesville. Widowed a year ago. Three children, oldest son's in his fifties."

I laughed. "Good for her." Mary referred to herself as a *player*. According to her, no man could measure up to her dear departed husband, so no more wedding bells for her. But that didn't mean she couldn't have fun. Since—again according to her—men couldn't help falling in love with her, they only got thirty days with her before she moved on to her next flavor of the month.

Connor put his hand on my back as we headed to the bar. Jenn noticed and raised a brow. I'd definitely be getting a phone call from her, but I didn't know how I was going to explain something I didn't understand myself.

Tonight Mary's hair was . . . well, I guess turquoise was the best word for it. Who knew there was even turquoise dye? Her leather pants and knee-high boots matched the color of her hair, and her blouse was shocking pink. As usual she was loaded up with jewelry. I doubt there was another woman in her late sixties who could pull all that off, but somehow Mary did. Either that or our love for Mary blinded our eyes.

The moment Mary saw us, she shrieked. Mr. Ferguson, sitting on one side of her, and Dylan, sitting on the other, jerked their heads around to see the cause of her outburst. Actually, everyone at the bar turned their attention on us. Vincennes's bar was where the locals preferred to sit, leaving the tables for the tourists. It had become a meeting place of sorts and also where you got to hear the latest valley gossip.

"Our heroes are here," Mary shouted.

I looked behind me.

"I think she means us," Connor murmured.

"Oh."

Mary bounced off her seat and clapped, everyone else at the bar joining in. Okay, this was embarrassing. Even the tourists were craning their necks, trying to see what was going on.

"Where's Beauregard?" she said when we reached her.

"Um, home."

"Well, he's the true hero. He's the one that went after the bear. I've already posted about him on *Happenings in the Valley*, and you should see all the comments. Someone said Hollywood should make a movie, so I had a contest to name Beauregard's movie. My favorite so far is Beauregard Saves the Senator's Sister. Don't they call that an alliteration, where the letters are all the same? So clever. If you changed Beauregard's name to Sam, then it would be perfect."

My head was spinning, but that wasn't unusual around Mary. And I wasn't changing Beau's name. I glanced up at Conner. Amusement glittered in his eyes, and I could tell by his twitching lips that he was doing his best not to laugh.

"Oh, and don't make plans for Sam on Saturday, sweetie." Her eyes widened, and then she clapped. "Oh, I did it again. Sam, Saturday, sweetie. Get it?"

"You're just too clever, Mary. What's happening on Saturday?" I asked, although I was afraid of the answer.

"We're having a hero's parade for Sam." She tapped her flavor of the month on his shoulder. "Come along, Gerald. I have much to do before Saturday. You can help. Do you by any chance know a movie producer?" she asked him as they walked away.

"His name's not Sam," I muttered to her retreating back. Connor and Dylan burst into laughter. "Not funny." That only made them laugh harder.

"Doesn't take much to amuse boys," Jenn said, but I could see that she was having trouble holding it together herself. "Dylan told me what happened out there today. Sam really is a hero."

"It's Beau!"

She laughed, then went off to do whatever it was the manager of a restaurant did. I slipped onto the empty bar stool between Conner and Dylan. No sooner was I seated than Gloria Davenport, reporter at large—the only one—for *The Valley News* popped up at my side.

"Naomi's going to give the entire front page to Sam on Saturday," she said breathlessly. "We've never had a dog hero before. We need you go bring him in tomorrow so we can take pictures and interview him."

Had I heard her right? Naomi owned *The Valley News*—which was mostly gossip she and Gloria imagined in their heads—and sure, Naomi was sometimes batty, but she wanted to interview my dog?

From down the bar, Shelly, the chamber of commerce director, said, "Why don't we give Sam honorary mayor status on Saturday?"

The whole town had gone crazy.

And his damn name was Beau.

CHAPTER TWENTY

~ *Connor* ~

SWEAR TO GOD, I TRIED my best not to laugh. Failed at that and got a narrow-eyed glare from Autumn. Unable to resist, I leaned over and said into her ear, "You'll want Sam to be all shiny and sweet smelling before his interview. I'll help you give him a bath." Wouldn't mind helping her bathe, either.

She stabbed her elbow into my ribs, getting an "oomph," from me.

On the other side of her, Dylan laughed. "Daisy's really proud of her son, Sam."

Autumn elbowed him, getting an "oomph."

"Y'all"—she swept her hand around to include the entire bar people—"are all idiots."

Because she was the cutest thing when she was mad, I couldn't help it. I leaned over and kissed her before I thought better of it. And that was apparently a big oops, because conversations ceased and it got so quiet that I froze with my lips pressed against Autumn's.

"They're looking at us," Autumn mumbled against my mouth.

And I didn't care. I kissed her again, giving them something to talk about, because talk they would. She sighed, sounding wonderfully like she didn't care either. If I didn't get her to bed, sooner than soon, I would likely combust.

Jenn returned with a platter of Angelo's chicken scarpariello—chicken pieces, sausages, onions, mushrooms, spicy pepperoncinis, and kalamata olives, and one of my favorite Vincennes meals—putting the plate in front of Dylan.

"Here you go, babe," she said, giving him a kiss on his cheek.

When Autumn turned on her stool toward me and crossed her legs, my gaze lowered to those sexy boots. The need to be alone with her burned a hot fire through my blood.

"Autumn and I'll take a large pepperoni and sausage to go," I said, knowing that was her favorite pizza.

"We will?" Autumn said.

"We will."

She must have seen right into my male brain and what I was thinking because she smirked, but it was an I'm-on-to-you-and-I'm-good-with-it smirk.

After cocking her brow at me—a what's-going-on-be-tween-you-and-Autumn brow raise—Jenn stole an olive from Dylan's plate, then headed for the kitchen. Autumn would definitely be getting a phone call later.

I planned for Autumn to be too busy to be answering any phone calls.

☙

"I guess we outed ourselves with that kiss," Autumn said after we'd finished off the pizza.

"Sorry about that." I gave her my best I-screwed-up smile. "You're adorable when you're mad, and I kind of forgot myself." On the way back to her place I'd cooled down a little, and my brain was able to think again. Before we went any further, I needed to make sure we were on the same page. She'd just given me the opening to talk about what was between us and where we were going with it, but I wasn't sure how to start the discussion.

She'd changed out of her sexy dress and those hot little boots, and I was sorry about that, too. I'd had plans for her in those shoes. The yoga pants with the frolicking puppies on them and the yellow tank top were sexy in a cute kind of way, though.

"Now everyone's going to think we're dating," she said.

"You have a problem with that?" I didn't like the shrug she gave me, as if she might want us to stay a secret. Why did that bother me? We weren't a couple, just two people wanting to enjoy each other for a time or two. Maybe longer. But we were both single and free, so there wasn't any reason we couldn't be seen out together.

"Not so much a problem," she finally said. "But I don't want everyone thinking there's something serious going on between us. You know how this town is. After that kiss they'll start watching the mail for a wedding invitation."

"That's not going to happen." I must have said that too harshly because she jerked a little.

"What, you don't think I'd make a good wife?" Her laugh was too bitter for my liking. "Don't answer that. I wouldn't. Not anymore. You're a man, and I no longer trust the male species. I'd be suspicious every time you were out of my sight, and I'd hate myself for that."

"We're not all Brian or your father, Autumn." Adam had taught me that being in love wasn't worth the hurt, but if I did have a wife, I'd never cheat on her. If I ever reached the point where I wanted to, I'd end the marriage first.

Autumn sighed as she rubbed her foot. "I know that. It's my judgment in men that's obviously lacking. The only male I'm sure I can trust is Beau, so he's the only one I'll let in my life."

At hearing his name, Beau's ears perked up, and he tilted his head, his adoring gaze on Autumn. When she didn't look at him, he pushed up from his doggy bed, made two full turns, then plopped back down, but kept his eyes on his mistress.

"Go to sleep, Sam," I said to get a rise out of Autumn. This conversation was veering offtrack. She kicked me. Before she could tuck her foot back under her, I wrapped my fingers around her ankle. "Are these red marks from those boots?" I rubbed my fingers over the top of her foot.

"Yeah. They're killer boots, but man, they cripple me after an hour of wearing them."

"Then don't." They were totally hot, but what was it with women wearing shoes that made their feet red or gave them blisters? I pulled her foot onto my lap and massaged it. She laid her head back on the sofa, letting out a moan that sent desire barreling below my belt.

She opened her eyes and gave me a grin. "That's another thing about men. They'll never understand women and their shoes."

I loved that sparkle in those blue eyes that were starting to haunt my dreams, and I was pretty sure Autumn wearing nothing but those boots would show up soon in my nighttime fantasies.

"Here's the thing." It was time to lay my cards on the table. I pressed my thumb into her heel, then moved it up to her toes, and this moan from her was deeper, throatier. Autumn Archer was killing me.

"What's the thing?" she murmured, sounding half-asleep.

"That I want you. If I'm not mistaken, the feeling is mutual."

She pulled her foot away and sat up. "I'm listening."

"Neither one of us is looking for long-term. So you and I"—I waved my hand between us—"can have a little fun without worrying about one of us getting hurt."

"It doesn't feel odd to you that we've been good friends for, like, forever, and now we're talking about jumping into bed together?"

"Are you saying you're not interested?" Because if she was, I was going to be one disappointed man.

"No, I just don't want to feel all weird about it."

She hadn't seemed to mind me kissing her. "Come here." I patted my leg. "Let's experiment a little."

A flirty smile curved her lips as she scooted across the sofa and straddled me. "Now what?"

"I'm going to kiss you." I started at one corner of her

mouth, teased and nibbled a little, then moved to the other side. When her breath hitched, I angled my head and took possession of her mouth. Our tongues tangled, and she really was the most delicious thing I'd ever tasted. She squirmed, rubbing against my lap. I put my hands on her hips to still her. Much more of that and the control I was holding on to by a thread would be broken.

After a few minutes I pulled away. "How did that feel?" Her lips were damp, her eyes unfocused, and that look on her was so hot that I could just eat her up.

"Good. Really good. Amazing, actually."

"But not weird?"

CHAPTER TWENTY-ONE

~ Autumn ~

IBLINKED, FEELING LIKE I WAS floating up from a fog. When I could think again, I lowered my gaze to Connor's mouth. "I'm not sure yet. You need to kiss me some more before I can decide."

He softly chuckled. "Okay, let's try this again."

As our lips met, I braced my hands on the back of the sofa. Connor reached behind his head and moved them to the back of his neck. Once my hands were where he wanted them, he put his back on my hips. There was something sexy about him holding me still, as if my slightest movement tortured him. I liked the thought that I could drive him a little crazy.

When I combed my fingers through his hair, he sighed into my mouth. Connor's hair was soft and silky and so lovely to play with. He deepened the kiss, his tongue invaded my mouth, and his arousal pressed against the confines of his pants, the feel of him on my sex driving me crazy.

"Please," I whispered, needing more. So much more.

He pulled away, then leaned his forehead on mine, our harsh breaths mingling between us. "Did that feel weird?" he finally said.

I gave a breathless laugh. "If the throbbing ache going on here"—I took his hand and pressed it against my yoga pants–covered sex, and boy, did I ever want those off— "isn't weird, then no, so not weird."

"That's all I needed to know." He stood with me wrapped around him, and then he put his hands on my thighs and pushed my legs down until my feet landed on the floor. His eyes snared mine. "I'm going to give you tonight to decide if you and I are a good idea." He cupped his hand under my chin. "I doubt you have a clue how hard it is for me to walk away from you right now, Autumn, but that's what I'm going to do."

"Because I said it felt weird? It doesn't anymore." *Don't go* was what I really wanted to say. His kisses had wiped any thought of weird from my mind.

"If you still feel that way tomorrow . . ." He brushed his lips over mine. "Then I'm all yours for as long as you want me."

As soon as he realized Connor was leaving, Beau scrambled up to escort him to the door. Right before he walked out, Connor glanced back at me and winked. What was it about a man winking at you that was just downright sexy?

Beau trotted back, sat in front of me, and looked up as if to say, *Now what?*

"Never tell a man it feels weird—well, in your case, a girl—to be with him."

Beau barked in agreement.

While I readied for bed, one thing Connor had said stayed on my mind. "I'm yours for as long as you want me." What did that mean? Were we dating? Just fooling around? He knew my view on love and marriage, so he wasn't expecting us to get serious. And he'd even said that like me, he wasn't looking for long-term. So we understood each other. But I kind of liked that he would be mine as long as I wanted.

I wasn't one for jumping in and out of men's beds, no matter the dumb words I'd spouted about playing around. It would be nice to have someone like Connor to keep company with. But wait, was he going to see other women while we were getting it on? That wasn't going to work for me.

Yeah, it seemed that I wanted to have my cake and eat it,

too, and that was kind of a surprise. Nothing was secret in Blue Ridge Valley, and if Connor was messing around with me and others, everyone would know it. After the mess with Brian I wouldn't be able to handle being talked about again. I was going to have to address that with Connor. And it wasn't jealousy I was feeling at the thought of him with another woman. Okay, maybe a little.

My phone buzzed with a text. Connor? I smiled as I picked it up from the nightstand, but it was Jenn wanting to know if I was free for lunch tomorrow. "And the third degree starts," I muttered as I texted her back, agreeing to meet her.

I gave Beau his nighttime treat and then climbed into bed. By myself. What fun was that? Just as I was dozing off, my phone buzzed again. This time it was Connor texting me.

What time R U giving Sam a bath?

I laughed. Funny man. Sorry. U must have the wrong #. No Sam here.

Bummer. U need help with your bath then?

Now there was an interesting thought. R U sexting me?

Want me to?

Strangely, Brian and I had never sex texted. I wondered why. The thought of sexting with Connor sent a little thrill though me, but I wasn't ready for that with him yet.

Put that on your wish list ☺

It's #1 now

Not surprised

Ha ha! See U tomorrow. Sweet dreams

Nite

It was really nice that he'd texted me, but Connor had always been thoughtful like that. I fell asleep thinking of Connor, specifically how good he kissed.

𝒞

"So what's going on with you and Connor?"

I peered at Jenn over my menu. "Wondered how long it was going to take you to ask that." I glanced at my watch. "Exactly forty seconds from the time we sat down."

"You're lucky I didn't show up on your doorstep last night. Would have if I wasn't sure Connor was there. Was he?"

"For a while."

She scowled at me. "Am I going to have to drag it out of you? Start talking."

The waitress came and took our orders, giving me a minute to consider how much to tell her. Who was I kidding? Jenn was my best friend. I'd always told her everything, and would end up doing that anyway before lunch was over.

"After making out like teenagers, he said that I needed to decide whether I still felt weird about him before we went any further," I said after telling her everything, starting with that first kiss over a year ago.

"And do you?"

"Believe me, he kissed any feelings of weirdness right out of me." I grinned at her. "The man can kiss." I played with my Greek salad, moving around the little bit of lettuce still on my plate with my fork. "I . . ." I shrugged, not sure what I was trying to say.

Jenn pushed her empty plate to the side. "I hear a but."

"He's been my friend, our friend, since elementary school. I never thought of him that way until he kissed me the first time. Before that, Connor and Adam were like our adopted brothers."

"So, did it feel like you were kissing your brother?"

"God, no. I've never been kissed like that."

"Then what's the problem?"

That was Jenn, digging until she got to the bottom of something, which was why I'd told her everything. Maybe she could help me understand what was holding me back. As long as Connor was kissing me, I had no reservations. I'd fallen asleep thinking about him, and I'm pretty sure there was a smile on my face as I drifted off. In the light of day, though, the doubts were there.

"I don't know. For one thing, I don't want to lose him as a friend, and that could happen."

"That's a legitimate concern, but I don't think that's what's holding you back." Jenn brushed long strands of auburn hair away from her face. I'd always envied her hair. Dylan liked to call her Red, and I loved his nickname for her.

The only thing that would make our girl lunch better was if Savannah were here. But Savannah was back in New York. Other than her attendance at our weddings, the only way we got to see her was her face plastered all over the place. It was kind of strange to stand in line at the grocery store and see one of your best friends on the cover of a magazine.

"Well?"

"What if he falls in love with me?" Hearing me say that aloud sounded conceited, as if any man couldn't help falling for me, but it could happen, and that would be a disaster.

"What if you fall in love with him?"

I blinked at that. "You know that's not in the cards."

"Why? Because both your father and Brian are douche-bags? That excuse doesn't grant you immunity from falling in love with Connor." She shrugged. "That could happen whether you want it to or not."

I sputtered a laugh. "Wrong. Because of my dad and ex-husband I have full immunity from ever falling in love again."

"Keep telling yourself that, but the heart is a contrary organ and seldom listens to its host's wishes. Anyway, so what if Connor falls in love with you? That's his problem, not yours. If you want him, I say go for it. If you don't think you can handle the fallout that might or might not happen, then don't."

"You make it sound so easy."

She reached across the table, putting her hand over mind. "Autumn, you know I love you like a sister. I just want to see you happy, and if Connor makes you happy, then awesome. He's a good man, one of the best. No matter what you decide, he'll respect that. I think the bottom line is, do you want him?"

All I could do was nod.

"Then get out of your own way and go for it."

And that was why I loved Jenny Conrad. She knew me better than myself, pointing me right where I wanted to go. And Connor was definitely where I wanted to go.

"You're right, but I'm saying it here. I'm not going to fall in love with him."

A smile appeared on her face, and then she laughed. "We'll recall this conversation at your wedding."

"Stop it. So not going to be a wedding."

"Uh-huh," she said and then grabbed the check before I could.

There. Was. Not. Ever. Going to be another wedding in my life. And no, those were absolutely not famous last words.

CHAPTER TWENTY-TWO

~ Connor ~

"YOU HURT HER, AND I'LL never forgive you."
I stared at my twin. "Whose side are you on, anyway? What if she hurts me?"

"Then I'll have to kill her."

That settled me down a little. I grinned at my brother. What good was a twin if he wouldn't kill for you?

"She's not going to let me hurt her," I said, leaning forward and dangling my hands between my legs. "Between her father and Brian, she's developed a real distrust in men. Swears the only thing we're good for is to scratch her itch."

Adam choked on the beer he'd just tried to swallow. I'd stopped by his house—a beautiful log cabin, much the same as mine—to watch a game with him after Autumn had called, begging off tonight. Seemed her mother was in the middle of another meltdown or something, and Autumn's presence was required. What else was new? I'd wanted to tell her to stop letting the woman yank her chain but had managed to resist.

It was Autumn's decision as to when enough was enough. I just hoped that happened soon. It bugged the hell out of me to stand by and watch Melinda Archer treat her daughter like a bouncing ball, pushing her away one minute, and in the next pulling her into all the drama that was Melinda and Ray's lives. Although Ray pretty much ignored the existence of his daughter, which also pissed me off, at least he was consistent. Autumn knew where she stood with him.

Melinda on the other hand was a parasite, doing her best

to suck the life out of Autumn. I had a theory about that. If Melinda wasn't happy, no one else in the world should be happy, especially her daughter.

Before I got too angry thinking about all the crap Autumn was probably listening to about now, I went to the kitchen and grabbed a beer. Although neither one of us cooked much, Adam and I had state-of-the-art kitchens. We'd built our homes on ten acres of land that we'd divided right down the middle, where a fast-moving river tumbled over rocks and beaver damns, creating the best sounds in the world. Sometimes when I needed to think, I'd go down to the bank on my side and listen to the soothing, fast-moving water.

Every once in a while I'd look up and see Adam on the other side, as if he knew I had things on my mind and needed him. That worked both ways, because there were times when I felt drawn to go to that spot between us and would see him on the opposite bank. We were so busy these days that we didn't do that so much anymore.

I missed those quiet moments with my brother. Even though we'd built a bridge over the river, connecting our properties, we'd each stay on our side, talking across the water. Our land was in a pretty valley surrounded by the Blue Ridge Mountains, our slice of heaven.

"I don't think you and Autumn are a good idea, but what do I know? I thought Savannah and I were, and look where that got me," Adam said when I returned.

"This conversation's getting depressing." I'd go forward with Autumn if she was willing, Adam's thoughts on the matter be damned. I wanted her too much. And I wasn't getting into a discussion about Savannah, which would only put Adam in a bad mood. He swore he was over her, but I had my doubts.

"You hear there's a parade on Saturday for Beau?"

"You mean Sam?" He smirked. "Stopped by Mary's for coffee and a muffin this morning, and that's all she could talk about. Sam the Hero this. Sam the Hero that. Said she knows someone who knows someone who knows a Hollywood movie producer."

Mary was a scary lady. Once she got something in her head, you'd better get out of her way. "Don't let Autumn hear you call him Sam. She'll knock you silly."

"True. All I'll say is I sure hope you know what you're doing, bro." He set his empty bottle on a side table and then propped his feet up on the coffee table. "Time for the game."

I'd come over to watch the hockey game with him. The Nashville Predators had made it into the playoffs, and since Nashville wasn't all that far from Blue Ridge Valley, we considered that we had a team to root for. Plus, we'd graduated from the University of Tennessee, so that added another layer to our loyalty to Tennessee sports teams.

"Sure hope we get some rain soon," he said. "Not liking how dry it's getting."

"Yeah, we're going to start seeing wildfires if we don't." The brief rain the night Autumn and I had gone to see Taren Blanton hadn't helped much. It had been the driest winter and spring on record, and one cigarette tossed carelessly out a car window or someone letting a trash burn get out of control, and we'd have trouble on our hands.

Adam and I were not only on the volunteer rescue team, but we were volunteer firemen. Partly because we believed in giving back to the town where we'd found so much success, and partly because our parents had died in a house fire. It had happened during our first year of college, and one question would always haunt us: if we'd been home, would we have been able to save them? We'd never know, but fighting fires, maybe saving others, helped to deal with the grief.

"You give any thought to what we talked about?"

I had my head resting on the back of the sofa and rotated it to face Adam. "The old grocery store property?"

"Yeah."

"It has potential for what we want." At present our show-case homes were mine and Adam's, which meant we took prospective buyers looking for a custom-built log home on tours of ours. We both hated people tramping through where we lived. Our idea, now that we were in a position to afford it, was to buy a property large enough to build three model homes.

Right now one section of my three-car garage had been converted into a sales office. And although selling our homes was my main business, I was a licensed real estate agent and had listings all over the county. Operating out of my garage wasn't the best setup, and along with the model homes we'd build on the property, we'd have a sales office. I couldn't wait to get my house and garage back to myself.

"Potential is an understatement, Connor. It's perfect. Plenty of land for three model homes, along with more than adequate parking. And it's right on Main Street, so we couldn't get more visible than that."

"True. Any problem with getting building permits that you can see?" We'd have to tear down the existing building, which shouldn't be a problem for the town council since the old grocery store was an abandoned eyesore.

"No. Old Man Humphrey's asking too much, but I think you can sweet-talk him down on the price. He's had it for sale for six years now."

"I'll approach him next week, tell him there might be an offer. I won't tell him it's us until we can agree on a price."

"Good thinking. He thinks we have more money than God. He knows we're the ones interested, he'll double the price."

I snorted. "No doubt."

We settled in to watch the game. Toward the end I glanced at my watch. It was getting late. Autumn had promised to call me when she got back home. Either she had forgotten or she was still at her mother's. I didn't like either option

CHAPTER TWENTY-THREE

~ Autumn ~

MY MOTHER GREETED ME AT the door with red eyes and a splotchy face. I was expecting that, though, since she'd been sobbing on the phone when she'd called. No matter how much I tried, she'd refused to tell me what was wrong, but I knew it would be the same old, same old.

"What did he do this time?" I asked, walking past her. To say I was peeved was putting it mildly. I was supposed to see Connor tonight. After my lunch with Jenn I'd given it a lot of thought and had come to the conclusion that I wanted more Connor kisses and whatever else he had to offer, and there would be no weirdness about it at all.

I shouldn't have answered the phone when I saw Mom's name on the screen. Truthfully I almost didn't, but then she would have continued to call me every five minutes until I answered. Anytime I tried to put her off when she demanded I come over, she'd hint that her life wasn't worth living, and there would be a thinly veiled threat that she would do something drastic.

Although I was pretty sure it was her usual dramatics, I'd never forgive myself if she actually did do something horrible because I wasn't there when she needed me. So here I was, for like the millionth time, bringing along my shoulder for her to cry on. I was so tired of it.

"He wants a divorce." She threw herself down on the sofa and wailed.

It was going to be one of those kind of nights. I dropped my purse on the coffee table, then headed straight to the kitchen and poured myself a glass of wine. How much more of my parents' drama was I supposed to take? Some of my earliest memories were of their fights, how they'd thrown accusations at each other, the tears, the slamming of doors.

Not that I blamed my mother for my father's affairs, but I'd once overheard him tell her that she was a cold fish. I'd decided right then and there that when I got married, my husband would never have reason to sling those words at me. That accusation had stuck in my mind when I'd showed up at Brian's dealership wearing nothing but a raincoat. I wasn't a cold fish, and it occurred to me that possibly my mother wasn't either, that maybe it was my father's way of putting the blame for his weakness back on her. The same way Brian had blamed Lina for his cheating.

Early in our relationship I'd told Brian about my father's infidelities and how it had sucked the life out of my mother. I'd told him I would never tolerate cheating because I would never allow myself to become my mother, withering away a little each time she caught him screwing around on her. Brian had claimed to understand and had sworn he would never do that to me. I'd wanted so badly to believe him—to be in love with a man who would never treat me like that—that I'd ignored the warning signs.

Well, never again. I put my hands on the counter, taking deep breaths, seeking calm before I went back to the living room. It was getting harder and harder to deal with my parents.

"He's said that before," I reminded her when I returned. "Often."

"Well, he means it this time."

And I'd heard that before, more than once. He never followed through because usually his latest squeeze would get tired of him for this reason or that and kick him out before anything could come of it. Mom would then welcome him back with open arms.

"Let him get the damn divorce, Mom. In fact, you divorce him." She'd never threatened to leave my dad, and I had a feeling that if she did, if he had to worry about her not sitting home, miserable without him, he'd change his ways. I think in his warped way he loved her. He just didn't know how to keep his pants zipped.

"But I love him." Her lips trembled as she gave me an accusing glare. "You don't understand."

"You think not?" Leftover anger from a year ago surged through me. Unable to sit still, I set my wineglass on the table, then stood, going to the window, and looking out into the night. "You think it didn't kill me when I caught Brian screwing around on me? Do you know why I refused to give him another chance?" I turned, and at her blank face, I realized she'd never get it, never change. But I had to try.

"Because of you and Dad. I don't remember a time when he wasn't either moving out or moving back in. Frankly I think it's pretty amazing that I'm not more screwed up than I am. But I promised myself years ago that I'd never let myself be you."

"That's a mean thing to say, Autumn."

"If that's how you see it, I'm sorry." I moved back to the sofa, sitting close to her and taking her hand in mine. "I do remember that there was a time when you used to smile. You were happy and so pretty. I think that was probably when I was around five or six. Then as the years passed, you changed, Mom. Each time he left or you kicked him out, you got more miserable, more bitter. You stopped laughing. And this is going to sound really mean, but I'm going to say it anyway. You stopped being pretty."

Her lips thinned, and she snatched her hand away. "I didn't ask you to come over to tear me to pieces with cruel words. You're my daughter. It's your job to be here for me when I need you."

Seriously? Long-held rage and hurt stormed to the surface—the uncertainties during my childhood, dreading coming home at the end of a school day, never knowing if my dad would be living with us or not, never sure what condition my mother would be in—and I let the words tumble out that I'd never said but had always wanted to.

"No. You have it backward. A mother's job is to be there for her children, and you never have. It's always been about you. Maybe that's why Dad doesn't stick around. Perhaps he gets just as tired as I do of all your drama." And it was true. Even during the times he was with us, it was like living onstage in a Broadway farce. It drained the soul.

She slapped me.

"Maybe I deserved that," I said, putting my palm on my stinging cheek, shocked that she'd hit me, something she'd never done before. What hurt more than the slap, though, was that she didn't seem sorry she'd done it. "But honestly I don't think I can go on like this, dropping everything no matter what's going on in my life and running to your side when you demand it. You need to talk to someone, a professional. Will you let me look into that, find someone who can help you find your way back to being happy again?"

"I'm not crazy, Autumn, and I resent you implying that I am. If anyone needs to see a psychiatrist, it's your father."

"Actually, you both do. So the answer's no? Because if it is, then I'm done with both of you." Nothing else I'd ever said had worked, so maybe it was time for some tough love. That and I really couldn't keep on like this with her. I was also coming to believe that I was enabling her by being the dutiful daughter, presenting myself on demand and commiserating ad nauseam with poor Melinda Archer.

"You've changed since Brian left you and not for the good. If this is how you're going to be, you can leave now."

"First, I left Brian. Second, I think going now is a good idea. If you want to put on a pretty dress, do something with your hair, and go out tomorrow for a nice mother-daughter lunch, call me. If you pick up the phone in the future to ask me to come over for more of this, please don't. I won't do it."

I took my wineglass to the kitchen, washed it, put it away, then picked up my purse and walked out. She didn't try to stop me. My heart hurt, and the love I had for my mother in it wanted to go back inside and take back everything I had said. But I made my feet keep walking. At some point I had to stop letting her control me like a puppet, and tonight seemed to be that point.

As soon as I got home, I'd call Connor, and if it wasn't too late, maybe he'd come over, even if it was just to hold me. Beau greeted me at the door, grinning like a fool at the sight of me. "Hey, boy. Miss me?"

He barked a *yes!*

My phone buzzed, and I smiled. I wouldn't have to call Connor because he was calling me. It wasn't him, though; it was my father. I almost didn't answer it. Dealing with one screwed-up parent in a night was enough. But he rarely called me, and I couldn't resist the chance to talk to him.

"Hey, Dad."

"What's this about you upsetting your mother?"

And the drama queen strikes again. I bet I wasn't backed out of the driveway before she was on the phone with him. You'd think he could at least ask me how I was before jumping right in on me. I should have gone with my first instinct and not answered the phone.

"So you're going to take her side without even hearing mine?" I sat on the sofa and propped my feet on the edge of the coffee table. Even though he mostly couldn't live with her, he always had her back, which was one reason I believed he loved her in his own warped way. It would be nice once in a while to have him at my back, but that had never happened.

"You said some mean things to her, Autumn. That was uncalled for."

"What about me, Dad? Don't I get to have a life without being dragged into the middle of my parents' mess every time I turn around? It's sad and depressing, and I just can't do it anymore."

"Your mother is fragile. You know that, which is why I don't understand why you'd want to upset her."

He hadn't heard a word I said. Either that or he really didn't care what their fights and their messed-up parenting skills did to me. "If she's so fragile, then why do you treat her the way you do? This isn't on me, Dad, and I'm not going to let you blame me for her misery. That's all on you."

There was a long silence, and then he said, "What's gotten into you, Autumn?"

What indeed? I lowered my feet to the floor, put my phone on speaker before setting it on the coffee table, then leaned forward and rested elbows on my knees. I was hurting, and my father didn't care.

"Why is it my responsibility to be Mom's caretaker?" I whispered. If she was sick, actually ill, I'd be there for her around the clock, but I couldn't play their games anymore.

"Speak up. You're mumbling."

I sat up, straightening my spine. "I said if you're so worried about her, then act like her husband for a change." Not wanting to hear how he'd respond to that, I disconnected.

For a good hour I sat with only the dim light of the lamp I'd turned on when I'd come home, staring at the wall in front of me. I'd thought my parents loved me, but I wasn't even sure about that anymore. Some of my earliest memories were of a happy home, a loving mother and father. But around the first or second grade things changed. The fights started, and neither of my parents tried to shield me from their anger at each other. Even at a young age I had been put in the middle, both of them expecting me to choose sides. That was one reason I'd spent so much time at Jenn's house, and I'd always love her parents for treating me like another daughter.

A sob escaped, and I angrily brushed away the tears. I couldn't change the past, and my tears were meaningless. Beau nudged his nose between my legs, his worried eyes focused on me.

"Am I a bad daughter, Beau?" It felt like I was. A part of me ached to call my dad and tell him I hadn't meant anything I'd said. Another part wanted to call my mother and take back all the spiteful words I'd spouted. Then there was the angry child in me that stomped her feet, crossed her arms, and refused to do either of those things.

I did call Connor, though.

CHAPTER TWENTY-FOUR

~ Connor ~

I'D JUST TURNED INTO MY driveway, a three-minute drive from Adam's, when my Bluetooth came on, Autumn's name coming up.

"Hey, beautiful." I hoped she was calling to ask me to come over, even if it was late.

"Hey."

That wasn't her happy voice. "Are you okay?"

"No."

"I'm on the way over."

"You don't have to. It's late."

"See you in twenty." I cut off our connection before she could protest. After I went into my house to retrieve something, I headed to her place, making one stop at an all-night convenience store.

Autumn opened her door, and I could tell right away that she wasn't okay. Her smile seemed forced, and her eyes were red-rimmed from crying. Since I knew she'd been to visit her mother, I added another black mark against Melinda Archer for making my girl cry.

"Brought you something." I held out the bottle of wine in one hand that I'd taken from home, and in the other was the gallon of chocolate fudge ice cream I'd bought on the way over.

"Pity-party food and drink. Awesome."

"So what are we pitying?" As I followed her into the kitchen, my gaze strayed to her ass. The girl wore jeans very well.

"Me." She glanced over her shoulder, catching me. "Stop

checking out my butt."

"I'm a man. It's what we do. And I have to say that yours is perfection, so it's not my fault that I can't stop looking. It's yours."

"Have to tell you, not fond of the men checking out women's butts thing."

I gave my forehead a mental slap. *Idiot.* I'd just reminded her of Brian. "I'm sorry, Autumn." I set the wine and ice cream on the counter, then moved in front of her. "I wasn't thinking."

She slipped her hands into mine. "No, it's okay. I actually like that you appreciate my butt. It's just been a bad night, and I'm touchy right now."

"I gather your visit with your mom didn't go well?"

"You could say that." She let go of my hands, fished a wine opener out of a drawer, and handed it to me.

I opened the bottle and filled our glasses while she grabbed two spoons, then took them and the ice cream to her kitchen island. After we'd settled on the bar stools, I said, "How does this work? We just eat right out of the carton?" I grinned at her eye roll. "Seriously, this is only my second pity party, and I want to get it right." I'd pity-partied with her every day of the first week after she and Brian had split, but I didn't think she remembered much of that time.

"Yes, Connor, that's how we do it."

We finished our glass of wine and made a sizable dent in the ice cream while she told me what had happened. I didn't say anything as I listened, but I was getting angrier by the minute. What sorry excuses for parents her mother and father were. It was hard to relate to that because mine had been pretty awesome.

Sure, Adam and I got into trouble and were punished, but the punishment always fit the crime. We never doubted they loved us, and they never put us in the middle of any arguments between them. Not that I remember them fighting much. If they had, they did it out of our sight and hearing.

It seemed to me that her parents were determined to suck the life out of their daughter. Autumn had always been defensive of her parents, especially her mother, so I was going to have to carefully choose my words. But I was proud of her for finally standing up to her mother. It was about time.

"I told my mother not to call me unless she wanted to dress up and have lunch with me while wearing a smile on her face."

I paused with a spoon loaded with ice cream halfway to my mouth. "Do you mean that?" Was Autumn finally going to remove herself from a toxic situation? God, I hoped so.

"Yeah, but… Well, I've never told anyone this before, but she's hinted that she'll do something, you know, like swallow a bottle of pills or sit in her car in the garage with the motor running." She looked at me with the saddest eyes I'd ever seen. "What if someday I refuse to come when she calls and she follows through on her threats? I'd never be able to forgive myself for that."

Hell. I had no idea what the right thing to say here was. Although I thought Melinda's saying things like that was just another way of controlling Autumn and she had no intention of killing herself, the woman was unpredictable.

"Do you really see her not sticking around, if for no other reason than to torment you and your father?"

Autumn shrugged. "Not really, which is why I'm not too worried. On the other hand, I can see her doing that simply to punish Dad or even me."

I set my spoon down. "I get what you're saying about feeling guilty if something like that ever happened, but Autumn, you're not responsible for her or her actions. Anything stupid she might do is on her, not you."

"I know that in theory, but I'd still never forgive myself.

It gets even better. As soon as I left, she called my dad, and then he called me. The gist of the conversation was that I'm an awful daughter to treat my mother that way."

"What I'd like to know is how you managed to become an adult with her act together after growing up in that house?" I took her spoon out of her hand, sticking it into the ice cream. "I'm so angry right now for you that it's a good thing your parents aren't here, or they'd get an earful."

I tugged on her hands, pulling her off the stool until she was standing between my legs. "As much as I want to tell you to cut them out of your life unless and until they start treating you right, I won't. How you go forward with them is your decision, but I hope you really mean that you're going to stand your ground with your mother. Who knows, that might be exactly what she needs to wake up and see what she's doing to you. As for your father, to hell with him. He hasn't earned the right to say those things to you, and furthermore, he's dead wrong."

"Thanks for that and for being here, Connor. You make a pretty good pity-party partner." She leaned into me, resting her face on my chest.

"Careful, you're starting to sound like Mary with all the alliterations."

She laughed. "God help me, I did."

"That aside, anytime you need a pity partner, I'm your man. I've got the hang of it now. Ice cream, wine, and a pair of good listening ears."

"Just so you know, the ice cream was great, but cake is a better pity food. In my opinion, anyway."

"Duly noted." I lowered my chin, resting it on her head. This close to me, I could smell her scent, feel the softness of her body against mine—especially her breasts pressing into my chest—and that was about all it took to get aroused. I wanted her so badly that it hurt, but above all else, she was my friend. And that was what she needed right now, a friend.

"Can one divorce their parents?"

I smiled into her hair. "I think it's been done." Before she felt what was going on below my belt against her belly, I put my hands on her waist, picked her up, and set her a few feet away. "Why don't you go change into those cute little puppy pants you had on the other night, and I'll find us a movie to watch. Is it a pity-party rule that it has to be a sappy one?"

"Most definitely, but it's late. You're probably wishing you were home, asleep in your bed."

"I'm right where I want to be. Go." Although we weren't doing what I wanted, and for sure it wasn't sleeping, I was beginning to wonder if Autumn and I would ever manage to get naked under the sheets together. Over a year now I'd been in a holding pattern, waiting for her and the right moment. I was starting to feel like a monk, and my man parts were extremely unhappy with me.

"Connor?" she said, pausing at the entrance to her hallway.

"Yeah?"

"Tonight didn't go like I wanted it to. The first thing I was going to tell you when you came over was that I don't feel weird about kissing you. Or anything else we might do." Her cheeks blushed pink. "Are going to do."

"You can't begin to imagine how happy I am to hear that." And that pretty smile she gave me before she disappeared down the hallway felt like an arrow had zinged my heart. A little arrow, but one all the same.

I wasn't falling for her exactly. Not like in love or anything, because I don't and won't do love, but I was liking her a whole lot in a more than "just a friend I was hopefully going to have sex with" kind of way. That was a mouthful, not to mention heavy on my mind. I just hoped to hell Autumn and I knew what we were doing.

CHAPTER TWENTY-FIVE

~ Autumn ~

AFTER PUTTING IT OFF FOR a day, I arrived at the *Blue Ridge Valley News* with Beau for his interview. I was still trying to wrap my head around the fact that my dog had an interview. It had been tempting to blow it off altogether, but I'd be hounded out of town if I hadn't shown up with my dog, so here we were. I told Beau to sit, which he did, I'm happy to say—he didn't always obey my commands—then I stepped out of view of the camera Naomi was snapping pictures with.

As soon as we left here, I planned to call Connor and apologize. He'd found *Pretty Woman*, one of my favorite old movies, playing on a cable channel. I'd snuggled up to him to watch it and had promptly fallen asleep. At some point he'd carried me to bed, tucked me in, and then let himself out. I had to be the worst date in the world.

"Ask him the questions we wrote up," Naomi said to Gloria as she knelt in front of Beau to get a close-up face shot. Naomi, somewhere in her seventies, had owned the gossip rag forever, since before I was born, anyway.

Gloria pulled over a metal chair, placing it in front of Beau, then sat. She opened a steno pad, where I assumed the questions were listed, glanced at it, and then said, "Were you afraid of the bear, Sam?"

I stared at her in disbelief. Did she actually think Beau was going to answer? His butt on the floor, a grin on his face, and his feathery tail sweeping across the wood, he barked, happy to be meeting a new friend. Beau wasn't choosy. He considered everyone his friend, even gossipy reporters.

"That was a no," I drily said. "And his name is Beau or Beauregard if you prefer." I watched her write *no* on her pad.

"Did you see the little cubs? Baby bears are so cute."

Beau barked twice.

"That was a yes." This was getting ridiculous, but what the heck. Beau was having fun.

Gloria clapped her hands. "I get it. One bark for no and two for yes."

Sure, why not? It was really hard not to roll my eyes, but I settled for giving her an affirmative nod instead.

"Have you heard there might be a movie about you?"

Two barks.

"We've decided on the perfect title. Sam Saves the Senator's Sister. Don't you just love that?"

One bark.

Gloria looked at me with alarm. "He doesn't like the title?"

"Apparently not." And my dog was freaking me out. Like, he really couldn't understand a word she was saying, right? "He's fond of his name, which is Beau. How about Brave Beau Battles a Bear?" Any minute now my eyes were going to start rolling around in my head without my permission.

Beau barked twice.

She glanced at Naomi—who was still busy circling Beau, taking pictures—getting a nod. "Okay, that could work, but I'll have to run it by Mary and the movie committee."

There was a movie committee now? This was getting entirely out of hand. "You do that." I stood, got Beau's leash, and clipped it onto his collar. "Well, it's been fun, but Beau and I have another appointment." At the crazy farm.

"Oh, before you go, I need to tell you our exciting news," Naomi said. "Senator Blanton has agreed to ride in the parade. We've arranged for two convertibles. The Blue

Ridge Valley High School band will lead the way with the cars following. The senator, you, and Sam . . . er, maybe Beau now, depending on approval from the committee, will be in the first car. Connor will be in the second one."

By himself? "No."

Both women frowned. "What do you mean no?" Gloria said.

"Um, no as in no? Beau and I will ride with Connor in the second car." They were lucky I'd even agreed to participate in this stupid parade. Senator Blanton wasn't getting to dictate the seating arrangements. And why was he coming to Blue Ridge Valley for this silliness, anyway?

Naomi pulled Gloria off to the corner. They whispered among themselves for a minute, then both turned and looked at me, way too pleased expressions on their faces for my liking.

"What?" I said, although I dreaded their answer.

"He's a senator, Autumn," Naomi said as if I didn't already know that. "He can do great things for our town. He specifically asked that you ride in his car. This parade is for Sam, so we would think you'd want him to have a place of honor. You're being unreasonable about this, but we'll let Beau or Sam, whichever name the committee decides on, ride with Connor." They each smiled as if I'd be pleased with that solution.

"Again, no." And why was the senator requesting that I ride with him? "Either figure out how to get the senator, Connor, me, and Beau in the same car, or it's Connor, me, and Beau together. Give the senator the lead car for all I care."

I was still raw after spending the evening with my mother two nights ago, and maybe I wasn't in the best of moods to deal with their silliness. I felt a little badly about that but not too much.

Ignoring the hurt expressions on their faces, the ones that said I didn't appreciate what they were doing for me or for Sam—damn it, Beau—I said, "See you Saturday."

My guess, they'd figure out how to get all of us in the first car, because who wanted to slight a senator? As for him doing anything for our little town, I had my doubts that would ever happen.

☾

"Seriously I'm beginning to think Beau understands English, all of it," I said after relating the details of his so-called interview with *The Valley News.* Connor and I, along with Jenn, Dylan, and Adam, were having late drinks at Fusions.

"He really barked the right answers?" Jenn said through her laughter.

"Accidently. You get that, right?" I smirked at Dylan. "No more wine for your wife."

"You hear that, Red? She just cut you off."

He smiled at her with so much love in his eyes that my heart gave a little trip. That was what I'd once thought I had, but in hindsight I could honestly say that love really was blind.

"Why is Blanton getting involved in this?" Connor said.

Adam glanced at me and then at his brother. "Maybe he likes the scenery around here."

"Yeah, well, he can find some other scenery to look at," Connor said, scowling.

"Why don't you want him looking at our scenery?" Was there a sub-conversation going on that I wasn't following?

Connor and Adam exchanged a glance, some kind of message passing between them. They did that a lot, talked without words. Even more confusing, Dylan was smirk-smiling as if he understood their twin talk.

"What?" I said, getting exasperated.

Jenn's gaze darted from Dylan to the twins, then back to Dylan. She shrugged. "I have no clue either. Want me to get it out of Dylan later?"

"My lips are sealed," Dylan said, winking at her.

"Uh-huh." She trailed a finger down his arm. "Bet I can get you to unseal them."

It was fascinating to watch the way Dylan's eyes heated as he followed the progress of her finger. Sometimes, watching them together, I thought that I'd be willing to fall in love again if I could find a man like Dylan. One I could trust.

"Why don't we go test your claim," Dylan said. He tossed some bills on the table. "That should cover our drinks."

Almost before I could blink, he had Jenn up and both of them gone. "Okay. One of you tell me what you were talking about."

"The scenery," Adam said, standing. He picked up the bills Dylan had left. "I'll take care of the tab on my way out." He squeezed my shoulder. "Good night, Autumn."

"Night." Adam had changed since Savannah had left. He didn't smile as much anymore. Didn't laugh much, either. We'd all been a tight group growing up, but I'd always been closer to Connor and Savannah closer to Adam. Savannah and Adam had taken their relationship to the next level during our senior year, though. At the time I'd thought they were the perfect couple, but she'd left a damaged man behind when she'd moved to New York. I hoped someday he'd find a way to be happy again.

Although Adam now had a reputation as a serial dater— as had Connor a while back—I believed Adam still carried a torch for Savannah. And speaking of men with a long list of booty call numbers in their contact list, I needed to have a talk with Connor.

CHAPTER TWENTY-SIX

~ *Connor* ~

IT TOOK A LITTLE PERSUASION, but I convinced Autumn to come back to my place and leave from here for the parade tomorrow. We'd stopped by her house so she could pack an overnight bag and pick up Beau. I'd spent a lot of time at her place, but she was rarely at mine.

I wanted her at my home, and that was worrisome—like I had this bizarre urge to nest. Autumn was seriously messing with my mind if I was having crazy thoughts like that. I shook my head to clear it. The only reason I wanted her here was so there wouldn't be any interruptions.

As soon as we entered, Beau took off, exploring and sniffing everything. I set the tote with Beau's supplies and Autumn's overnight bag on the counter. She stood in the middle of the living room, her interior designer's eye assessing my decor. I bit back excuses for the lack of any kind of style, instead letting my gaze roam over her.

The blue and white silk blouse—the top two buttons undone, showing a hint of cleavage—was tucked neatly into black pants, black heels peeking out from under the hem. She was one classy woman who didn't try to be sexy on top of the classy, but she was both those things.

"I've told you before that I love your log home," Autumn said, twirling in a circle, taking in the wood beams, ceiling-tall stone fireplace, and floor-to-ceiling windows that in the daytime framed a beautiful view of the river and the mountains surrounding us.

"Thanks. I hear a 'but,' though."

She glanced over her shoulder and smiled. "You need a

decorator."

"Mmm, I might know of one." She was right. Other than a brown leather couch and matching chair, a coffee table, and a large-screen TV, the living room was pretty bare. "Decorating isn't one of my talents. Would you be interested?"

"Are you kidding me? I'd love it. If you're serious, I'll start putting together some ideas to show you."

"Great. Do it. Want something to drink?"

"No, I'm fine."

"You certainly are." I held her eyes captive as I prowled toward her. Every time things started to heat up between us, something had happened. But not tonight. There weren't going to be any disturbances tonight, no parents interfering or hikers needing saving. I didn't care if the world crumbled around us; we weren't going to pay attention to anything but us.

When I reached her, I cradled her face with my hands, then brushed my lips over hers, once, twice, before claiming her mouth. She leaned into me, and I slid my arm around her back and pulled her flush against me.

She gripped my upper arms, digging her fingers into my skin. Before I deepened the kiss, before we passed the point of no return, I had to ask one more time. "Still not weird?" I said after pulling away and staring down at her. Something flashed in her eyes that I couldn't decipher, but it didn't seem good. "Autumn?"

"Definitely not weird, but . . ." She glanced at my couch. "Can we sit? Talk about something a minute?"

This was where a caveman at the beginning of time would toss the object of his desire over his shoulder, carry her to his lair, and have his way with her, because talking was overrated. Since I liked to think I'd evolved, even if only a little, from my long-ago ancestors' days, I refrained from using Neanderthal tactics, although my lower half thought that was an idea worth considering.

"Yeah, sure," I said a little belatedly. It really was true that men's attention spans alternated between when they were going to have sex and when they were going to get to eat. Somewhere in between those two things, we slept.

I followed her to the sofa. "What's on your mind?"

She toed off her heels, sat, and faced me, curling her feet under her. "I'm not sure how to put this."

"Saying it straight out usually works best."

"Um, okay. We're going to have sex, right?"

God, I hoped so. "I'm voting a resounding yes, but it's up to you."

She glanced at me, and then her eyes shifted away. "Are you going to see other women while we're together? I mean, I'm not saying we're a couple or anything like that. It's just that I wouldn't be comfortable if you did."

It rubbed me wrong that she didn't see the possibility of us being a couple. And when had I gone from wanting a little fun with Autumn to wanting to date her? It wasn't so much that I was changing my mind about falling in love, but I didn't want to hide the fact that I was seeing her as if she were some kind of dirty secret. She deserved better than that.

Before I could answer, she said, "Admit it, Connor. You're a player. Maybe not lately, but..." She shrugged.

I hated that word. So what if I went out—had sex with, if we're going to get technical—with my fair share of women? I was young, single, financially secure, and liked having a good time. What was wrong with that?

Yet I hadn't *played* in too long a time, and the blame for that went straight to the woman staring at me with her gorgeous blue eyes. If I admitted that, she wouldn't believe me. The couple thing was bugging me, so maybe we could make a trade.

"How about this? I promise on my word as your friend that while we're together, you'll be the only woman in my life, if you'll agree to openly date me. Everyone's already talking about us after that kiss, so we might as well give them something to gossip about."

"Why? I mean, I thought this was just sex. You know, friends with benefits."

I picked up a lock of her hair, curling it around my fingers. "Is that all you want from me, Autumn?" I didn't understand why I was pushing for more when she was offering me a no-strings-attached bed partner, but something inside me was rebelling at being nothing more than her itch scratcher.

"I thought that's what you wanted."

I dropped the curl and put my hand on her neck, swallowing a smile when she leaned into my touch. "I like hanging out with you, and I want to go out, just the two of us."

She didn't say anything at first, and then she smiled. "Would you like to know my answer?"

"I'm on pins and needles here, Autumn."

The woman attacked me. I fell back against the sofa when she landed on my lap, straddling my thighs.

"I take it that's a yes?"

She nodded. "It's a yes. Just promise you won't let it mess up our friendship when this is over."

"I promise. I think you should kiss me to seal the deal."

"Do you now?"

I nodded, maybe a little too eagerly. "You do all the work this time."

That made her grin. "You think I've been slacking with my kisses?"

"Yep, so you have some catching up to do, beautiful." Even though I was itching to touch her, I kept my hands on the sofa. I was definitely curious to see what she'd do.

Copying my earlier move, she put her hands on my cheeks, stared at my mouth for a few seconds, then touched my lips with hers. She played at flicking her tongue from one corner of my mouth to the other. Then with a little sigh and a puff of air, she pushed her tongue past the seam of my closed lips. It was damned difficult not to flip her onto her back and take over, but I wanted to see where she'd go with this.

She tasted and explored every part of my mouth, scraping her tongue over my teeth, along the insides of my cheeks, and then as she tangled her tongue around mine, she began to unbutton my shirt. Her fingers fumbled with the first button, but when I attempted to help her, she slapped my hands away. That was downright sexy.

Never letting go of my mouth, she finally managed to get all the buttons undone. When she tried to tug my shirt over my shoulders, I lifted up so she could slide it off. We were still joined at the mouth like wet on rain. There had never been a make-out session in my life that had sent me to this hot and bothered this fast. What was this girl doing to me?

Once my shirt was off, her hands roamed all over my chest. My nipples seemed to fascinate her the most, and when she pinched one, I let out a low moan. At hearing it, she unfused our mouths, then kissed her way down to my other nipple and sucked on it. The pleasure that ripped through me was so intense I almost shot off the couch.

I put my hands on her hips, and she slapped them away again, making me chuckle. "I never knew you were such a demanding little thing."

She lifted her head and smiled at me. "Correct me if I'm wrong, but I'm thinking you like it."

"You're not wrong." Her lips were swollen and damp from kissing me, and her eyes were a few shades darker, shimmering with desire. Total turn-on. I waved my fingers at her. "Carry on."

The next thing on her agenda turned out to be getting off my pants. "I want your blouse off," I said as she unbuckled my belt.

"Not yet." She slid my zipper down. "Lift your butt up."

"Yes, ma'am." While she was sliding my pants down, I kicked off my shoes. "How come I'm going to be naked and you're not?"

"Because that's how I want it." She twisted around on my lap, giving me her back. "Hold your feet up."

She tugged off my socks, then resumed her position, facing me. All my clothing was gone except for my boxer briefs. She eyed those, gave them a considering look, then said, "We'll leave those on for a minute."

"You're the boss." There was no hiding how hard I was for her, not that I had a problem with her knowing what she did to me.

"Put your hands on the back of the sofa and leave them there." She nodded in approval when I clutched the back of my couch.

This was a side of Autumn that I'd never known existed. I liked it. Who was I kidding? I loved it. Her gaze roamed over me, pausing on my tented briefs. And damn, if she didn't lick her lips.

"You're killing me, Autumn, looking at me like that."

CHAPTER TWENTY-SEVEN

~ Autumn ~

"GOOD. BY THE TIME I'M done with you, you're going to need CPR." I lifted my eyes to Connor's. He was looking back at me, his eyelids hooded, his lips parted, and his hands were gripping the top of the sofa. I don't know what had gotten into me tonight with this bossy thing. Maybe it was because it had been a long time since I'd been with a man, but I was feeling naughty. I also think that my friendship with Connor had a lot to do with it. I could be myself with him.

A wicked smile curved his lips. "Do your best."

"Challenge accepted." I tapped my fingers over his erection. "What little prize are you hiding from me?"

He snorted, a strangled-sounding snort. "Little? You wound me."

"Mmm, maybe I should see for myself." I was having fun teasing him, and he was obviously enjoying it. But like a man who couldn't take any more, he glared at me with both fire and impatience. I wrapped my fingers around him over the cotton of his briefs, and he hissed a long breath.

"In sixty—or not even that long—seconds you're going to be as naked as me," he said, standing with me wrapped around him as if I weighed no more than his favorite blanket.

I yelped, slinging my arms around his neck at suddenly being lifted into the air.

"I'm taking over." He stared hard at me, daring me to argue. "I've wanted you too long, waited too long for this to happen. You can play with me all you want later. Right now, though, my rules." He slipped his hands under my bottom. "I'm going to touch you and taste you until you're begging me to make you come. And Autumn?"

"Yes?" That came out in a whisper, and something like satisfaction flashed in his eyes. With my legs wrapped around his waist, he headed up the stairs. Because I was facing him, my gaze roamed over his face, taking in the dark stubble on his jaw, the way he looked at me out of those blue eyes, and then to his mouth, waiting for his next words.

"I might let you."

"Might let me what?" Somewhere along the line, I'd lost the thread of our conversation.

"Let you come."

"Oh," I whispered. "That."

He laughed. "Yeah, *that*, but it depends." At my raised brow, he said, "On whether you're a good girl and do everything I say."

A fever started low in my stomach, spreading its warmth through my bloodstream, heating my body like never before. He didn't talk as he carried me into his bedroom, but his eyes never left mine. I was aching for him, for whatever he was going to make me do.

He stopped at the edge of his bed, and with his gaze still intent on me, he let go and I slid down his body. "Should I—"

He put a finger on my lips, hushing me. So I waited.

"Take off your pants." He sat on the edge of the bed, his gaze intent on me. "Take them off, Autumn," he said when I just stood there.

This was a different Connor, one I'd never met. Excitement, the thrill of the unknown, raced up my spine. I unbuckled my belt, then lowered my zipper. His eyes tracked my every move as I let my pants slide down my legs. I stepped out of them and then waited for my next instructions.

"Blouse."

That was all he said, just that one word, but it was the roughness in his voice that skittered through me, sending a shiver rippling under my skin. Holding his gaze, I started on the first button, taking my time. At the last button I paused, completing my task as slowly as possible, doing my best to torture him. When I let go, my blouse would fall open. Would he like what he saw?

Nerves hit. Connor, my friend, would be the first man to see my body in over a year. The boy whose tree house I'd invaded. The boy who liked to throw spitballs at me because it made me giggle.

"Let go of your blouse."

My fingers refused to obey.

He studied me for a moment, then reached up and put his hand over mine.

"Let go. Let me see you."

"What if…"

"What if?" he said.

"If you're disappointed."

The corners of his mouth curved up. "How will I know if you don't show me?"

Connor was slaying me. One minute he was a demanding lover, commanding me to his wishes. Then in the next he morphed into a man whose gentle smile and soft eyes assured me that I wasn't going to disappoint him. I dropped my hand to my side.

"Good girl," he whispered, drinking me in.

He slipped his hands under the top of my blouse and slid it down my arms. I closed my eyes at the feathery touch of his fingers over my skin. I hadn't known until this moment how much I missed being touched by a man who wanted me.

"Don't close your eyes, Autumn. Watch me. See how much I want you. How beautiful I think you are."

My eyelids popped open, and I caught my breath at the hunger I saw in his eyes, at the heat shimmering in their depths. "Connor," I breathed. I felt liquid, like melted gold.

"So beautiful," he answered. He trailed the back of his hand over the lace edging of my bra. "So damn beautiful." He pulled me down next to him, leaned over, and put his mouth against my ear. "If you remember your name by the time I'm done with you, it will be a miracle."

He wrapped a strong arm around my back, bringing me against him. His free hand found its way into my hair, and he gave it a gentle tug, forcing my face to lift up.

"Open your mouth, Autumn. Let me taste you."

He was still issuing commands, but he'd softened his voice, gentling me like one would a wild animal. My lips parted, and he wasted no time diving in. I think an eternity passed before he lifted his head and stared at me with eyes that were wild and possessive.

"Do you know how long I've wanted you in my bed? Under me? Over me? Wrapped around me?"

I shook my head since words had escaped me.

"Too damn long." He reached behind me and unhooked my bra with the ease of a man who'd had a lot of practice undressing women, a reminder that when he got bored with me, he'd move on. It both reassured me that this was only a game we were playing, while sending a little pang through my heart that I didn't understand.

He kissed me hard again, his tongue and teeth and mouth claiming me. My hands lifted to his neck while his lowered to my breasts, and when he flicked both of his thumbs over my nipples, I moaned into his mouth. Without warning I was flat on the bed with Connor kneeling above me.

"Those sounds you make are driving me crazy."

"Sounds?"

"Those little sighs and moans, the way you whimper."

"You like that?"

"Oh yeah. I'm going to spend all night listening to you."

Still on his knees between my legs, his gaze traveled over me. "Damn beautiful." He lifted his eyes to mine. "What do you like? Gentle? All slow and easy? Fast and hard? Rough?"

What did I like? I wasn't sure anymore, nor had any man ever asked. That Connor was asking sent warmth through me because it made me feel special and protected. "I want to do what you like," I finally said.

He smiled. "Ah, beautiful. That tells me everything I need to know."

CHAPTER TWENTY-EIGHT

~ Connor ~

MY BEAUTIFUL GIRL WAS A fascinating mix of sultry woman and innocence, one minute gifting me with a sexy striptease and, in the next, going all shy on me. She couldn't even tell me what she liked, but that was okay. I would have fun finding out.

I put my hands on her thighs and circled my thumbs over her skin. "Do you want me to taste you, Autumn?" When she nodded, I tsked. "No, you have to tell me what you want." She chewed on her bottom lip, drawing my gaze to her mouth. I loved her mouth.

"Maybe I'll go get a beer while you're thinking about it." I lifted my hands.

"No! Yes."

"Hmm, no, you don't want me to taste you, and yes, I should go get a beer?"

"Connor . . ." She squeezed her eyes shut. "Yes, please taste me."

"Look at me when you say it." I put my hands back on her thighs and inched my fingers to the edge of her panty line. I was going to enjoy teaching her to play.

Her eyes opened, and she stared straight into mine. "Please taste me. There, are you happy?"

"Deliriously." I swallowed a smile at the glitter of irritation in her eyes. She was anticipating my mouth on her, wanted it, but she needed to learn that anticipation heightened the senses, fueled the desire. I flattened my palm over her mound, and damn if her damp panties didn't have me almost throwing my lesson out the window.

"Here? Do you want me to taste you here?"

"Connor," she wailed.

I swallowed another smile. Instead of giving her what she craved, I crawled over her, holding myself above her. "Oh, I'm going to get there, make no mistake. But I think I'll start here." I kissed the tip of her nose. "And work my way down. What do you think of that plan?"

"I think you're a cruel man, Connor Hunter."

"Trust me, that's not what you're going to be saying soon." I covered her mouth with mine. What was it about kissing this woman that had me thinking I could do it forever? She grabbed ahold of my waist and tried to pull me down. When I refused to budge, she slid her palms over my stomach and abs, then to my ass, and tried again.

There was no place I wanted to be more than nestled into the vee of her legs, but we were playing by my rules tonight. And maybe she didn't realize it, but her heavy breaths and her moans into my mouth gave her away. She was loving it.

I kissed my way to her ear. "Anticipation, Autumn," I whispered, then lifted my head and looked down at her. "It's a good word. Means a feeling of excitement about something that is going to happen. The longer you have to wait for it, the better it will be." I trailed my tongue down to the valley between her breasts. "Promise."

She tangled her fingers in my hair and pulled hard. "You're mean *and* cruel."

I pinched her nipple as punishment. A low moan rose from her throat. "Panties off." For the next ten, fifteen minutes I kissed and nipped and tongued every inch of her body, not satisfied until I had her screaming my name as she shattered.

With the taste of her on my mouth, I crawled back up her body and kissed her hard. "Are you liking our word for the night any better now?" I asked after pulling away.

She pressed her lips together, refusing to answer, but her

dilated eyes and heaving chest betrayed her.

I laughed. "Beautiful and hardheaded. You hate admitting I'm right. Don't move." I rolled over, shed my boxers, and then reached into the nightstand drawer, grabbing a handful of condoms, dropping all but one on the table. Autumn watched me put it on, her eyes going liquid again.

"Have you thought of us together?" I asked, moving over her.

"Yes."

"You've imagined how it would feel to have me inside you?" At her nod, I said, "Don't just nod. Tell me." I lowered my body, covering her. "Don't ever feel shy about saying what you want, Autumn."

She grinned up at me. "I never would have guessed you'd be so talkative in bed."

"I'll talk all night long about the naughty things I'm going to do to you as soon as you tell me what I want to hear."

"I've thought of how it would feel to have you inside me ever since the first time you kissed me."

Rewarding her, I slid halfway in, choking back a moan at how good she felt. "That's a long time to be thinking about me"—I pushed a little farther into her heat—"doing this to you."

"I know." She lifted her hips, urging me deeper. "I couldn't get you out of my mind no matter how hard I tried."

"Did you think about me late at night when you were in bed and couldn't sleep?" Damn, she felt good.

"Yes," she whispered.

"Did you touch yourself, imagining it was my hand touching you?"

She whimpered when I thrust fully into her.

"Did you, Autumn?" I said when she didn't answer.

"Yes."

"Good girl." I began with slow strokes, letting her get

used to me. She was so incredibly tight, felt so insanely good, and this first time wasn't going to last long. But we had all night. I never expected that I'd lose myself in her, and as I made love to her, our bodies joined, our eyes locked on each other, a stray thought flittered through my mind. *This is where I belong.* It was there long enough to make me freeze for a moment, and then she moaned and cried out.

"Connor!" she said, my name a rasp of their two syllables. And then she shattered in my arms.

Whatever had given me pause was gone, and the only thing in my mind was Autumn. All Autumn.

❧

Much later we sprawled in my bed, me leaning on the headboard and her using my chest to pillow her back, eating macadamia nuts out of the jar and sharing a bottle of root beer.

"Can I ask you a personal question?"

Autumn handed me the jar after dumping a half dozen or so nuts into her hand. "I guess. Might not answer."

"Fair enough." I shook some macadamias into my palm, then set the jar on the nightstand. Maybe I shouldn't pry into her sex life with Brian, but I wanted to know if I'd read her right. "You and Brian, your sex life was pretty vanilla, right?"

She leaned forward and peered over her shoulder at me. "Wasn't expecting that question."

"You don't have to answer." Although I wanted to know the answer. It would make a difference in how I went forward with her.

She popped the last macadamia into her mouth and then brushed the salt from her hands. I stayed quiet, listening to the crunch of the nut she was eating, waiting for her to speak. She had the sheet pulled up over her breasts, and I made it one of my goals to get her to stop hiding from me.

She was gorgeous, and she shouldn't feel shy about letting me see her. All of her.

"What made you ask that?"

After a short debate with myself, I decided to answer truthfully. "Because even though you were with Brian for a little over two years, and before that there was Paul— I assume you slept with him?"

"It that a problem for you?"

"Not at all. I'd be a hypocrite if I thought that." She was hugging her knees now, giving me the back of her head. I put my hands on her shoulders and pulled her back against me, then wrapped my arms around her chest. "It just surprised me a little that you're shy in bed, because in all other parts of your life you're fearless. I guess I wondered if that's something else I can blame on your douchebag ex."

She shook her head, then said, "I'm sorry."

"For what?"

"For being a lousy lay."

"Hush. You are not a lousy lay, and that's not even close to what I'm saying." I was saying this all wrong if that was all she was getting out of it. "Believe me, beautiful, I'm going to thoroughly enjoy teaching you how to have fun in bed. I'm a little confused, though. The day you drove off the mountain—which took about ten years off my life, by the way—you had gone to Brian's dealership wearing nothing but a raincoat. Did you do that for him or yourself?"

"I don't know. At the time I thought I was doing it for him. When we were dating, before we got serious, he made a comment in passing that he'd like to bend me over his desk and . . ." She waved a hand in the air. "You know."

What I knew was that Brian was a class A ass, and I wasn't sure why I'd even brought him up. Or maybe I was. I was pissed that for whatever his reasons were, he'd taught Autumn that she had to hide her sexuality. "You're a sensual woman, Autumn. Be proud of that."

"Yeah?" She twisted to face me, keeping the sheet pulled over her breasts.

"Oh yeah." I'd had enough of her hiding herself, so I yanked the sheet from her clutches. "You don't need that. You're too beautiful to be hiding yourself." Her blush was adorable, but she didn't try to cover herself again. Since she didn't seem to know what to do with her hands, I linked our fingers before she decided to cross her arms over her breasts.

She stared down at our joined hands, then lifted her eyes to mine. "Maybe I wasn't lacking something to hold his interest?"

I hadn't planned to tell her what Brian had said to Dylan, but her thinking she was lacking anything was ridiculous. Hearing the douchebag's opinion on fidelity might help her put those doubts to rest.

"Brian said something to Dylan shortly after you caught him cheating. I didn't tell you before because I didn't think you were ready to hear it, but it's time you did." She looked over her shoulder at me, and honest to God, I could drown in those blue eyes hanging on my every word. "I don't remember his exact quote, but it was something along the lines of it being different for men, that a little pussy on the side didn't mean anything." And there was the fire I loved seeing in her eyes.

"The rat bastard. He never planned to be true to our vows despite all the things he said claiming otherwise?"

"I think that's pretty obvious. You're not lacking one damn thing, beautiful girl, nor are you the reason he's a sorry excuse for a man. And before you storm off to knock down his door and beat him senseless, let me prove it to you." I put my hands on her waist, turning her and pulling her up to straddle me. "Only one rule this time around. You're in charge."

There wasn't another woman I knew or had been with who I would have pushed this hard to see for herself how desirable she was, and it was only because Autumn had been close to a lifelong friend that I cared enough to put this much effort into restoring her faith in herself.

"To hell with Brian," she said. "I've got something much better right here."

"Have at me," I said, laughing at the unholy glee lighting up her eyes. I thought I might have created a sex-loving monster. I hoped so.

CHAPTER TWENTY-NINE

~ Autumn ~

I COULDN'T THINK STRAIGHT THIS MORNING. Connor took me to a world I never knew existed with his kisses and touches, with how his deep blue eyes had held mine prisoner as he filled me in a way I'd never before known to even wish for.

Then he'd torn me open, exposed my deepest secrets and fears word by eye-opening word, forcing me to see that I'd suppressed my own needs and desires to accommodate what Brian—the jerk face who thought it was perfectly okay to have a little pussy on the side—wanted from me.

Gray light filtered in through the edges of the bedroom blinds. Unable to go back to sleep, I looked at Connor, but in the darkness all I could see was the outline of his body. That was a shame since I would have enjoyed feasting my eyes on him when he was unaware. Instead I eased out of bed.

As soon as I stood, Beau was at my side, his wagging tail beating against my legs. "Let's go watch the sunrise," I whispered. I couldn't remember the last time I'd seen the sun come up, and this morning seemed like the perfect day to do that.

After I pulled leggings and a T-shirt out of my overnight bag, we made our way to the kitchen. I opened cabinet doors until I found Connor's coffee stash. He had a K-Cup machine, and I picked a mocha-flavored one. Minutes later, coffee in hand, Beau and I went out onto Connor's back deck.

"Don't run off," I said to Beau as he raced down the steps. I leaned on the railing, watched him for a few minutes in the dim light, and satisfied he would stay close, I turned my gaze on the sun beginning to peek over the mountaintop.

I thought about Brian and my father. Were they two peas in a pod? Did my dad not see anything wrong with cheating on my mother the same way Brian had with me? And what made my mom and me vulnerable to men like that? Our environment? Mom never talked about her parents, so I didn't know much about them. I'd never even met them. Had her dad been a cheater and she'd learned to believe that was just how men were? Had I subconsciously sought out a man like my father even though I'd sworn that would never happen? Sworn that I'd never be my mother, yet I had been, if only briefly.

If so I'd broken that mold by not tolerating even one cheat. For that I was proud of myself. I wished I could sit down with both Brian and my dad and have an honest discussion. I wanted to understand how their minds worked, how they could claim to be in love with a woman yet not stay faithful. Since I doubted either one would be honest, confronting them would be pointless. I was over Brian, completely and totally. But my dad still had the power to hurt me and my mom.

Both had excuses for their behavior, and truthfully, I felt sorry for them. Rationally I knew not all men were my father or my ex-husband, but my trust in men had been destroyed, and I didn't ever see that changing.

So while I felt lighter of heart, I still didn't trust my judgment, mostly because I didn't have a blueprint for a marriage filled with love and fidelity thanks to my parents. Love wasn't for me. And that was okay. Better to just have fun out of life than to have your heart ripped out of your chest.

"Beautiful," Connor said, slipping up behind me and

wrapping his arms around me.

I looked up at the sunrise. "Yeah, it is."

"That's not the beautiful I was talking about." He nuzzled my neck. "I woke up with naughty thoughts in my head about you and would have showed you what was in my mind, but you weren't there."

He sounded miffed. I chuckled. "Stop pouting. You can show me those naughty thoughts right here."

"I like how you think. In fact, I came prepared."

"Yeah?" I turned in his arms, leaned back, and perused his body. All he had on was a pair of well-worn jeans that he'd left unzipped. My gaze fell on the tantalizing arrow of black hair pointing down, and I traced it with my finger.

I grinned. "You've gone commando on me. I like it."

He grinned back. "Seemed a wasted effort to put on underwear when I was hoping for a little outdoor activity."

"I've never made love under a sunrise before."

"We'll have to correct that."

"Have you?"

"Don't go there, Autumn. Our pasts have nothing to do with you and me."

Meaning he had, and a streak of jealousy streamed through me, which was stupid. He lifted me onto the railing, causing me to yelp in surprise. I wrapped my legs around his thighs.

"I won't let you fall." He gave me an odd look, then said, "Ever."

Before I could translate his meaning, he tugged on my leggings. "These need to come off. In fact, jump down. You need to sit on them so you don't get any splinters in that perfect ass of yours."

Once I was settled back on the railing to Connor's liking, he pulled a condom out of his pocket and set it on the railing, then pushed his jeans down and stepped out of them. Looking at a naked Connor took my breath away. He was perfection, and I feared that he set the bar very high, that any man after him wouldn't measure up.

"I would have thought after last night that you would've needed more time to recover," I said. We'd made love half the night, with short breaks in between for a snack or a drink.

"You'd think so." His mouth curved in that wicked grin I was learning to love. "But apparently not."

"You're insatiable," I said as I picked up the condom and handed it to him. "But I'm not complaining."

Under a beautiful mountain sunrise Connor showed me how it felt to be cherished by a lover. Although I didn't trust my choices in men, I'd lucked out with Connor, both as a friend and as my first itch scratcher. Even as that thought entered my head, I inwardly cringed at putting him in the latter category. Where it had once sounded amusing, it now felt vulgar and not fair to Connor.

Still pressed against me, he toyed with my hair. "I'm not sure I'll ever get enough of you, beautiful."

"Not sure I want you to." I almost bit off my tongue after saying that because it just wasn't true. I wouldn't allow it to be.

CHAPTER THIRTY

~ Connor ~

"CUTE." I EYED THE RED bandanna tied around Beau's neck. We were at my garage door, ready to head to the festival grounds. After the earlier time on my deck, Autumn had withdrawn into herself. I wondered the same thing every man did when a woman avoided his eyes. *What the hell did I do wrong?*

"Everything okay?"

"Sure. Why wouldn't it be?" She knelt in front of Beau, leaning away as she studied her dog. "I should have gotten him some sunglasses. That would have been the perfect finishing touch."

I squatted next to her and Beau, looking the dog in his eyes. "Do not let her start dressing you, Beauregard. You do and I'll have to take away your man card."

Beau barked twice.

"Did he just agree with me?" I asked.

Beau barked twice again.

Autumn smiled, but it didn't reach her eyes. She'd been quiet ever since we'd come back inside, and she was starting to worry me. Was she regretting being with me?

Last night and again this morning on my deck had been amazing. If not for this ridiculous parade, I'd pick her up right now and carry her straight back to bed, where I'd prove to her that we were good together. After the hours we'd spent exploring each other numerous times, I should be sated and satisfied. I wasn't. I wanted her more than ever.

Without thinking better of it, I kissed her. I was in serious trouble.

"Okay, no sunglasses," she said after I let go of her mouth.

I stood, and she followed me up. "After that kiss, that's all you've got to say?"

She wrinkled her nose. "What, you need to hear what a great kisser you are?"

"Yes, please." I winked.

"Yes, Connor, you're a great kisser. You can kiss me whenever you want to, and I'll try not to swoon."

"If you do, I promise I'll always catch you." We both kind of froze at that one word. *Always.* As if I'd just said the equivalent of *forever.*

"Good to know." She squatted again, fussing over Beau's neckwear. Clear avoidance going on there. "I guess we should head out."

She'd as good as dismissed me, and I didn't know what to make of the disappointment I felt. It wasn't like either one of us were looking for a forever. I sure wasn't. Yet I had the urge to kiss a different response out of her. Exactly what I wanted from her, I hadn't a clue.

We rode to the Blue Ridge Festival Grounds where the parade was staging. I had no idea what to expect, maybe the few convertibles Autumn had told me we were to ride in, along with our local high school band. I should have known, considering it was Mary and her cohorts organizing this, that I was underestimating them.

Along with the convertibles and our high school's band, were the members of our local Elks Club and, behind them, a rowdy group of five- or six-year-olds wearing masks that looked eerily like Beau—where the devil had Mary come up with those?—and a float with Blue Ridge Valley's Pets for Life letters on the side. The float held around twenty cages filled with dogs, all barking or yelping. I couldn't see what was lined up past them.

The Pets for Life—our local no-kill shelter—float wasn't new. It was in every parade we had, and many of the dogs would find families before the day was over. Three clowns ambled around the grounds, some of the younger kids screaming in fear at the sight of them. Then there was Senator Blanton standing off to the side with a young man dressed in a suit, a leather satchel strapped over his shoulder. His aide?

"There you are," Mary said, rushing up to us.

I blinked, wondering if my eyes were deceiving me. Nope, they definitely saw what I thought they saw. Mary's hair was dyed black—the first time I'd ever seen her with close to a normal color—and perched on her head was a headband with furry black ears sticking up. And where in the world had she found a black, adult one-piece? I leaned back, peering behind her. Yep, that was a tail. The kicker was the black-furred boots with little red-painted toenails.

"Um, that's an . . . interesting costume, Mary."

Beau barked twice.

A tiny sniff, barely audible, sounded next to me. I glanced at Autumn. Her lips were pressed firmly together, and laughter danced in her eyes. Tearing my gaze away from hers before we both lost it, I focused back on Mary.

"It's amazing what you can find on the Internet these days," Mary said, then twirled, almost tripping in her furry dog boots.

"Easy there." I grabbed her upper arm, stabilizing her.

"We need to have a meeting with Senator Blanton to review today's events," she said, grabbing Autumn's hand.

I fell in line on the other side of Mary as we headed for the senator. "Why is he here, anyway?" I still didn't understand that.

Mary peered up at me, her dog ears flapping with every movement of her head. "Think what a senator can do for us, Connor. He'll be an asset to the team."

The team? What team? But I didn't ask, too afraid of hearing what Mary might have up her sleeve.

"Naomi told me your suggestion for a new title for our

movie," Mary said to Autumn. "It's doable, although I still think Sam Saves the Senator's Sister has a better ring."

Over Mary's head, I rolled my eyes at Autumn, getting a lip twitch from her. "What was your suggestion?" I asked.

"Brave Beau Battles a Bear," she answered, amazingly straight-faced.

I covered my laugh with a cough, then cleared my throat. "I don't know, Mary. I like the ring of that one. Very catchy and easy to remember."

"Maybe we should ask the senator's opinion," Mary said.

And didn't that sound like loads of fun? Senator Blanton saw us approaching, and I didn't like the smile on his face when he saw Autumn. Going full-blown territorial, I stepped around Mary, and when I was next to Autumn, I put my arm over her shoulders, getting an odd look from her. Yeah, male brain sending out the universal signal. *Mine.*

Most men paid attention, but not all, and I wasn't sure about the senator. Would a man like him interest Autumn? I mean, comparatively speaking, I wasn't in his league. Not as much money, not as much power, and not on *People Magazine's* Sexiest Men Alive list.

"Hello again, Mary," the senator said as if greeting a tiny woman dressed as a dog was an everyday occurrence.

"Senator," Mary gushed. "I've brought our heroes." She glanced at Beau. "Sam, this is Senator Blanton. You saved his sister."

"Sit," Autumn said. Beau sat. "Shake." Beau lifted a paw.

The senator squatted. "I thought his name was Beau."

"It is," Autumn said.

"We haven't decided yet," Mary said.

"Well, Beau or Sam, it's very nice to meet you."

And wasn't that a politician for you? Straddling the fence.

"You look very dapper in that neckwear." Blanton held out his hand, and Beau rested his paw on the senator's palm. "My family's indebted to you, so if you ever need anything, all you have to do is ask."

Clever bastard. The man was speaking to Beau, but his eyes were on Autumn.

"How's Taren doing?" I asked to get his attention off Autumn.

He rose to his feet. "Much better, thank you. We're bringing her home, to our Asheville house. Perhaps you and Autumn can come visit her once we get her settled in? She's asked to see you both."

"We'd like that very much," Autumn said.

"Lovely." He turned to the man standing next to him. "Jason, give Autumn my card that has my cell number on it."

"Yes, sir," Jason said, promptly pulling out two card cases from the leather man purse strapped over his shoulder. He eyed them, then opened one, handing a card to Autumn.

Senator Blanton glanced at me. "Give Mr. Hunter one, too."

Either he'd intentionally let me know that Autumn was his focus, or I had simply been an afterthought for the senator. I took the card Jason gave me, folded it in half, and then stuffed it down my jeans' pocket without looking at it. Something like humor flashed in Senator Blanton's eyes. As much as I hated admitting it, the man was sharp.

"Please call and let me know when you can come see her, hopefully sometime next week, since she might wish to relocate to our main home in Raleigh soon."

"We will," I said before Autumn could respond, reminding him that Autumn and I were a *we*. After last night I wasn't going to stand by and watch him make a play for her. Autumn had called me a player—and I can't tell you how much I hated hearing that word on her lips—and sure, I'd had more than my share of bed partners, but none of them, not one had me wanting to come back for more the way Autumn did. It might be weeks, months before this thing between us sizzled out, which was both worrisome and intriguing.

"The parade starts in twenty minutes," Mary said, pushing between us. "We need to review the agenda for the day." She peered adoringly up at Blanton. "Senator, you, Autumn, and Beau will be in the first car." She darted a glance at me. "Connor, you will be in the second car with the mayor."

Sneaky little woman. Autumn had nixed that plan, and Mary knew it, but to protest in front of the senator would make me look like a poor loser.

Autumn frowned. "Connor's supposed to be with me."

A warm feeling traveled through me, and I shot her a smile.

"Here's the mayor now," Mary said, ignoring Autumn to plop off in her dog feet toward Mayor Jenkins, who was shaking hands with one of the clowns.

"We can probably squeeze Mr. Hunter into our car if that's what you want, Autumn."

Yep. Very gracious of him. I had no doubt the man knew what I'd say to that before the words left my mouth. Nor would we have to squeeze me in. The convertible would hold the three of us, Beau, and the driver just fine.

"No problem," I said through gritted teeth. "I have some things to discuss with Mayor Jenkins, so riding with him will give me the opportunity."

"But—"

Impulsively I brushed my lips over Autumn's, cutting her off. "It's okay, beautiful." I hated the thought of her riding with Blanton, but I refused to get in a pissing battle. It would only take about twenty minutes to get from one end of town to the other, and so what if the man made a play? I knew Autumn. She was not a woman who jumped from one man's bed to another's. All of Senator Blanton's dazzle and multiple homes wouldn't faze her. I hoped.

Mary got everyone lined up and then blew the whistle hanging around her neck. The high school band led us off, followed by the convertible carrying Autumn, Blanton, and Beau. They had perched themselves on the top of the back seat, Beau in the middle. Next came the mayor and I, and I followed Mayor Jenkins's lead by actually sitting on the seat. The clowns were running all over the place, tossing candy to the crowds lining both sides of the street. It looked like every resident of Blue Ridge Valley had turned out.

As we rolled out of the festival grounds, I glanced back. Directly behind my car was the Pets for Life float, the barking dogs almost drowning out the band marching in front of us. Mary stood at the front of the float, her dog ears flapping in the breeze. Behind the float about a dozen tractors followed along, and then came the 4-H Club members, some waving their club flags, some with cows on leads, and—I squinted—yes, that was a pig trotting alongside one of the boys. Bringing up the rear were eight girls on horses, their glittery western shirts sparkling in the sun.

I turned my gaze back on the car ahead of us, scowling at seeing Blanton leaning his head next to Autumn's as he talked with his mouth next to her ear. I should have put a bug on her so I'd know what he was saying.

CHAPTER THIRTY-ONE

~ *Autumn* ~

"YOU'RE ALMOST AS PRETTY AS Beau, but I'm sorry to say that his bandanna gives him the edge," Senator Blanton said, his dimples showing when he smiled. "But forgive me, Autumn, that wasn't something a man should say to a woman, that her dog is prettier than her."

I laughed. "Too late, Senator. You've already put your foot in it." The man was amusing and clever. And that dimpled smile would make any girl's heart go pitter-patter. Or it should. It wasn't working on me. Connor was the only man on my radar right now.

For however long it lasted between us, I reminded myself. I was still rattled by the intense longing I'd experienced after Connor and I had made love on his deck. I wasn't sure why or exactly what I longed for, and honestly I thought I would be better off not trying to figure it out.

"Lucas," he said as he waved to the crowd.

"Right. Lucas." I lifted one of Beau's paws, waving it at the people we passed.

"Beau! Beau! Beau!" The chant rose in the air, causing him to bark in answer.

Lucas chuckled. "Maybe I could borrow him when I go out on the campaign trail. Pretty sure he could get me votes."

"Probably, but I'd miss him too much." Lucas was easy to talk to, I'd give him that. On TV senators always seemed so stuffy and opinionated.

The right side of his mouth quirked, bringing one dimple along with it. "That's an easy fix. You could come, too."

"Ha! That would make a great headline. Who's the mystery woman following Senator Blanton around like a stalker?" He had a nice laugh, a genuine one.

"Well, there is that." He glanced at me, seemed to hesitate, then said, "So, you and Connor Hunter?"

"That would be a yes." I almost added *for now* but decided that wasn't information he needed to know. Nor did I want to encourage him by admitting that Connor and I were a temporary thing. I couldn't help liking the man, but he still didn't make my stomach twitchy the way Connor did.

"My loss then."

We both continued waving as we talked. "How about a consolation prize? I'll vote for you in the next election." Actually I'd voted for him the last time around, but I didn't want to feed his ego. Not that he had one that I could see.

"I'll accept that prize even though it's not the one I would have wished for."

Lucas was a charmer all right, and although it made me feel good to have the attentions of such a hot-looking, powerful man, I couldn't help wondering why. Surely he could have just about any woman he wanted—beautiful, sophisticated ones—so what was his interest in me, a small-town girl who had no clue how to play in the political world?

"There's something else I want to talk to you about," he said. "A business proposal that would be right up your alley as an interior designer."

That got my interest. "What's that?"

He glanced ahead. "It looks like we're at the end of the line. I have a few loose ends to tie up first regarding what I want to discuss with you. As soon as that's done, I'll be able to lay it all out for you. I'll call you, set up a meeting at your convenience."

"Sure, that works for me." I stifled my curiosity, but the excitement refused to be crushed. Was he buying a house in Blue Ridge Valley he wanted my interior design talents for? Decorating a senator's house would be a huge feather in my cap.

"I'll need your phone number."

"Oh, right." He pulled out his phone and entered my number in his contacts as I gave it to him.

"One other thing, Autumn. This is confidential for now. I need your word that you won't tell anyone you might be working for me. It would cause too much speculation."

"You have my word." That was easy. I knew how to keep secrets.

"Thank you. And by the way, that includes Mr. Hunter."

"I understand." Brian had never been interested in my career—I guess decorating homes was boring—so I was used to not discussing my work. My own parents never even asked how I was doing, but then they were too wrapped up in their own messy lives to care. A little flicker of unease flittered through me that I couldn't tell Connor, but we weren't a couple, not really. All we wanted from each other was sex, and sharing our day-to-day lives wasn't on our agendas.

Our car came to a stop behind the band. Lucas hopped over the door, then opened it. He lifted his hand to help me out. "I'll be in touch." He gave Beau an ear scratch, sending my dog's eyes rolling back in his head. "You're a good dog, Beau," he said. Then he turned to greet the people rushing up to him, eager to meet their senator.

I smiled at seeing several young and single women I knew pushing their way to the front, hoping to get noticed. I'd probably be one of them if not for Connor.

"So, what did you two talk about?"

Speak of the devil. I wrapped my arm around Connor's. "He asked me out. I said yes." I don't know what made me say that, other than I'd been suddenly possessed by the devil. Connor made a noise that sounded like a growl, and Beau, hearing him, joined in with his own growl.

"You both are too funny." I pulled Connor away from the admirers surrounding Lucas. "We just talked about the parade and the crowds, stuff like that. Honest."

Was he jealous? I shouldn't hope that he was. Not when we had no claim on each other. Yet the way he was looking at me with a possessive gleam in his eyes made my knees weak. That wasn't what I wanted, was it? I had to wonder exactly what we really were about.

"What?" I said when he didn't say anything, only kept staring at me.

His gaze shifted over to Lucas, then back to me. "He's interested in you."

I shrugged. "So? Do you see me standing over there with him?" I narrowed my eyes at him. "You're not jealous, are you?"

He huffed out a breath. "I don't know. That wasn't the deal, was it?" His gaze shifted to something over my shoulder. "Incoming."

"Autumn, didn't you see us? We waved to you."

At hearing my mother's voice behind me, I squeezed my eyes shut. She'd said *us* and that could only mean my father was with her, and they were back together. I loved my parents, both of them. I just didn't love them together, because it wouldn't last, and I'd be left to pick up the pieces when my dad walked out on her again.

Connor put his hands on my arms after I turned around. "Should I toss you over my shoulder and run away with you right now?" he murmured into my ear.

"You have no idea how tempting that is," I whispered back and then pasted on a smile. "Mom, Dad, didn't know you would be here." Much less together.

"Oh, honey, we wouldn't have missed your parade for the world, would we, darling?" my mother gushed, darting a glance at my father, needing approval that she'd said the right thing.

I wanted to shake her until she agreed to stop being

his doormat. She had on a pretty sundress, her lips were red stained—my father's favorite color of lipstick—and her hair was shiny clean. Her pity clothes would be tucked away in a drawer until she needed them again. But her smile was brittle, because she was always waiting for the other shoe to drop. Again.

From as far back as I could remember, I'd been told I was the spitting image of my mother, and I used to love that. Not so much anymore. I never wanted to look in a mirror and see eyes that had lost their light like hers had, even now with my father home. Her eyes were dull and joyless because she knew there was a time stamp on his being back home. There always was.

"We sure wouldn't have, sweets," my dad answered, giving her that easy smile that charmed all the ladies.

Darling and *sweets*, their pet names for each other... Well, until the fighting started again, and then it would be words like *jackass* and *cold bitch*. Connor moved his hands up to my shoulders, his thumbs massaging my tense muscles. I leaned my back against his chest, needing his touch.

"Mr. Archer, Mrs. Archer," he said, "it's nice to see you. It's been a while."

My dad nodded. "Too long. Looks like you and your brother are doing well. Every time I turn around, I see a new log house going up with one of your 'Built by the Hunter Brothers' signs in the yard."

He hadn't addressed Connor by name because he'd never been able to tell the twins apart, even after I'd told him countless times about their earrings. I wanted to squeeze my eyes shut again because I knew what was coming, and when Connor's thumbs stilled, I knew he did, too.

My dad made a decent enough living buying run-down homes, fixing them up, and then selling them. For a while now he'd been after Connor and Adam to partner with him so he could buy more expensive homes to resell. He wasn't one of the twins' favorite people, not only because of the way he treated my mother but more so because of how he kept forgetting he has a daughter. Like now. We'd been standing here for five minutes and he'd yet to acknowledge my existence. I should be used to that by now, but it still hurt.

If you asked me to describe my relationship with my father, it would be me doing stupid things to get his attention and him forgetting he had a daughter except on the holidays when he gave me money to spend. What I clung to were the early years when I knew for a fact that he loved me.

"Hi, Dad," I said belatedly, getting wound up because he'd yet to say a word to me.

His gaze landed on the arm Connor had around my shoulders. "I could bring a lot of business to the Hunter brothers, don't you think, baby girl?"

It's great to see you, Autumn. How are you, Autumn? Those are things he could have said to me, but obviously I was of more use to him as a means to get in with Connor and Adam. Conner pulled me closer, probably knowing I was about to lose it.

My father was a self-centered man. Everything was always about him. I knew this, so why did I still let him get to me? Connor's touch calmed me, and I swallowed the biting words on the tip of my tongue. They would accomplish nothing.

"Hey, guys," Jenn said, jogging up to us, her timing totally awesome.

My dad frowned at Jenn, then said to Connor, "We'll talk later."

Connor didn't answer.

I hugged Jenn. "Hey, yourself. Where's Dylan?"

She rolled her eyes. "Where do you think? Traffic control, crowd control, Mary control, or at least attempting that one." She laughed. "The woman's driving him crazy."

Beau barked, getting her attention.

"Well, hello there, sweet boy." She knelt and scratched his muzzle, getting a lick on her chin. Beau loved Jenn. Actually, he loved everyone except my parents, and around either one of them—or both when they were together—he tended to stick close to me, staying quiet. I think he always picked up on my tension when I was near them.

When Jenn stood, she smiled at my parents. "You must be so proud of your daughter."

Jenn also didn't like my parents much, having comforted me through the years when I'd cry on her shoulder because my dad had left again. But she was always respectful toward them, more so than Connor and Adam were.

"Of course we are," my dad said. He smiled at my mom. "I think Melinda filled up her phone with pictures of Autumn riding with Senator Blanton."

Mom giggled. "I did." She glanced at Jenn. "Did you see the way he looked at her? I'm sure he's interested in her. Here, I'll show you." She fished in her purse, then brought out her phone.

Connor's fingers tightened on my shoulders.

"Um, I'll look at them later. Connor and I have a meeting with Mary we're already late for." I grabbed Jenn's hand. "She wants you to attend, too."

"Right, the meeting," Connor said. "Enjoy the rest of your day," he said to my parents.

"Bye." Jenn waved to them as I pulled her away.

Beau tugged on the end of his leash, apparently as anxious to get away from them as the rest of us. Maybe I should feel guilty for taking off and not spending more time with them, but I was done with having guilt trips where my parents were concerned.

"Did you know they were back together?" Jenn said once we were out of hearing range.

"Nope. But I'm usually the last to find out." They'd be

reconciled anywhere from six months to a year before my father fell madly in love with the next woman.

"What's this about how Blanton looked at you?" Connor said.

CHAPTER THIRTY-TWO

~ Connor ~

I'D WANTED TO GRAB THAT phone out of Melinda Archer's hand and see for myself how Blanton looked at Autumn.

Autumn shrugged. "My mother's delusional. You know that."

True, but I'd seen the man's head leaning close to hers during the parade. Not to mention the vibes I'd picked up before the parade started. I wasn't imagining that Blanton was interested in her.

If she returned that interest, she'd tell me. I think. It wasn't like I had a claim on her, not exactly. She was the one who'd asked that I not see other women as long as we were together, and I assumed that applied to her, too. As much as I wanted to, I couldn't deny that I was jealous, a new feeling for me. I didn't like it.

Bluegrass music filled the air. "That's Hamburger," Autumn said. "Let's go listen to him."

Jenn glanced at her. "I thought we were going to a meeting with Mary."

I leaned around Autumn's back, getting Jenn's attention. "Catch up with us here, Jenn. There is no meeting. That was just to get us away from the crazy parents."

"Oh, right." She slapped her forehead. "My dumb."

That was one of the reasons I loved Jenn. She'd always been able to go with the flow. The biggest reason, though, was that she'd always been there for Autumn, whether it was to assure Autumn that her parents loved her, no matter how much they ignored their daughter, or the way she could make Autumn laugh.

Autumn grinned. "I always said you were the dumbest of us all."

Jenn snatched Beau's leash out of Autumn's hand. "Just for that, I'm stealing your dog." She trotted backward as she and Beau headed away from us. "Dylan will never forgive me if I don't bring Daisy's son to see him. I'll catch up with you guys later."

"I love her," Autumn said, her eyes on her dog and her friend as they disappeared among the people heading over to the festival ground's stage.

"Impossible not to." I put my arm around her waist, pulling her next to me. "Let's go do some feet stomping to Hamburger's fiddle."

"I wish Savannah was here," she said out of the blue.

"Hmm," was all I could say to that. Personally I hoped she stayed far away. I no longer considered Savannah Graham a friend, but I knew better than to say that to Autumn.

I'd once liked her as much as I had Autumn, Jenn, and Natalie. I still remembered the day the four of them had stormed the tree house our father and Adam had built together. Autumn's head had poked up in the opening first, and looking back, that wasn't a surprise. She was the instigator of all their pranks and shenanigans. And believe me, there had been more than their fair share of both those things.

"Hello," she'd said, grinning and waving at Adam and me as if it were perfectly acceptable to invade a boy's secret hideout, even though there was a sign at the bottom of the ladder that said NO GIRLS ALLOWED. Both of us had stared in shock at the girl who'd dared to risk our wrath when we had water guns. We grabbed them and fired, drenching her. The crazy girl only laughed.

Her face and hair wet and dripping water, she climbed in. "Shoot them, too." She pointed at her friends as they followed her in. We knew the girls. Jenn's house was next door to ours. Still, they were girls, so we soaked them, too. Unfazed, Autumn, Natalie, Jenn, and Savannah had relentlessly moved in on our territory. They'd turned out to be cool girls, though, up for anything, and the six of us had become lifelong friends. And then Natalie had died, and Savannah had gone to New York, taking Adam's heart with her.

That left four of us still in the valley, and here I was, lusting after Autumn. I never saw that one coming. But where Adam had fallen in love with one of the girls, that wasn't going to happen to me.

Hamburger Harry walked onto the stage wearing his signature overalls and carrying his fiddle. For any tourist in town who'd come out to watch the parade, they were in for a treat. Hamburger played a mean fiddle. I didn't much care for bluegrass music, unless it was Hamburger playing it.

"Don't let us leave without a jar or two of moonshine," I said to Autumn. Hamburger always had his canvas tote filled with mason jars of flavored moonshine.

"Definitely. He better have a jar of peach."

"You know he always has a peach flavored for you." And he'd have an apple pie one for Jenn. Since I wasn't as high on his favorites list as Autumn and Jenn, there may or may not be a jar in his tote of straight moonshine with cherries in it for me.

"Seriously, this is their entertainment?" someone behind me said.

"Whadda you expect from a one-horse town?"

I glanced behind me to see two guys looking at Hamburger with smirks on their faces. "Actually, if you watched the parade, you know we have eight horses."

One of them snorted. "I stand corrected. I shoulda said hick town instead."

His friend seemed embarrassed by the insult, so I gave him a nod, then, not looking for a fight, turned my attention back to Hamburger as he began to play. His feet, encased in well-worn black lace-up boots, began their shuffling dance. Within minutes the crowd was clapping in time to his music, some couples breaking out in dance.

"Hot damn! Look at that old man go."

I recognized the voice of the one who'd insulted my town and grinned. No one could entertain a crowd like Hamburger Harry. He was somewhere in his eighties, which made the energy he had onstage even more impressive. I put my arms around Autumn's chest and swayed to the music with her. She tilted her face up and smiled. My heart did a funny bounce. What was up with that?

"You'll have to meet him at his truck to get your jar of moonshine," Dylan said, coming up next to us.

Jenn peeked around from his other side. "Yeah, our meanie chief of police wouldn't let Hamburger bring his tote inside the festival grounds."

I scowled at Dylan. "We need to find a new chief. Clearly this one's not gonna work."

Dylan laughed. "The rules are the same for him as anyone else. No liquor brought inside."

"All I got to say is no one had a problem with it before you came to town, copper."

"And he's not telling you that Hamburger said there's a mason jar of moonshine with cherries in it for him," Jenn said, then smirked at her husband.

He crossed his arms over his chest. "I take the fifth."

"Whoa. Back up. Any moonshine with cherries in it belongs to me," I said, glaring at Dylan. "I have prior claim."

Dylan slapped me on the back. "Then you better hope there are two jars, my friend."

"Two jars of what?" Adam asked, joining us.

"Nothing," I said. Adam had the same taste buds as me, and he was always stealing mine if he found any of Hamburger's moonshine in my fridge.

"Connor and Dylan are fighting over a jar of moonshine," Autumn said helpfully, then smirked at me.

I spanked her butt. "Hush, woman. He's the evil twin. Don't be talking to him."

"With cherries in it?" Adam asked.

Autumn shrugged. "Apparently I'm not to talk to you, so I can't tell you yes."

"Just whose side are you on, beautiful?" Without thinking, I kissed her, a quick smack on the lips. When I glanced up, Dylan was looking at us with amusement, Jenn had about a thousand questions in her eyes, and Adam was frowning.

"So, what's everyone doing for the rest of the afternoon?" I said.

CHAPTER THIRTY-THREE

~ *Autumn* ~

JENN GLANCED OVER AT ME while holding her hands under the dryer. "Is this thing between you and Connor getting serious?

I adamantly shook my head. "No. I swear. We're just having some fun."

We were in the restroom at Fusions. Connor, Dylan, and Adam were waiting for us in the lounge. Connor and I had met them here after dropping off Beau and our two jars of moonshine at home. As soon as we'd walked in, Jenn had herded me off to the ladies' room to give me the third degree.

"I just don't want to see you get hurt again. You know I adore Connor, but he's not long-term material."

"You think I don't know that?" I sighed, knowing that she was concerned for me, but it bothered me that Connor's friends saw him as a player. But then so did I, which made my irritation unreasonable. "I do know, and that makes him the perfect man for a post-divorce fling. When I said I was done with husbands and forevers, I meant it. Besides, weren't you the one who told me to go for it?"

"I only meant that you should have some fun, not give him your heart."

"Why would you even think I would?"

"I see how you look at him. There are stars in your eyes, Autumn." She touched up her lipstick, then dropped the tube into her purse. "We better go before the guys send a search party."

"My heart's still right where it should be. In my chest."

And she was imagining things if she thought there was anything in my eyes.

She glanced back at me as I followed her out. "I hope so."

Both Connor and Dylan stood when we neared the table, pulling out the chairs next to them. "Let's mess with them," I whispered to Jenn. "You sit next to Connor and I'll sit next to Dylan."

She put her hand behind her back, giving me a thumbs-up. Connor's eyes were tracking my approach, and I gave him a flirty wink. Then I glanced at Dylan. I was pretty sure he saw nothing but Jenn coming his way. The man was so in love with her, and I couldn't be happier that she'd found her perfect mate. I also felt a little sad that I'd never experience a man looking at me like that.

Because Jenn and I were so in tune after years of pulling pranks on our friends, we crossed in front of each other at the same time, her going to the chair Connor held out, and me going to Dylan's side.

"Thank you, sir," I said to Dylan as I lowered myself into the chair next to him.

Jenn plopped down in the chair Connor held out. "She made me do it."

"Tattletale," I said.

"Cannot tell a lie here," she snapped back, her eyes twinkling with mischief.

"What are you, George Washington?"

She looked pointedly at her chest. "Do I look like George?"

"If George had breasts like yours, Red, I would have married him, too," Dylan said. He winked as he slid into his chair.

Adam choked on his beer. "TMI, man."

"Just saying it like it is," Dylan answered, his gaze still on his wife.

Connor smirked. "Even without Jenn tattling, I would

have bet my life that it was Autumn's idea."

I blinked my eyes at him. "*Moi*? Why am I always the first suspect?"

Everyone else at the table snorted.

"Remember that time she stole Mrs. Rahall's lesson plans and left a ransom note?" Jenn glanced at Dylan. "Mrs. Rahall was our seventh grade math teacher."

"I'd forgotten about that," Connor said, laughing. "She demanded a dozen chocolate fudge cookies be left under my desk in exchange for the lesson plans. Naturally Mrs. Rahall thought I was the culprit."

"Well, I did confess when she pinched your ear and tried to haul you off to the principal's office." I'd wrongly assumed Mrs. Rahall would be smart enough to realize the thief wouldn't choose their own desk for the drop-off.

Connor met my eyes. "I knew it had to be you. Who else would try to pull a prank like that? I was going to take the blame for you, though."

I think my heart just melted. "You never told me that."

He just smiled, and yep, my heart definitely melted.

"What about the time she put her house up for sale?" Adam said.

Dylan grinned. "How old were you?"

"Thirteen. I called the classified line, deepened my voice, and convinced the person on the other end I was the owner." My friends still thought it had been another one of my pranks. What I'd never explained was that I had this idea the house would sell that very week, and then my mother and I would move somewhere my father couldn't find us. I did it one of the times he'd left her, and I just couldn't bear her crying. If we moved to someplace new, she'd forget about him, or so I'd hoped.

"Yeah, her mom couldn't understand why people started calling, wanting to make an appointment to see the house," Jenn said.

Dylan leaned back and narrowed his eyes. "Any shenanigans occur on my watch, you'll be my prime suspect, Autumn Archer."

He sounded so serious, but his twitching lips gave him away. "I'm a reformed prankster, Chief. No need to suspect me."

Everyone at the table snorted, including our new chief of police.

❦

After returning home, I slipped into a pair of leggings and a cropped T-shirt. When I returned to the living room, I found Connor on the floor on his back playing with Beau. For a minute I stood at the end of the hallway watching them.

"Stay," Connor said.

Good thing he didn't command Beau to stay still. My dog's butt was on the floor, but he bounced with excitement, his gaze glued to the ball Connor held above his head.

"Stay," Connor said again as he threw the ball. Beau's eyes followed his favorite toy as it sailed through the air. After the ball came to a stop in front of the fireplace, Beau looked at Connor with a silly smile on his face, as if to say, *Can I go now? Can I go now?*

"Get it." At Connor's words Beau scrambled to get his feet under him, then raced to the ball. He trotted back with the yellow tennis ball in his mouth, dropping it on Connor's chest. He sat and barked.

"You're torturing him," I said, sitting on the floor close to Connor and crossing my legs under me.

Connor's eyes landed on the two-inch space between the waistband of my leggings and my cropped shirt. "Only fair since his owner appears intent on torturing me." He reached up and traced his finger across my stomach. "This little bit of skin peeking out from under your shirt? It's driving me crazy. I want to put my tongue there and lick my way from one side of your waist to the other. You're one sexy girl." Then his gaze moved up to my face, and I sucked in a breath at the heat in his eyes.

"I might sell my house," I blurted. The idea had been brewing for a few days. I had a new life, and I wanted a home that belonged to me, not one I'd lived in as someone's wife. I'd thought that a few changes such as a new bed and Brian taking his stuff away would have made it feel like mine. But it hadn't. There was still a part of him in the things surrounding me, like the beautiful wood horse carving on the wall. Brian and I had bought that together when I'd thought he was my forever. Even with him gone there was just too much of him in these rooms, and I didn't want to live here anymore.

"I tell you that you're about the hottest thing I've ever seen, and that's what you have to say?" He sat up, catching the tennis ball as it fell from his chest. "Get lost, Beau," he said, dropping the ball in front of Beau.

"Am I?" I wanted to be Connor's hottest thing.

"Seriously, Autumn," he said, then tackled me, landing on top of me. "How do you not know that, beautiful?"

"Am I? Beautiful to you?" I asked as he settled himself between my legs. I wanted to be that to him. His beautiful, even if it was temporary. Thinking of Connor as a brief lover passing through my life made me want to cry. That wasn't how I was supposed to think of him.

"Damn it, Autumn," he said. "We're going to make love right here on this floor until you get how much I want you, how sexy hot I think you are." He slid down until his face was opposite my stomach. "And I'll start here since this little strip of skin is calling my name." He dipped his tongue into my belly button, and when I shuddered, he lifted his head and smiled. "Have I told you I love how responsive you are?"

"No."

"My bad."

He'd barely touched me and already I was aching for him. It was true, I was crazy responsive, but it was for him. Even when I'd thought Brian and I were happy and had a good sex life, he hadn't made me ache and shudder with a mere touch of his tongue on my stomach. I could have been happy with Brian if he'd been faithful, but I honestly hadn't known what I was missing until Connor. It only confirmed what I was beginning to believe. Lust beat love hands down, especially with a man like Connor who paid attention to a woman's pleasure.

"Ah, no panties," he said after slipping his hand under my leggings.

"I was wondering how long it would take you to discover that."

He chuckled against my stomach, and the vibration traveled over my skin, teasing another shudder to ripple through me.

"Please, Connor. I want you."

"You have me, Autumn."

You have me. Those words bounced around in my mind as he made love to me, disturbing yet somehow perfect. Words I'd remember Connor said to me long after we went our separate ways.

CHAPTER THIRTY-FOUR

~ Connor ~

SITTING AT CLYDE HUMPHREY'S KITCHEN table, I sipped on the cup of coffee his wife had made before excusing herself so the "menfolk" could talk business. His property had been for sale long enough that I was confident we'd get the deal done. He might want to counter just for the fun of it, and if so, Adam and I were prepared to go a little higher.

"Well, son, that's a decent enough offer. A week ago I'd have jumped on it. Seems I got a better offer just yesterday for the land and building." Old Man Humphrey gave me a sly look over the top of his glasses. "Haven't accepted it yet. Planned to do that in a day or two, if you want to sharpen your pencil, come up with a more attractive offer."

That was not what I'd expected to hear. I set my coffee cup on the table. Who else wanted that property? I couldn't think of another soul who would be interested. "Just how sharp does my pencil have to be, Mr. Humphrey?"

"Somewhere between sharp and sharper."

That was a lot of help. Not. I stood. "I need to talk to my brother. I'll be back in touch no later than tomorrow."

He rose from his chair and walked around his table. "I'd rather see local boys get that property. You and Adam come up with something I can't refuse, ya hear?"

"I hear." He'd deliberately told me it was an outsider wanting his land and implied that it was someone with money. Our pencil would have to be sharper than we'd wanted.

After leaving the Humphreys', I got hamburgers at a

drive-through, then drove to the construction site of a log home we were building for a couple retiring to the Blue Ridge Mountains from Minnesota. I found Adam perched at the top of a twenty-foot ladder braced against the stone fireplace. Peering up, I saw that he was installing recessed lighting.

My twin loved building things, had from as far back as I could remember, and the things he built, like our luxury log homes, were beautiful. He was a true artist. I couldn't build something as simple as a doghouse if my life depended on it. But I could negotiate my way out of a paper bag and sell sawdust to a lumber mill.

We had three crews, the one at this house and at two other log homes we were building. How Adam managed three crews and kept everything on schedule was beyond my understanding. On the other hand, clients, contracts, and keeping the books made him want to crawl into a hole and pull the dirt over him. We were both happy with our roles, and that was all that counted.

"Yo," I called up to him. "We need to talk." I held up the bag of burgers. "I brought lunch."

"Almost done here. Give me a minute."

The pallets of wood flooring had arrived and were stacked in the middle of the living room. I grabbed two bottles of water from his cooler, then walked over and perched on top of the pallets. A few minutes later Adam hustled down the ladder. He unbuckled his tool belt, dropping it next to me.

"What's up?"

I handed him one of the burgers and one of the fries. "We have a problem."

"What's that?"

"Someone wants the land. Made an offer for it yesterday."

"Damn. Who? Did he say?"

"Nope, only that whoever it is isn't a local."

I finished off my hamburger, wadded up the paper, and dropped it in the bag. "He hasn't accepted yet, so we still have a chance at it. I told him I'd get back to him by tomorrow. What do you want to do? Go back with a higher offer or forget it?"

"We've looked. Nothing else is suitable. That land's perfect for what we want."

"I know. So how much should we up it?"

He shrugged. "You decide."

"Figured you'd say that." I threw a French fry at him. "You better hope I never run away and join the circus. You'd never manage the business side without me."

"You join the circus, I'm coming with you."

"Deal." I hopped off the pallet. "Old Man Humphrey said I needed to sharpen my pencil, so I guess I'll go do that."

"Haven't seen much of you lately."

And here we go. I'd been expecting a little brotherly talk. "Been busy."

"Yeah, with Autumn. She's our friend, Connor. I don't want to see her hurt." Eyes the same blue as mine looked at me with concern. "Or you either."

"We're just having a good time together. Neither one of us is going to get hurt." I understood where he was coming from. Savannah had seriously messed with his head, and he didn't want to see the same thing happen with me.

"I hope you're right. Let me know how things go on the land."

"Of course."

Adam kept women at a distance, except for Autumn and Jenn. That was only because we'd all grown up together, and he was comfortable with them. He dated as much as me—or as much as I had in the past—but since Savannah, he never went out with the same woman more than once or twice. We used to go carousing in Asheville together, but I hadn't had the desire to do that since hooking up with Autumn. I'm sure he missed that.

Walking out to my car, I started feeling guilty that I hadn't spent much time with my brother lately. I called Autumn.

"Hey, beautiful," I said when she answered.

"Hey, yourself. What's up?"

"I'm going to invite Adam over tonight. How would you like to have pizza and a movie at my place with us?" I'd actually like Adam to spend some time around us, let him see that we were just having fun together. That there was nothing serious going on.

"Wouldn't you rather have a night with just the two of you?"

"Nope. In fact, I'll call Dylan, see if he wants to join us. Jenn can come over when she gets off."

"Sounds like fun. What time should I come over?"

"Five if you're free. You can ride with me to pick up the pizzas."

"That works. See you then."

"Oh, and bring Beau." I was going to try to talk her into spending the night, which would be easier to do with her dog there. Besides, I liked the silly boy.

On the way home I called Adam and then Dylan, inviting them over, but didn't mention to Adam that Autumn was coming, too. They were both up for a night of pizza and beer. Then I stopped at the store and loaded up on beer, sodas, and snacks.

After getting back to my house, I put the beer and sodas in the fridge, then went to my office and worked on a new offer for Humphrey's land. Adam and I badly wanted that place, so I made it for the most we'd pay and hoped that was enough. I signed it, scanned it, and then e-mailed it to him.

As soon as I hit send, I rubbed Luke Skywalker's head for good luck. He'd been my hero as a boy, and my parents had given me all the *Star Wars* toys one Christmas. I don't know what happened to the others, but Luke was a permanent fixture on my desk.

That same Christmas Adam had gotten his first tool chest, loaded up with everything a boy could want to build shit. I smiled, remembering my parents' laughter as their sons screamed with excitement over their presents. It still hurt to think of them, but the good memories were there to help take away the pain of losing them.

"Miss you, Mom and Dad," I said aloud, then headed for the shower. By the time I heard Autumn's car in my driveway, I'd showered, shaved, and dressed.

Beau pranced up the sidewalk with his yellow tennis ball in his mouth. He dropped it at my feet, then expectantly looked up at me. "You bring me a present, Beauregard?"

He barked once.

I tossed the ball inside, then glanced past him at Autumn. "Did he just tell me I can't have his ball?" She had on a pair of black skinny jeans and a pink T-shirt that said *Badass*. She sure was.

"Sounds like he did." She handed me a bottle of wine.

"Thank you, but you didn't have to bring anything. Only yourself." I pulled her to me. "Come here and give me kiss, badass girl."

She put her hands on my shoulders, lifted onto her toes, and put her mouth on mine. "You taste like cherries," I murmured. We'd kissed before, but each time I discovered something new about her, and always something I liked.

"That's . . ." She lifted her head. "That's cherry-flavored lip gloss."

"Delicious." I slid my hand around her neck and pulled her back to me. She sighed into my mouth when our tongues met and tasted each other, and, damn, I loved those sighs of hers.

I was seconds away from not caring that we had company coming over and hauling her to my bed. Before I got so lost in Autumn that Adam and Dylan arrived to find us naked on my living room floor, I pulled away from her mouth and kissed her nose and then each eye.

"We have to go get the pizzas," I said. "But we'll get rid of everyone as soon as we can and continue this."

"I'll hold you to that." She snapped her fingers. "Let's go for a ride, Beau."

Beau barked, grabbed up his ball, then spun in circles. I took her bottle of wine inside and set it on the counter. We loaded up Beau, then set off to get the pizzas. On the way I almost told her about the land Adam and I were making an offer on, and that we'd like her to design the interiors of our three model homes, but thought better of it. I didn't want her to be disappointed if we didn't get the property.

"You still interested in redoing my house?" I asked after we'd picked up the pizzas.

She pulled her seat belt away from her chest and twisted to face me. "Definitely. I brought some pictures and samples to show you later."

"No doilies or girlie figurines, right?"

"I do not do doilies. Jeez, Connor."

"Just checking." I winked, getting a punch in return. That was one of the things I loved . . . that I liked about Autumn. Her sass. It made me want to kiss her silly.

Back at the house I stuck the pizzas in the oven on warm while Autumn rummaged through my cabinets, collecting plates and bowls. For a minute I watched her, thinking how much I liked seeing her in my kitchen, playing hostess. I glanced at Beau, sitting at her feet, his intent gaze on her. He was probably hoping a chip or pretzel would fall. I liked him here, too. I shook off those crazy thoughts and opened a bag of chips, sneaking Beau one.

CHAPTER THIRTY-FIVE

~ *Autumn* ~

"WHAT ONE OBJECT IN YOUR home are you most embarrassed about owning?" I read aloud and followed it with a groan. "Why me?" Jenn had managed to get away from Vincennes early and had arrived around nine thirty. We were playing Loaded Questions, and I read the card again, hoping I'd read it wrong. I hadn't. The only thing that came to mind was my vibrator.

"Spit it out, Autumn," Connor said, his lips fighting a grin.

Of course he knew what I was thinking of, as did every-smirking-one else sitting around the table. "Obviously, y'all know my answer, so I don't see why I have to say it."

"Them's the rules, my friend," Adam said, his grin matching Connor's. "From your mouth to our ears."

"It's my vibrator, okay?" I rolled my eyes. "Satisfied?" It wasn't that I was embarrassed I owned one, but that I had to say it in front of three men.

Sitting next to me, Connor leaned over and whispered, "Not yet."

I kicked him under the table, getting a chuckle.

"What color is it?" Jenn asked.

I stared at her in disbelief. "What happened to us girls sticking together?"

She laughed as she held up her wine. "My second glass happened."

"Red gets loose-lipped around that second glass," Dylan said, smiling at his wife. "That's why I haven't told her I'm a spy in my secret life. Ply her with wine and all bets are off."

"So, what color is your vibrator?" Connor said.

"It's awesomely big and purple." It wasn't oversize, and it was pink, but that got the laughter from my friends that I'd been going for.

Connor, next to answer a question, flicked the card he'd just picked up into the air. "I think I'm in trouble."

"We're identical twins, so I know you're not awesomely big and purple," Adam said. "You are in trouble, brother."

It was impossible to play a serious game with these guys, but who cared? There was nothing better than laughter with the people I loved and counted as my friends.

I grabbed the card Connor had tossed. "It says—"

A nails-on-the-chalkboard screech filled the room as the emergency radio on Connor's kitchen counter blared. Immediately three cell phones—Connor's, Adam's, and Dylan's—emitted an alert signal.

"I'll call in," Dylan said as he punched numbers into his phone.

Jenn and I shared a worried glance. All three of our guys were on the volunteer rescue team, the reason each of them had been paged. Someone was in trouble. It was approaching eleven, and whatever this was about, they'd head out into the dark to try and save whoever it was. That could be all kinds of dangerous.

"A five-year-old boy's missing," Dylan said after tucking his phone back into his pocket. "His family's camping out at Mountain Pines Campground. They went for a short hike before it got dark. One minute the kid was with them, the next he wasn't. The parents looked for him for a while, and when they couldn't find him, the mother made her way back to the campground to call for help. The dad's still out there somewhere."

"And now we probably have a lost father along with the boy," Connor said as he stood. "We can take the Jeep."

"I've got my bag in the car," Dylan said, heading for the

door.

"Me, too." Adam followed him out.

Everyone on the rescue team kept a bag in their cars with suitable clothing and emergency supplies. Dylan and Adam returned, and they all went up to Connor's bedroom to change.

"I hate when they have to go out at night," Jenn said.

"Yeah, me, too. And it's supposed to rain soon."

The guys came back down, dressed in cargo pants, white long-sleeved T-shirts with our volunteer rescue squad logo on them, jackets with the words *Blue Ridge Valley Rescue* in neon yellow on the backs, and hiking boots. They were all business now, the laughter from our game forgotten.

I exchanged a glance with Jenn, knowing she was thinking the same thing as me. These three were men who cared about our town and the people who lived here. Pride swelled that they were my friends. My gaze fell on Connor, and he caught me looking at him and winked. Long-dormant butterflies woke up, fluttering their wings like crazy in my stomach.

"Why don't you both stay here?" Connor said. "Hopefully we'll be back in a few hours. If not, make yourself at home. You're welcome to the guest bedroom, Jenn."

"Thanks," she said. She and Dylan walked out, their arms around each other, and Adam followed.

Connor pulled me to him, giving me a quick kiss. "My bed for you, beautiful."

I walked out with him, and when I noticed Adam standing a few feet away from Dylan and Jenn, who were in a lip-lock, I tugged Connor over to him.

"Stay safe, okay?" I gave him a hug. It was the first time I'd ever hugged Adam, and it was strange because although he was Connor's identical twin, he smelled and felt different. I liked knowing that if I were blindfolded, I could still tell them apart.

"Always," he said, hugging me back.

Then I turned to Connor. "That goes for you, too."

"Don't worry about us. We're trained for this, and we're always careful."

I would worry about him, about all of them. He put his hand under my chin, lifted my face, and kissed me again, and then he jogged to the driver's side of the Jeep. Jenn and I watched until they disappeared from view. In the distance thunder rumbled.

Jenn looked up at the sky. "I hope they find the little boy and his father fast."

So did I. The temperature was already dropping, and when that storm got here, it would be wet and cold. "Let's go clean up the kitchen."

"You and Connor getting serious?" she asked as she loaded plates into the dishwasher.

"I keep telling you that we're just having fun together."

"That's what Dylan and I said." She flashed her wedding ring at me. "And look at us now."

"Not going to happen with us. I meant it when I said I was never getting married again, and you know Connor. He'll get restless soon and move on." It was what we wanted and had agreed on. We weren't long-term, but lately, every time I thought that, I felt like crying.

Before Jenn could grill me any more on Connor, I said, "Let's call Savannah."

She glanced at the clock. "You don't think it's too late?"

"Eleven in New York City is like sundown to us."

"You're right." She grinned. "And even if we wake her up, too bad. Her fault for not keeping in touch better."

"Exactly." I got my phone and punched in Savannah's number, then put it on speaker.

"Hello," a male voice said.

Her boyfriend, I mouthed to Jenn, wrinkling my nose.

"Hi, Jackson. This is Autumn, Savannah's friend. Jenn's here with me, too. Is Savannah available?"

"No, she isn't. I'll tell her you called."

I met Jenn's eyes. "The jerk hung up on us."

"A hundred bucks says he doesn't tell her."

"Not only that, but why is he answering her cell phone?" I didn't at all like how Savannah had become inaccessible to us. We were her longtime friends, but she rarely called us anymore, and when we tried to get in touch with her, we usually got her voice mail but no return call.

"He's cutting her off from her friends," Jenn said.

"We don't know that. I mean, it feels like maybe he is, but Savannah's stronger than that. I can't see her allowing a man to control her like that."

Jenn shook her head. "I don't think she is. Think about it. What's the real reason she left for New York to pursue a modeling career?"

"That's all she ever talked about from the time we met her. From first grade on, she never wavered from that, while you and I wanted to be ballerinas one day and airplane pilots the next. It's what she's always wanted."

"I'm not so sure." Jenn opened a cabinet door. "Where does Connor keep his coffee?"

"He has those K-Cup ones. They're in the cabinet right above the coffee maker. I'll have one, too."

She pulled down a box and peered inside. "There are all kinds of flavors here. I think I'll have an amaretto-flavored one. What's your pick?"

"Is there a chocolate? If not, then hazelnut."

"Mocha swirl work?"

"Yep." After we made our coffees, we settled on the sofa in Connor's living room. "So what are you saying? That Savannah didn't want to be a model?"

"Think about it, Autumn. Who told Savannah she wanted to be a famous model, probably from the day she was born?"

"I know it's what her mother wanted, but I just thought Savannah was on board, too. I never saw any indication that she wasn't."

"Me either, until Adam. I thought at the time, and I still do, that she didn't want to leave him. Did you know her mother went to Adam and told him that he was standing between Savannah and her dream?"

Surprised, I shook my head. "No! She did? How do you know that?"

"I stopped by the twins' house one night to drop off some CDs I'd borrowed. Mrs. Graham was leaving as I drove up. When I went inside, it was obvious Adam was upset. Their parents were out to dinner, and Connor was out on a date. I didn't want to leave Adam alone."

She glanced down at Beau, sleeping at our feet. "I'm breaking that confidence now because I think Savannah's in trouble. Adam finally told me that Savannah's mother had said, among other things, that Savannah would end up hating him if Adam kept her from going to New York to pursue her dream. The next day he broke up with her."

Tears were burning my eyes by the time she finished. "I never knew. I always thought she'd broken up with him, but now that I think about it, neither one said exactly what had happened."

"I know. Everyone, including Connor, thinks that Savannah was the one who broke up with Adam. The real truth is that her mother made that happen. He swore me to secrecy, said he didn't want anyone to know, including Connor. He said his brother would ask a thousand questions he didn't want to answer."

"As sad as all that is, her mother might have been right. Savannah could have ended up resenting Adam if she'd stayed here with him."

"I guess we'll never know, but it should have been left to them to decide their future. I think the reason Mrs. Graham paid that visit to Adam was because Savannah was having second thoughts about leaving him. When he told Mrs. Graham that he would go to New York with Savannah if she asked, she laughed, telling him that he was just a small-town mountain boy and that he would be both an embarrassment and a hindrance to her career."

"That's awful. Adam would have never stood in Savannah's way or been an embarrassment to her. I mean, just look at him. He's drop-dead gorgeous. She'd have been the envy of any woman who laid eyes on him."

"Yeah, well, it's all spilt milk now. The question is, what are we going to do about Savannah? If she's in trouble, then she needs us."

"And if she's not and is perfectly happy with the way things are?" I thought about it for a moment. "There's only one way to find out. We pay her a surprise visit."

"My thoughts exactly. Either she needs us or she's putting her past life, including her childhood friends, behind her. If she's moving on and we don't matter to her anymore, then I want to know so I can stop worrying about her."

I nodded my agreement. "Talk to Angelo, see when you can get a few days off, and then I'll rearrange my schedule." Thunder boomed, shaking the house and startling me.

Jenn and I both looked out the window when lightning flashed. "I hate that the guys are out in this storm," I said, hoping they'd find the boy soon.

CHAPTER THIRTY-SIX

~ *Connor* ~

THE WEATHER WAS MISERABLE. IT was pouring rain and cold. Any tracks the dogs might have been able to follow had been lost in the deluge. But there was a lost boy out here somewhere, and he didn't have warm clothes and rain gear on like the searchers, so we'd keep looking until we found him. It was unfortunate that the much needed rain had decided to make an appearance tonight.

"Rusty," I called, then listened. Nothing. We'd called out his name until we were almost hoarse.

The father had been located an hour ago and reunited with his wife, so at least we were only searching for the kid. I couldn't imagine how scared he must be, and I hoped we found him soon. The temperature had dropped considerably, and in this weather hypothermia could happen fast, especially for a child. Would a five-year-old be able to find ways to stay warm and dry? Probably not, which only increased the urgency to find him.

Adam and I had buddied up. We always did on searches. It was raining so hard that even with headlamps on our helmets and the heavy-duty flashlights we both held, we couldn't see more than a few feet ahead.

"I'm not even sure where our grid is anymore," I grumbled. If it was an adult lost in the woods, the search probably would have been called off until the morning to protect the safety of the volunteers. But everyone on our team, along with the other searchers—probably close to a hundred men combined—refused to give up until we found the boy. I wasn't worried about getting lost. Along with our GPS trackers, we both had a compass, satellite radios, and other emergency supplies.

Adam stopped in a clearing, making a full circle. "I can deal with the rain, but I hate the damn lightning. Which way?"

"How far are we from the campsite?" I don't know why I bothered trying to see ahead. There was nothing but rain and blackness.

"No more than a mile, I'd guess."

"Let's work our way back. I doubt a child would have made it this far. Pay attention to any rock outcroppings or such that he might have taken refuge under."

Adam called Rusty's name as we pushed past bushes and tried not to stumble in slippery mud. Hopefully we weren't waking up any bears. With this weather they should be tucked away, nice and warm in their lairs. One bear experience was already one too many. Had that been only last week when Autumn and I had gone to the waterfall?

I'd had a moment back at the house, two of them actually. The first was when I'd winked at Autumn and a brilliant smile had appeared on her face, one meant just for me. I'd gone all warm and fuzzy inside. Then she'd noticed Adam standing off to the side when we were getting ready to load up, and she'd gone over and hugged him, telling him to stay safe.

It was impossible to ignore what was happening. I was falling for her. That wasn't good. It was the last thing she wanted from me, and if I gave her the slightest hint that I might want more with her than a fling, she'd run for the hills. Maybe that would be for the best, stop before I ended up like Adam with a broken heart. Yet the thought of not having her in my life hurt. I had some serious thinking to do.

Until we found Rusty and could go home, I needed to concentrate on our search, along with not slipping and ending up with a sprained ankle or worse. Later I'd think about Autumn and what I wanted to do.

"We should be about halfway back by now," I said.

Adam glanced over his shoulder. "What would you do if you were a boy lost in the woods at night?"

"Cry."

He chuckled. "Me, too, but after that?"

"At his age he probably doesn't know to stay put until someone finds him, and even if he was told to do that, he'll be scared and forget. He'll be trying to find his parents, which means he could be anywhere."

Adam let out a sigh. "That's what I was afraid you'd say."

"The other option is that because of the rain he found a place to take shelter. If he's curled up under a rock outcrop or a fallen log, we could walk right past him and never see him in this weather."

"Yeah, his mother said he was wearing jeans and a dark blue T-shirt, so he'll blend into the night," Adam said.

"Parents should dress their kids in neon yellow if they go hiking in the woods." We trudged on, calling Rusty's name. From the updates on our radios, the other searchers hadn't found a trace of him either. It was becoming worrisome.

Lightning flashed again, and out of the corner of my eye something caught my attention. I aimed my flashlight at the object. "Adam, hold up." Almost hidden under a bush was a boy's blue and white sneaker, the size about right for Rusty.

"What is it?"

I held up the shoe. "Did we get a description of his shoes from the mother?"

"Yeah, blue and white."

We searched all around the bush, but the other sneaker wasn't there. "Okay, he's been here but no way to know how long ago. Let's call it in, get some others in this area to help us search."

"What's that?"

I looked to where Adam was shining his light, about ten feet higher up the mountain. We headed that way. Dangling from the top of a bush was a soaked sock. "Smart kid. He's leaving signs for us to follow. Keep going," I said. "He's got to be around here somewhere."

Adam called in our report and GPS location. We started moving in a circle, widening our search pattern as we went. We were on the side of the mountain, and between the steep incline and the slippery mud, it wasn't easy going.

Not five minutes later we came to a large boulder. I shone my flashlight under it, and sure enough, there was a small cave-like indentation. Falling to my knees, I poked my head underneath.

"Shit," I exclaimed, jerking away.

Adam was instantly next to me. "What?"

"Quiet." I grabbed his arm. "He's under there, but we have a big problem." I pulled him down with me. "When I shine my light, look right behind his knees."

"Fuck," Adam whispered.

We quietly backed away. The boy was curled up, asleep, or I prayed he was only sleeping. Coiled behind his legs, as if seeking the boy's warmth, was a rattlesnake. The snake's head was tucked under his body, so at least he was also sleeping. For the moment.

"We need to wait until the others arrive," Adam said. "Maybe one of them has a gun on him."

"And we shoot the snake, the bullet goes through his body, then ricochets off the rock into the boy? Too dangerous."

"Well, a fucking rattlesnake ain't exactly a tea party, Connor."

"Tell me about it." I knelt again and peered under the overhang, hissing a breath at what I saw. Staying on my knees, I leaned away. "The snake's awake." The bastard had his head up, flicking his tongue in the air. We had to get the boy out of there before he woke up and moved.

I pulled off my backpack, handing it to Adam, and then gave him my flashlight. "I'm going to jerk the kid away."

"You be damn careful, brother. You get bit, I swear, I'm going to leave you out here to rot."

"Yeah, yeah." In an effort to stay out of the snake's line of sight, I fell onto my belly, then inched my arms along the ground toward the boy. I prayed he didn't wake up and make any kind of movement.

When I got to Rusty, I slipped my fingers into the waistband of his jeans. A warning rattle, like rice being shaken in a paper cup, sounded. Closing my eyes, I said a little prayer, and then I yanked with every bit of strength I owned, pulling the boy with me as I rolled. He screamed and started kicking me.

"Easy, Rusty," was all I had time to say before I hit a small tree. It gave way, and then the ground under me crumbled.

"Adam!" Unable to find purchase, I tossed the boy to him, then fell, tumbling head over heels for what seemed like a hundred years. At one point my foot hit a rock, and pain sliced up my leg. Glad that wasn't my head, I managed to think. I don't know how far I fell, like my very own avalanche, but I finally came to a stop on my back, unable to breathe.

Rain filled my mouth as I struggled to inhale. I squeezed my eyes shut, grimacing against the pain in my leg and in my chest. At least I was alive. I thought. I hoped. Dead, I wouldn't be hurting this bad, right? Hopefully I didn't have a collapsed lung.

It took a few minutes, but breathing finally became a little easier. The agony in my leg, though, was increasing by the second. I'd lost my helmet, and without the headlamp or my flashlight, it was damn dark. The good news, my GPS tracker was in one of the pockets of my cargo pants.

My satellite radio? I patted my left side where it had been clipped to my belt. Gone. Once I'd ascertained that I was alive and breathing, my heartbeat calmed. Adam wouldn't leave this mountain until they found me. All I had to do was wait.

Something dripped into my eyes, something heavier than rain, blurring my vision, and a dull ache began to throb in my head. I swiped my hand over my forehead, then licked one of my fingers, the metallic taste of blood exploding on my tongue. The pain in my head grew, and between that and my aching leg, my stomach churned.

My vision grayed. "Damn," I muttered, then gave in to the blackness.

CHAPTER THIRTY-SEVEN

~ *Autumn* ~

"SLEEPY?" I ASKED JENN.

"No. I can't sleep until I know Dylan and the guys are okay and that they found the boy."

"Yeah, me either," I said although we were both nodding off at each end of Connor's sofa. I blinked my eyes open and looked around. I couldn't wait to start redecorating his house. It had so much potential. Unfortunately I hadn't had a chance to show him my ideas before the guys had been called out to the search. I was a little nervous about him liking my design, but I thought it was pretty spectacular.

To pass the time and keep my mind off Connor, I went to my car and retrieved my briefcase. "Connor asked me to redecorate his house. I'm curious what you think of what I came up with," I said when I came back in. Opening my laptop, I pulled up my design.

I'd only finished the living room so far, wanting to make sure he liked where I was going before I started on the rest of his house. It had a definite masculine feel, but if, someday, Connor married, all it needed were a few feminine touches—some pretty throw pillows, a few plants, things like that—to welcome a woman into his home. I narrowed my eyes at my design for his living room, suddenly hating it. This was my idea for his home, and some other woman shouldn't love living here.

"Wow," Jenn said, leaning against my arm as she looked at my laptop screen. "He's going to love it."

"So is she," I muttered. I'd gone eclectic, combining

modern with a touch of rustic that perfectly fit Connor's log home, and what woman wouldn't love this design?

Jenn glanced at me. "Who's she?"

I closed my laptop lid. "Whoever he falls in love with."

"Ah, her," Jenn said, looking way too amused. "That could be you, you know."

No, it couldn't. Love and I weren't compatible. "Nope. I'm just going to enjoy my time with the best kisser in the world while it lasts."

"I beg to differ. Dylan's the best."

"Ha! You have to say that since he's your husband."

She puckered her lips and made kissy noises, which Beau took as an invitation to attack her face with his tongue.

"I stand corrected," she said, laughing as she tried to avoid his licks. "Beauregard's the best kisser in the world."

"Well, now that we've established that, we don't have to beat each other up over which of our guys is the better kisser." I tapped Beau on the nose. "Down." He gave me a you're-no-fun look but settled at our feet again.

Conner's emergency satellite radio, which we'd moved into the living room with us, crackled to life. "We've found the boy." That was Adam's voice. I was suddenly wide awake.

Jenn sat up, leaning close to the radio. "Awesome," she said.

After he gave their coordinates there was silence for a few minutes before the radio came to life again. "There's a rattlesnake next to him. Connor's going to pull the boy away."

My heart fell all the way down to my toes, my stomach going along for the ride. Jenn and I looked at each other, and I could see my fear mirrored in her eyes.

More excruciating silence, and then Adam's voice screaming into the radio. "Connor fell down the mountain! Oh God. I can't see him."

I think I died just then. "Connor," I whispered. Jenn

grabbed my hand, and we sat, helpless, waiting for more information.

"Tell the parents we have the boy," Dylan finally said over the radio.

Relief at hearing her husband's voice flashed in Jenn's eyes, and I was jealous that she knew he was safe. I chided myself. That was a mean thing to think. Of course I was happy to know Dylan and Adam and all the rest of the rescue team were safe, and that the boy had been found. But I was physically sick with worry for Connor.

"What about Connor?" I said to the radio. It had gone silent again.

Jenn squeezed my hand. "I think we're going to be up all night. I'll go make us some more coffee."

"Thanks." As if sensing the stress in my voice, Beau came to me and put his chin on my knee. I scratched his head. "He's going to be okay, sweet boy." I hadn't changed my mind about ever marrying again, but when I wasn't paying attention, Connor had slipped his way past my walls. He'd become more than a good friend I was having fun with. Was there a word for between like and love?

"Here you go." Jenn set the coffee on the table in front of me. Beau lifted his head and sniffed and, not finding the smell to be of interest, put his head back on my knee and peered up at me.

"I wish they'd say something." I stared at the radio, willing it to come to life.

A few minutes later static sounded from the radio, and we both stilled. "Base, radio Mission Hospital to send MAMA. Instruct them to land in the clearing at the campground. Tell them we have a male, twenty-seven, unconscious, a deep cut in his forehead, probably a concussion, possible broken leg, and the beginnings of hypothermia. We've got an EMT here and can report vitals in a minute."

My stomach somersaulted at hearing Dylan's voice calmly listing all the things wrong with Connor. "How can he be so calm?"

"They're trained to be composed in an emergency, Autumn. You know that."

"I have to go to Asheville." MAMA was Mission Hospital's medical helicopter, and if they were taking him to Mission's trauma center, he was considered in serious condition. I stood, looking around. "Where did I put my purse?"

"It's on the counter. I'll drive, though." She picked up her phone from the coffee table. "Give me a minute to text Dylan and tell him we're going."

"No, Beau, you can't go this time," I said when he raced to the door. On second thought, I didn't know how long we'd be in Asheville. "I should drop Beau off at home."

When we got to my house, although I wanted to toss him inside and haul ass, I walked him, letting him do his business. It took about forty-five minutes to get to the hospital, and I appreciated that Jenn left me to my thoughts.

What were my thoughts? I was so mixed up. I was physically sick knowing that Connor was seriously injured, so much so that I had to ask myself just what Connor meant to me. More than I wanted him to? But wouldn't I feel the same way if it was any of my friends?

"He's probably not here yet," Jenn said as she pulled her car into a parking space near the emergency room.

Whatever I felt for Connor could wait for me to figure out. Right now I just needed to know that he was okay. When we got inside, we found out that Jenn was right. The helicopter hadn't returned yet. After finding seats, Jenn called Dylan.

"Got his voice mail," she said, then texted him that we were at the hospital. A few minutes later her phone buzzed with a text. She read it and then handed her phone to me.

Helo lifting off. Driving Adam to hospital.

I texted him back. How is Connor?

Stable

That wasn't nearly enough information, but it was better than serious or critical. Or was he just saying that so we wouldn't worry too much? I was back to feeling sick.

I handed Jenn her phone. "How long will it take the helicopter to get here?"

Jenn shrugged. "Faster than a car, but other than that, I don't know."

"Let's walk outside so we can hear when it arrives." MAMA's landing pad was on top of the hospital. They probably wouldn't appreciate it if I went up to the roof.

Outside, I strained to hear the sound of a helicopter while staring up at the western sky in the direction of Blue Ridge Valley. At least it had stopped raining. Approximately twenty-five minutes later I heard it, the *whoop, whoop* of a helicopter.

I grabbed Jenn's arm. "He's here."

We returned to the waiting room, Jenn taking a seat and me pacing in front of her, watching the closed doors blocking my view from seeing when they brought him down. I went to the window. "Will you tell me when they bring Connor Hunter down?" I asked the woman behind the counter. "They just brought him in on your helicopter."

"Are you family?"

"No, a close friend."

"I'm sorry. We can only give information to family," she said with a kind smile.

What I'd expected her to say, but I tried again. "I'm only asking if you'll tell me when they bring him down."

"Give me a minute." She walked away.

"The doctor's with him now," she said when she returned.

"Thank you." I walked back to Jenn and sat on the edge of the chair. "The doctor's in with him. I wish Adam would get here so we can find out how he is."

She squeezed my hand. "He's going to be okay. He has to be."

"It's just the waiting to hear something that's killing me."

The revolving doors opened, and Adam and Dylan walked in. I ran to Adam. He opened his arms, and we hugged. "He's here, with the doctor. They won't tell me anything because I'm not kin."

He took my hand, pulling me with him to the counter. "My brother, Connor Hunter, was brought in by helicopter. Can you tell me his condition?"

"The doctor will come talk to you shortly. I'm sorry, but that's all I can tell you."

So we waited. An hour passed before a doctor appeared. His gaze traveled over the four of us, stopping on Adam. "You have to be his brother."

Adam nodded. "How is he?"

"The worst of his injuries is a concussion. We'll be keeping him overnight to monitor him. He has eight stitches across his forehead. As for his ankle, he's lucky. He has a severe strain, but it's not fractured. We'll fit him with a boot before he leaves. He'll need to stay off it for a few days."

"It probably would have been worse if the ground hadn't been soft and muddy," Dylan said.

"Yeah, I was hating the rain. Now I'm thankful for it. When can he go home?" Adam asked the doctor.

"Possibly tomorrow. Like I said, his concussion is the most concerning, and it depends on how he does tonight."

"Can we see him?" I needed to see for myself that he was okay.

"He's been moved to a room, and yes, you can go up. He'll probably be asleep, though."

He told us Connor's room number, and we headed to the elevator. "Jenny and I will say a quick hello, then get out of your way," Dylan said. "We'll leave her car here so the two of you will have transportation.

Adam took the keys Jenn handed him. "Thanks."

When we walked into the room, Connor was watching a nurse as she slipped a pillow under his ankle. "Don't see why I can't go home," he said, sounding both groggy and grumpy.

"Mr. Hunter, you have a concussion. That is not something to take lightly," she responded.

I smiled. "Stop harassing her, Connor."

He turned his head our way and then winced. "Hey, beautiful."

"Hello to you, too," Adam said.

Connor snorted, then winced again. "Note to self: Stop moving, laughing, or blinking."

"Even blinking hurts?" I asked, going to him. When I reached the bed, I put my hand on his. "You scared the holy crap out of all of us."

"Sorry. Wasn't my intention to take a slide down the mountain, believe me. And yeah, even blinking hurts."

The nurse handed him a small remote. "If you need anything, or if you start feeling nauseated or dizzy, just push this button."

"'Kay." He dropped the remote onto his lap.

Dylan and Jenn moved to the bed. "We wanted to make sure you were alive and breathing before we headed home," Dylan said. "The doctor said you might get to come home tomorrow. We'll stop by and see you when you're back in the valley."

"Aren't you going with them?" Connor asked me when they started to leave.

"I thought I'd stay."

"Don't want you to. Sleepy."

And just like that he was out. I told myself that it didn't mean anything that he didn't want me here, but it felt like a rejection and that hurt. In my head I knew he wasn't rejecting me, that he probably wouldn't even remember this conversation tomorrow. It was the ache that had sliced through my heart at his dismissal that had me backing out of the room. I was falling for a man who would eventually move on.

That wasn't good, not for me. I didn't do hurting any-more.

CHAPTER THIRTY-EIGHT

~ Connor ~

"HEY, BEAUTIFUL. ARE YOU AVOIDING me? Call me." I disconnected, frowning at the phone's screen. I'd been home—well, at Adam's house—for two days, and not a word from Autumn.

Dylan and Jenn had stopped by, Jenn's parents had paid a brief visit, Mary had shown up—blue hair this week—and even Hamburger had appeared with three mason jars of cherries soaking in moonshine. He'd taken them out one by one as if they were treasures—and hot damn, they were—setting them on Adam's coffee table in front of me.

"Three, Hamburger?" I'd said. "I might have to fall down a mountain more often if this is what I get."

He'd reared back, slapping his coverall-covered knee, laughing like a deranged man. "Connor Hunter, you're a funny man." Then he narrowed his eyes. "Don't ya do that again, ya hear me?"

"I hear you."

Adam, sitting on his sofa next to me, had snatched up one of the mason jars. "He has a concussion, Hamburger. The doctor said he can only drink two of these. I'll just take the third one. Don't want his doctor mad at him."

Hamburger had laughed so hard that his face had turned red. The man was easily amused.

Yeah, I'd had well-wishing visitors, but not the one I wanted. Adam had hovered over me like a mother hen since he'd brought me home from the hospital, and I'd finally convinced him to go to the jobsite for a few hours.

My head ached a little now and then, but it was my ankle

that bothered me. The thing throbbed like a sonofabitch. The good news, other than a slight case of hypothermia, Rusty was unharmed and back home in South Carolina with his parents. I'd do it all over again to save the kid. He'd sent Adam and me a nice e-mail, thanking us for finding him. Attached was a picture of him standing in his yard, waving to the camera.

But what was going on with Autumn? I couldn't drive yet, or I'd go see her. When Adam returned, I should get him to take me to her house. Her silence was driving me crazy.

I called Mr. Humphrey. With everything that had happened, I hadn't had a chance to follow up with him, and I hadn't heard a word from him. That was concerning. When I got his voice mail, I left a message and then fired off an e-mail to him from my phone.

Adam walked in just as I hit send. "Brought you lunch." He handed me a paper bag with Mary's Bread Company's logo on it.

"Thanks, man." Nothing beat one of Mary's sandwiches. "I'm moving back home today, but first I want you to run me by Autumn's."

"Don't think so." He filled a glass with ice and water and then gulped it down.

"Huh?" I said around a mouthful of ham and cheese on sourdough.

"You're not moving back home yet, and you don't need to be out running around."

"News flash, bro. Not your decision."

He let out an annoyed sigh. "You have a concussion. What happens if you're home by yourself and you pass out or something and no one's around? Make me happy and stay here for one more day."

"I need my office, and I need to see Autumn."

"Have you heard from her?"

"No." And that was the problem. It didn't make sense.

"You see her around the past two days?"

"Nope." He leaned back on the kitchen counter and crossed his arms over his chest. "I think you hurt her feelings."

I frowned. "How?"

"She wanted to stay with you at the hospital, but you told her to leave, that you didn't want her there."

"I said that? I don't remember. Honestly I barely remember her even being at the hospital. It's all kind of fuzzy." That didn't make sense, though. Autumn wasn't thin-skinned. She wouldn't have taken my words personally.

"You were loopy. Later that night you woke up and asked if I thought love was a dirty word. When I told you I did, you said, 'What if I like dirty?' Are you in love with her?"

"No. Of course not." And I wasn't. I was sure of that. But I did remember thinking I was falling for her before I fell off a damn mountain. "I need to see her. Now."

Adam humphed. "Sounds like a man in love to me." His expression softened. "She's a good woman, our friend, but she has issues, Connor. The men in her life have messed with her mind, especially her father. One of you is going to end up being hurt, probably you. Maybe it's better to back off now before that happens."

He was right, but the urge to defend her was strong. "She's not Savannah," I said before I thought better of it. Adam's face blanked, and I wished I'd kept my mouth shut. "Sorry. That was uncalled for."

"Yeah, it was."

The doorbell rang, and he went to answer it, returning with a vase of flowers. "These are for you."

"From who?"

"How should I know?" He set them on the kitchen island.

Yeah, he was still pissed at me. I opened the card and read it.

Connor,

Please take care of yourself and get better soon.

Autumn

"What's going on in that woman's head?"

"What woman? Autumn?"

"Yeah, Autumn." I handed him the card, then pulled my crutches to me. "Are you going to take me to her house, or should I just drive myself there?" I intended to get to the bottom of whatever was going on with her.

He grabbed his car keys from where he'd dropped them on the counter and walked out. I hobbled along behind him, feeling like the biggest shit in the world for throwing Savannah in his face like that. To this day he's never told me the full story of what went down, and it's the only secret he's ever kept from me.

Autumn wasn't home when we got there. I tried to remember if she'd told me what appointments she had this week, but honestly, my brain was still hazy on things that had happened recently. Then I thought about the flowers she'd sent. The note had been impersonal, not at all like her. Before we'd hooked up, if she'd sent flowers, the note would have been silly or snarky, something about my hard head or falling off a mountain.

If I'd hurt her feelings, I wanted to know so I could apologize and explain that I hadn't been myself when I'd sent her away. If her note was a kiss-off, I wanted to know that, too. And I especially wanted to know why. If Adam wouldn't take me back to her house later tonight, I'd drive myself there.

Halfway back to Adam's, my phone buzzed with an incoming e-mail. "Damn it," I said after reading it. "Humphrey accepted the other offer. Said it was too good to turn down."

What a craptastic day this had turned out to be. We'd lost the property, and I didn't know where Autumn was, much less what was going on in her mind.

CHAPTER THIRTY-NINE

~ Autumn ~

THAT WAS A COWARDLY THING to do, sending Connor flowers with that crappy message. But we weren't a couple, right? So it wasn't like I was breaking up with him because there was nothing to break up. But if I saw him in person, my resolve to put distance between us would melt away faster than an ice cube on a hot stove.

It was that one moment at the hospital, when he didn't want me to stay, that had me backing away. Armor surrounded my heart, and I liked it that way. That something as minor as Connor telling me to go away hurt was a sign my armor was slipping.

I would not give another man the power to hurt me, not even Connor, one of my best friends. He was smart, and he'd understand the message on the card. Our time was up. He'd probably be relieved. Now he could go have fun with all his girlfriends. That I wanted to scratch the eyes out of those miscellaneous girlfriends was another sign that I needed to end things.

From what Jenn had told me after she and Dylan had stopped by to see him, he was home and resting. I'd asked her if he'd mentioned me, and he hadn't. My disappointment was the third sign that I was starting to care too much.

After leaving the florist shop, I headed for Asheville. Lucas Blanton had called this morning to tell me that Taren was going to the family's home in Raleigh tomorrow. She wanted to see me before she left. Actually she'd asked to see me and Connor, but he was in no condition to be paying her a visit, so I'd made his excuses.

To keep my mind from straying to thoughts of Connor, which it seemed determined to do, I turned my radio to a rock station and sang my way to the Blantons' house. That helped until Lady Antebellum started singing "Need You Now." Connor's favorite song. I punched the knob, shutting off the radio. Then I turned it back on, and listening to the words, my eyes started to sting.

"Enough," I said, changing the station. I was doing the right thing, for both me and Connor.

Following the directions from my GPS, I turned up a winding drive shaded on both sides by tall maple trees. Behind a fence on my left several hundred Texas Longhorn cattle grazed, the ones closest to the road raising their massive heads, curiously watching my car pass. I'd never seen one in person before, and it was easy to see why they were called Longhorns. On my right were acres and acres of plowed fields waiting to be planted. Probably with corn to feed the livestock.

The drive took me up a gentle incline, and when I reached the top and the Blantons' Asheville home came into view, I let out an impressed whistle. "Welcome to Tara, Autumn." I was a classic movie buff and had watched *Gone with the Wind* numerous times. If Scarlett O'Hara walked out of the white, two-story plantation mansion with the tall columns and black shutters, I wouldn't have been at all surprised.

I parked in the circular drive in front of the house, and after touching up my lipstick and running a brush through my hair, I walked to the door. Within seconds of ringing the doorbell a man I guessed to be in his fifties, wearing black dress pants and a crisp white shirt, appeared.

"Miss Archer?"

"Yes."

"The Blantons are expecting you. Come with me, please."

They had a freaking butler? I followed him past the black-and-white marble-floored foyer into a parlor. This was the first parlor I'd ever been in, and my interior designer's eye wanted to take in everything, but I focused on the woman sitting on a gray linen sofa, her legs resting on a matching ottoman.

"Forgive me if I don't get up," she said. Her brother did stand.

"Of course you shouldn't." She wore shorts, and a bandage was wrapped around her right upper leg. Her right arm also sported a bandage. "Hello, Taren. I'm Autumn Archer. I can't tell you how happy I am to see you looking so well. May I give you a hug?"

She smiled. "I'd like that."

Careful not to touch her arm, I leaned down and gently hugged her. She was very pretty and had the same beautiful amber-colored eyes as her brother. I glanced at Lucas to see him softly smiling at her. There was no doubt in my mind that he loved his sister.

"I have to tell you that I love your name. Taren's unusual."

"Thank you. It's a family name," she said.

Lucas smiled at her. "Our maternal grandmother was Charlotte Grace Taren."

"I'm just thankful I didn't end up with two first names." She chuckled. "That's such a southern thing to do, but so is giving us last names for first. I'll take Taren over Charlotte Grace." She leaned back against the sofa and peered up at me. "How do I ever thank you? I wouldn't be here today if not for you and Connor. Oh, and your dog. What's his name again?"

"We were just in the right place and the right time, and his name is Beau, short for Beauregard."

"Another southern name. I love it. I wish you'd brought him with you."

Before I could answer, Lucas waved his hand toward the sofa next to Taren. "Have a seat, Autumn."

"Thank you." The man hot enough to make *People Magazine's* Sexiest Men Alive list looked right at home in a southern mansion. I bet his pants and tucked-in blue button-down cost more than three of Connor's outfits put together. Not that Lucas seemed to be hung up on money and status. He hadn't acted like he was entitled from the first time I'd met him.

And I had to stop thinking about Connor.

Connor had been texting me and leaving voice messages all day. I'd ignored them. I should go straight to hell for treating my friend like that, but what was I supposed to say to him? That I was afraid I was falling for him? If he knew that, he'd run so fast I wouldn't hear the door closing behind him. Connor didn't want forever. He'd been very clear about that, so I wasn't offended. Okay, I was a little sad, but I'd get over it.

"I'll leave the two of you to have some time together," Lucas said, his gaze on me. "I'd like to talk to you later, Autumn."

"Sure." He'd mentioned at the parade he wanted to discuss something with me, and he had my curiosity. I turned back to Taren and smiled. "Compared to the last time I saw you, you really do look great."

"I feel better, believe me." Her eyes shifted away, and she stared down at her hands. "You probably know I lost my husband and daughter recently?"

"Yes, and I'm so sorry for your loss. I can't begin to imagine how much you must be hurting."

"I was. I am. But until I almost died myself, I thought I wanted to."

"And now you don't?" This was not the conversation I'd expected to have with her. I'd thought we'd exchange a few pleasantries and then I'd take my leave. It seemed as if she needed to tell me these things, though. I just hoped I said the right words to her.

"No." She laughed. "Funny, isn't it? You think you want

something, but it turns out it's the last thing you want. I haven't told anyone else this, but I went there with the plan to jump off the waterfall so I could be with my family." Tears pooled in her eyes. "I miss them so much."

I almost said *I'm sorry*, but I'd said that already. Maybe she didn't need me to talk, only to listen.

"Then I stumbled on a mother bear and her cubs, and I almost got my wish. But I didn't wish it anymore. I didn't want to die, but I thought I was going to. And then there you, Connor, and your dog were, saving me."

I was too shocked by her admission to respond. As awful as being attacked by the bear had been for her, it was the reason she was sitting here today, telling me all this, instead of her family mourning her.

"What I didn't realize until I was clinging to that tree, knowing the bear would eventually shake me out of it, was that my husband would have been furious with me if I'd gone through with my plan. Stewart would want me to learn how to be happy again." She smiled. "That's the kind of man he was. I wish you could have met him."

"Your life is a precious thing, and if you think about it, you carry them with you in your heart, their memories and your love for them."

"I love that. I never thought about it like that." She put her hand on my arm. "And I do mean it. I don't want to die."

It was such a relief to hear her say that. "Do you have a picture of your husband and daughter?" I don't know what made me ask that, and I wanted to bite off my tongue. But she smiled again as if pleased by my question.

"Yes." She pointed to a bookshelf. "There's one of the three of us on the second shelf. It was taken shortly before Stewart and Chloe died."

I walked to the bookshelf, picking up the first photo I saw. "I recognize you and Lucas. This must have been ten or so years ago? I assume this is your parents and another brother?"

"Twelve years ago, to be exact, and yes, my parents and Grayson. He's the middle child."

He looked a lot like Lucas. "I don't know why I thought it was just you and Lucas. Maybe because I've never seen his name mentioned anywhere." I glanced over at her.

"That's because we don't talk about him. At least Lucas and my parents don't. He's the black sheep of the family."

That made him even more interesting, but she didn't volunteer any more information, so I set the photo back on the shelf and picked up the one of her family. "Your husband is... ah, was"—God, this was awkward—"a very handsome man. And what a beautiful little girl."

"Will you bring the photo to me? I've avoided looking at it since I lost them, but now I want to."

If she started crying, I was going to bawl right along with her. I handed her the picture, taking a seat next to her. She traced their faces with her finger. If I'd lost a family I loved the way she had, I don't know if I'd ever get over it.

"Thank you," Taren said.

"You don't have to keep thanking me. I'm just glad Connor and I were at the waterfall that day."

She shook her head. "That's not why I'm thanking you this time. I don't know how you did it, but I can look at their picture now."

I hadn't done anything and felt uncomfortable that she was crediting me with something that momentous for her.

Lucas walked in then, phone in hand, stilling when he saw Taren holding the photo. "Taren?" He glanced at me and frowned. "She doesn't like to look at their pictures."

My cheeks heated. "I . . . um, I . . ." I didn't know what to say.

"Oh, I asked her to bring it to me." She smiled at her brother. "I can look at them now, Lucas, without losing my shit. Isn't that wonderful?"

His stern expression softened. "Yes, it is." He walked to

her, kneeling in front of her. "And it's wonderful to see you smile. Mother's on the phone. She wants to know what time you'll arrive tomorrow. While you talk to her, I'm going to steal Autumn away to discuss some business." He handed her the phone.

"Thank you, Autumn." She touched my arm. "You'll never know how much I've enjoyed your visit."

"I wish you the very best, Taren," I said, then followed Lucas out of the room.

A short walk took us to a study. A massive mahogany desk held center stage, and matching cabinets lined the wall behind the desk, filled with what looked like law books. The drapes were a deep blue, the throw pillows on the dark blue sofa were gold, and the cushioned chairs in front of his desk were upholstered in a blue and gold print pattern. Everything spoke of money, lots of it.

Lucas gestured to a chair and then went behind his desk. "I don't know what you said or did, but that is the first time I've seen her smile since losing her husband and daughter. Thank you. My family owes both you and Connor in ways that we'll never be able to repay."

"I think she was ready to smile, and you don't owe Connor or me anything." I wished they would stop thanking me. It was embarrassing. Taren would probably never tell him what she'd planned to do at that waterfall, and it felt like a heavy burden to know her secret.

"Maybe she was, but it didn't happen until she spent time with you."

"What did you want to talk to me about?" I asked to avoid getting another thank-you. He had a way of looking at me that said I had his undivided attention when, as a senator, I knew he must have a thousand things on his mind.

"All business then." His mouth lifted in an amused smile as he opened a folder, pulling out two sheets of paper. "Before I explain, I need you to sign a nondisclosure agreement. It only means that you can't talk about what we discuss to anyone, but it doesn't bind you to accept what I'm going to offer you. There are two copies here, one for me to keep and one for you."

He handed me both pages. It was exactly what he said, an agreement that I wouldn't speak of anything he told me. "Can I ask what this is about?"

"After you sign."

I couldn't really see any reason not to, and he was giving me a copy signed by him, so he couldn't add anything to the agreement later. Besides, he had me really curious. After I signed, I handed him one of the copies, then folded the other one and stuck it in my purse.

"Okay, I'm all ears."

He sat back in his leather desk chair. "I bought the Humphrey land and building in Blue Ridge Valley."

"Really? That place has been for sale for a long time. What are you going to do with it?"

"I have a mystery dinner theater in Charlotte that's doing extremely well. With all the tourists you get coming to the valley, I think it's the perfect place to expand, so I'm going to open a second one."

"That will be an awesome thing for the town." And it would. It was exciting. "What does that have to do with me?"

"I want you to design the interior."

That left me speechless.

He chuckled. "Surprised you, huh?" I nodded. "I've seen some of your work—the country club, along with the Matthews' home. They're friends of mine. You're very good at what you do, Autumn."

My mind was already spinning with ideas. And what a fantastic opportunity.

"I'd like you to go see the one in Charlotte, but I want something completely different from that one. Are you interested?"

"Heck, yes!" Well, that didn't sound very professional. "Yes, I am interested. I'll make arrangements to go to Charlotte." I mentally reviewed my calendar. "Either this weekend or the next."

"Good, but first, I'd like to walk you through the building, give you an idea what I'm thinking. I have to return to Raleigh tomorrow night, so could you meet me there in the morning?"

"I have an appointment at eleven, but before that, yes."

"Nine sound good?"

"Perfect." I had a thousand questions, but I wanted to get my thoughts together. Tonight I'd do some research on dinner theaters and make a list of things to ask him in the morning.

"Would you like to stay for dinner? I know Taren would enjoy spending more time with you." He smiled. "As would I."

"I'm sorry, but I have plans." I didn't, but between Connor and my visit with Taren, I wasn't up to smiling through dinner. "Speaking of which, I really need to get going. Would you tell Taren that I'd love to see her again whenever she gets back this way?"

He stood when I did. "Maybe some other time."

"That would be nice. I'll see you in the morning."

"Autumn," he said when I reached the door.

I paused and glanced over my shoulder. "Yes?"

"Still you and Connor?"

"Yes, still me and Connor. Good night, Lucas." That was two little white lies I'd told him. It was better, though, that he thought Connor and I were still a thing. And as the butler opened the front door for me, I tried to ignore the pang in my heart that almost brought tears to my eyes. I willed them away. Allowing my feelings for Connor to deepen was the road to heartbreak. Been there. Done that. Couldn't go there again.

Besides, Connor probably wouldn't miss me. I was sure

he had all the booty calls he could possibly want stored away in his contact list.

CHAPTER FORTY

~ *Connor* ~

AUTUMN WAS NOWHERE TO BE found. I'd strong-armed Adam into going back by her house, but she was still gone. Then I'd talked him into driving by the Humphrey building to see if there was anyone there to give us a clue who'd bought the place. That was a ruse to get him to drive through town so I could see if I could spot Autumn's car anywhere.

Those flowers and the accompanying message were driving me batshit nuts. Her words and her ignoring my voice mails and texts couldn't have sent a clearer message. She was breaking up with me. But why? And doing it without even talking to me? I wanted answers, and one way or the other I was going to get them, even if I had to camp out on her doorstep.

"So explain something to me," Adam said.

"What's that?" I scanned the parking lot of Fusions as we drove by but didn't see her car.

"You and Autumn. Just friends having some fun, isn't that what you said?"

"Yeah." *Where the hell are you, Autumn?*

"If that's true, why are we trying to stalk her?"

"Say what?" I glared at my brother. "I'm not stalking her."

"You so are, dude."

Was I? Wanting answers wasn't stalking. "Let's go to Vincennes for a pizza." Maybe Jenn would know where Autumn was.

"Yeah, if anyone knows where Autumn is, it will be

Jenn."

There were times when I wished I didn't have a twin who could read my mind. "I just want a pizza. Any crime in that?"

He snorted. "Either you're trying to fool yourself or me." He turned his car into Vincennes's lot. "For the record, it's okay if you need answers. Just stop pretending you don't care for her."

Christ, I did care for her. That wasn't supposed to happen. I unbuckled my seat belt. "Maybe I do, but that's a problem. I don't want to be you." As soon as the words were out of my mouth, I wanted to snatch them back.

"Excuse me?"

When he didn't make a move to get out of the car, I said, "You haven't been the same since Savannah left you." I looked at my twin. "When she broke up with you, I felt like I lost my brother. You stopped being you. After that, I swore no woman would hurt me the way she did you."

"Meaning you'd never let yourself fall in love?"

"Yeah, that," I miserably said. "But Autumn . . . I don't know how to explain it. I need her."

"You're in love with her."

"I'm not. I just want her in my life. For now, anyway."

"You're an idiot, Connor."

"Thanks for understanding," I said, letting the sarcasm drip in my voice.

"Oh, I understand all right." He opened his door, and after he got out, he poked his head back in. "What you're refusing to grasp is that Autumn's afraid you'll hurt her. Get out and let's go find your girl."

"So you've been in her mind now?" He was wrong. I didn't mean enough to Autumn to hurt her.

He slammed the door as if he were fed up with me. I couldn't blame him. I was fed up with myself because of a stubborn girl. The very reason I didn't do love. Adam opened the passenger-side door, handed me my crutches, then stalked off, leaving me to struggle out of the car.

"What's your damn problem?" I called after him. And he was full of it. No way was I in love with Autumn.

He strode back to me. "My problem is you. You're going to screw things up with her just like I did Savannah."

I frowned. "What are you talking about? You weren't the one that screwed up with Savannah."

"The point is, you're in love with Autumn, but you're treating her like one of your booty calls."

"Where the hell are you coming up with this stuff? I am not in love with Autumn. Get that through your head. I like her a lot, but that's all."

"Maybe you're not there yet, but you're well on the way. And unless you want to lose her, you need to admit that so you can be what she needs. She's running scared, Connor, and you want to know why?"

"Fine, I'll play along. Why?" Autumn and I had an understanding. We were in it for the fun, no more, no less. Well, we *were*. Apparently she was done having fun.

"Because she's falling for you just as fast."

"And you know all this how?"

He let out an exasperated sigh. "Because I see the way you look at each other. You've never looked at another woman the way you do her, and then there's the way she looks at you. Like a woman in love. The problem is both of you have blinders on. I get both of your reasons for lying to yourselves about how you feel toward each other, but you're still an idiot, brother."

"You don't know what you're talking about," I said and then crutch-walked myself into Vincennes. There were only two seats left at the bar, and I slid onto one of them, then leaned the crutches against the back of the stool. I hated the damn things and couldn't wait to be rid of them.

"Connor!"

I glanced toward the voice yelling from the other end of the bar. Mary's hair was fire-engine red tonight, her eye shadow a matching red. I waved at her. I liked Mary, and usually she amused me, but right now I wanted to be left alone with my thoughts.

Mary hopped off her bar stool with amazing grace for someone her age wearing four-inch heels. She danced her way to me with her arms outstretched. Since it would be futile to resist, I leaned down for her hug.

"Connor Hunter, if you keep on saving people, we'll have to build a monument in your honor."

Her eyes brightened, and I groaned. The minute she got an idea in her head, there was no stopping her. "Don't even think it, Mary. There will be no monument. Besides, you're too busy getting Beau's movie made. How's that going?"

Her smile dropped. "I was sure by now that I'd be able to announce we had a deal. I don't understand it. It would be such a wonderful movie, and you would think a producer would snap at the project. Look how popular Lassie and Rin Tin Tin were. People love dog movies."

The diversionary tactic apparently worked as she seemed to forget about monuments. Adam slid onto the stool next to me. While he and Mary greeted each other, I scanned the room, looking for Jenn.

"I need to return to my date," Mary said, "but I'm glad you boys came in so I can give you your assignments."

"Assignments?" Adam said. We exchanged an alarmed glance. With Mary that could be anything from wearing sandwich-board signs promoting some event or other to cleaning the festival grounds' toilets.

"Yes, for the June Bug Dance next month."

Ah, that. I'd forgotten that was coming up. It was an annual dance to raise money for the high school football team's traveling expenses. It was a worthy cause as some of the parents couldn't afford the overnight trips.

"And our assignments are?" I said even though I probably didn't want to know.

"You're going to love it. We're doing a June Bug hot guy

calendar this year." She grinned, very pleased with herself.

"No," I said.

"No," Adam said.

"It will be a heroes calendar, featuring some of our firemen, police officers, and the rescue team," she continued, ignoring our refusals. "You boys are the June pinups. Gemini. Twins. Get it?" She bounced on her feet, delighted by her cleverness.

Adam and I let out identical groans, both of us knowing that saying no to Mary was useless.

"I'll be in touch with the details." She stepped away, then stopped, coming back. "I almost forgot. You'll need to make an appointment to have your chests waxed before the photo shoot. Renee at Hair for All Seasons is expecting your call."

And with that bomb dropped, she was off.

Jenn walked up, a huge grin on her face. "I see Mary gave you the news."

"So not happening," Adam and I said in unison.

She laughed. "Those were Dylan's exact words. He's Mr. February."

"I am not getting my chest waxed," I said. "No way. No how."

Adam nodded. "Goes for me, too."

"I wouldn't make bets on that. Mary always wins," Jenn cheerfully said. She called the bartender over. "Diane, I think these boys need a strong drink. Make them each a Cape Cod, heavy on the vodka."

As the former bartender Jenn probably knew what every resident of Blue Ridge Valley's drink preferences were.

"Where's Autumn?" Adam said. "We stopped by her house earlier, but she wasn't home."

"Oh, she went to Asheville to visit Taren Blanton."

She went without me? And was the senator there? Was she moving on to him for some fun? Hurt and angry with how she was ignoring me and that she'd hauled herself off to see the Blantons without a word to me, I fired off a text.

Flowers and a lame message? That's how you end things? Have a great life.

It didn't take the passing of three seconds to regret the text, but I didn't send an apology.

CHAPTER FORTY-ONE

~ Autumn ~

I FROWNED AT THE DARK CIRCLES under my eyes. Connor's fault that I'd tossed and turned all night. His text had hurt, but he was right. Sending him flowers and that stupid message really had been lame. It was better this way, though. Neither one of us wanted our relationship to turn serious, which made it puzzling why there was a big hurt in my heart.

The generous amount of eye cream I applied helped a little. Since I'd be touring an abandoned building with Lucas, I dressed in jeans and a blouse instead of my customary business attire.

"No, you can't go today," I told Beau when he stood at the door with his leash in his mouth. I was beginning to be sorry I'd taught him to get it whenever we were going out. He looked up at me with the saddest eyes. Poor guy. He'd been left at home all day yesterday. What would it hurt to take him?

"Fine, have it your way. In the car, Beauregard." He bounded out when I opened the door, and I shook my head. When I had kids, I was going to be an awful mom, letting them do whatever they wanted because I wasn't going to be able to say no.

I paused on my porch. What was I saying? There would not be any kids for me since I never intended to have another husband. Weird that I hadn't considered that when I'd made that decision since I'd always wanted kids. Three or four of them. That had been my dream. A happy marriage and a home filled with the laughter of children. As opposite of the home I'd grown up in as I could get. I'd thought I found that with Brian, but by cheating on me, he'd stolen my dream.

Beau dropped the leash and barked, and I blinked, then pushed my thoughts out of my mind. Maybe I should get another dog or three. I could be a crazy lady, but instead of cats I'd collect dogs.

"Let's get this show on the road, Beau my man."

His tail sweeping the air, he picked up his leash and jumped onto the passenger seat when I opened the door.

It only took fifteen minutes to reach the property, and Lucas's car was already there. "You be a good boy," I said when I clipped the leash onto Beau's collar. He barked twice, making me smile.

"Good morning, Autumn," Lucas said when we walked inside. He handed me one of the two cups he held.

I sniffed it. "Mocha hazelnut. How'd you know?"

"I stopped by Mary's place. She knew what you liked."

"Well, thank you."

"Welcome. And how is Beau today?" He bent down and scratched Beau's head.

Beau loved the attention, of course. "I hope you don't mind me bringing him."

"Not at all. He's an honorary member of our family now."

That was a sweet thing for him to say. I turned in a circle, checking out the building. I'd been inside when it had still been a grocery store, but that had been years ago. "It's going to need some structural repairs."

Lucas straightened, his gaze following mine. "I know. I'm meeting with a contractor later this morning. I'm hoping it has good bones. So what do you think?"

"Plenty of room for a dinner theater." I gestured with my coffee cup. "I'd say you'd want the stage located at the middle of the long wall. Then you can place tables all around it."

"Agree."

"I'll get to your Charlotte location this coming week to see it, but I pulled up the website. I love the Victorian theme. You said you wanted something different, so what would you think if we made this one look like the inside of a castle?"

He made a full circle, his gaze taking in the interior of the building. "I like that idea. My Charlotte location is geared toward adults. Blue Ridge Valley is a tourists' destination, and I'd like this one to be kid-friendly. Kids would love a castle, don't you think?"

"I do, and I think a family-oriented destination will be great for you and our town. This is going to be so much fun." I couldn't wait to get started. "When do you close on the property?"

"In two weeks. Then I'll get whatever repairs done that are needed. After that, it's all yours."

"Okay, I'll start working on some designs to show you. Are you coming back for the closing or doing it by mail?" I still had trouble believing he'd chosen me to do this, considering I had no experience with what he envisioned. But that would only make me work harder to prove myself.

"I'll be back. I've already scheduled a meeting with the contractor for right after closing to get things started."

"I'll have a portfolio ready to show you then, but I'm going to need to be able to get back in for a few hours to take measurements and check out some things."

His smile was smug. "I thought you'd say that." He pulled a key out of his pocket and handed it to me. "I got Mr. Humphrey to give me two."

"Great. I really appreciate the opport—"

His phone buzzed, and he held up a hand. After looking at the screen, he said, "I have to take this. Give me a minute."

He walked to the far end of the building, then disappeared into what I remembered was the store's office.

While he was on the phone, I took mine out and started snapping pictures. When I returned to take measurements, I'd bring my work camera and get better ones, but these would give me a start.

I always got excited about starting a new project. The design creation was what I loved the most, and when I'd told him this was going to be fun, I'd meant it. It was also going to be a challenge, but I knew I could pull it off.

Beau's ears perked up, and he wagged his tail, his gaze focused on the door we'd come in. I glanced over to see Connor on crutches, struggling to enter. My heart took a hard bounce in my chest. This was the first time I'd seen him since leaving his hospital room. I raced over to hold the door for him. What was he doing here?

Beau barked a greeting, getting Connor's attention. "Hello, Beauregard, my friend. What are you doing here?"

"Are you talking to me or the dog?"

Connor's eyes lifted to mine, and there was something in the way he looked at me that had me sucking in a breath. So not good. I did not want to need air pumped back into my lungs because of any man.

His expression blanked. "Either one of you can answer. I was driving by and saw your car."

"Just checking out the building." Although true, I couldn't tell him the real reason since I'd signed a non-disclosure agreement, but I hadn't thought ahead when I'd done that. I hadn't considered how much I would hate keeping secrets from him. I wanted to ask him if he'd really meant what he'd said in his text, but of course he had or he wouldn't have sent it.

"Sorry, Autumn," Lucas said, walking toward me. "Had to take care of some senate business."

Connor glanced at Lucas, then at me, and his face and eyes turned downright cold. "I see."

What did he think he saw? "Connor?"

He ignored me, his attention back on Lucas as he came

toward us.

"Connor, it's good to see you, man," Lucas said, coming to a stop and putting his hand on Connor's shoulder. "I heard about you and Adam saving that boy. You sure have a knack for being in the right place at the right time. Taren was sorry you couldn't come with Autumn for a visit."

"Sorry I missed seeing her. I would have come if some-one had told me," Connor said with an accusing gaze on me. What the hell had I done wrong? "Why are you both in this building?" he said, still looking at me.

What was his problem? He was being embarrassingly rude. Lucas glanced at me, and if Connor's attitude was bothering him, he didn't let it show. Connor was staring at me, waiting for me to explain, but it wasn't my business to share.

"I guess it's not a secret any longer," Lucas said. "I bought the building."

Connor's gaze swung to Lucas. "You? You're the other offer?"

I frowned. "What do you mean?"

"What the hell do you want with this building?"

"What's going on, Connor?"

He ignored me, keeping his gaze on Lucas.

Lucas shrugged. "I'm sorry, but I'm not ready to divulge that yet."

"Obviously she knows."

The way he said *she* sounded like he had a sour taste in his mouth. Gazing up at Connor, Beau whined, not liking the tension in the air.

Lucas nodded. "She does. I hired her to work with me on my plans."

"What did you mean by other offer?" I asked.

Still refusing to acknowledge me, Connor said, "Adam and I made Humphrey an offer. We were outbid." He gathered his crutches under him and turned away, heading for the door.

"Connor?" He ignored me. "I'll be right back," I said to Lucas. I caught up with Connor at the door. "What's your problem, Connor?"

He lifted one of the crutches and pushed the door open with the end. "There's nothing to say."

"Really? You were rude to Lucas for no reason."

"So it's Lucas now? How sweet." He kept going, and I followed him out.

"You owe him an apology. He's doing something good for our town. And while you're at it, you can apologize to me, too."

"Yeah?" He stopped, and I moved in front of him. "For what, Autumn?"

"I didn't know you and Adam wanted this building. Is that why you're angry?"

He let out a harsh laugh. "Among other things."

"Like what?"

"Well, let's see. You send me a Dear John letter in the form of flowers and a shitty note. We were supposed to go see Taren together, but you took off without me. I can only assume you didn't want me tagging along because you hoped to spend time with the senator. You didn't tell me you were working for him. How long has that been going on?"

"I had to sign a nondisclosure agreement, so I couldn't tell you. You should understand that. And I resent your implication that there's anything going on between me and Lucas." We'd never had a fight before, and I hated that we were. But he was being unreasonable and ridiculous.

"What about the way you ended things between us?"

"We were supposed to be in it just for the fun. I didn't think it would hurt you. And what about your stupid text?" In all the years I'd known him, he had never looked at me so coldly, and it felt like a ball was expanding in my chest, making it hard to breathe.

"You don't have the power to hurt me, Autumn."

I flinched, but I wasn't surprised. He'd made it clear from the beginning where he stood. "Well, good. I'd hate to think that I broke your poor heart." It was a miracle that I'd said that without my lips trembling.

"No worries there." He glanced over my shoulder at the building. "Adam and I wanted the property to build model homes on. We were going to ask you to do the interior design. I guess you found a better offer."

With that he opened his car door, tossed the crutches over the seat into the back, then got in and drove away.

I hadn't known. They hadn't given the slightest hint that they wanted the place. Standing in the parking lot of an abandoned building as Connor drove away, I realized I'd lost a friend. But so much worse was the realization that he'd taken my heart with him. That wasn't supposed to happen. I put my fingers at the top of my nose and squeezed the tears away. I wanted my heart back.

CHAPTER FORTY-TWO

~ Connor ~

WE WERE IN IT JUST for the fun. Right. Got it. Adam hadn't been happy when I'd demanded my freedom this morning, but he'd taken me to my house, giving me all kinds of admonishments to rest. As soon as he'd left, I'd gotten in my car and gone to Autumn's. She hadn't been home.

I'd decided to take a drive through town, and I'd been surprised to see her car parked outside Humphrey's building. The bigger surprise—and not a good one—had been finding her there with Senator Blanton. She hadn't known we wanted that property, but finding out she was working with Blanton felt like a betrayal.

That burned, but it was her words that I couldn't get out of my head. Was this how Adam had felt when Savannah left, like a piece of him was missing? If this was love, then I didn't want any part of it.

You're the one who sent her that dumb text. True, but it had been my knee-jerk reaction to getting brushed off with flowers and her stupid note. It burned that she couldn't tell me to my face that she was done with me.

Still, I'd said things to her that I shouldn't have. I knew there was nothing going on between her and Blanton, but my jealousy had gotten the better of me. It was an emotion I'd never experienced, and I hadn't known how to deal with that other than to act like an ass. I'd told her an outright lie when I'd said she didn't have the power to hurt me. I wish to hell it was the truth, though.

Without thinking about it I ended up at our jobsite,

pulling to a stop next to Dylan's Mustang. We'd built a
log home for him and Jenn, and I wondered if there was
a problem he'd stopped by to talk to Adam about. Adam
took pride in his work, and we seldom had issues after the
owners took possession of their homes. I noted the progress Adam had made since I'd been here last. This one was
our grandest luxury log home yet. In three weeks we'd be
turning the keys over to the new owners.

I eased out of the car, got my crutches under my arms,
and carefully made my way over construction debris.
Tomorrow I was supposed to go back to the doctor, and I
hoped he'd tell me I could toss the crutches.

Inside I found Adam leaning against the kitchen counter,
talking to Dylan. "Chief," I said, greeting him. "You slum-
ming or here to cause trouble?"

Dylan chuckled. "Stopped by to invite you and Adam
over for steaks and a beer tomorrow night."

Adam frowned. "What are you doing out? You're supposed to stay off that foot."

I ignored his question. "You'll never guess who bought
Humphrey's building."

"Senator Blanton," Dylan said.

"You knew?"

"Just heard it this morning." He glanced from me to
Adam. "That a problem?"

I shrugged. "We had an offer in on the property."

"Yeah, we were going to build a couple of model homes
and relocate our office there." Adam glanced at me. "How'd
you find out?"

"Ran into Autumn there. With Blanton, I might add."
Dylan must have heard something in my voice, because he
raised a brow. "Apparently she's working for him."

"And I gather that's also a problem," he said.

"Yeah, it is. She refused to say what his plans for the
property are. Said she had to sign a nondisclosure agreement."

Adam studied me for a moment. "But that's not why you're upset."

"She said . . ." I glanced at Dylan. What the hell. He was a friend and a smart guy, so maybe he'd have some words of wisdom. "She said that she was just in it for the fun." Those words shouldn't hurt since I'd claimed the same thing, but apparently I'd only been fooling myself.

Dylan grimaced. "Ouch." His radio crackled to life, and he reached down, turning it off. "I'll step outside to answer so you two can talk."

I took his place, leaning back against the counter so I could rest my foot without the damn crutches. "How did you do it? Get over Savannah?"

My brother lowered his gaze and stared at his work boots. "I haven't." He raised his eyes to me. "So I can't answer that."

Although it was the last thing I wanted to hear, I'd long suspected that he was still in love with her. "This really sucks." I met Adam's gaze. "I really thought I was immune to falling in love thanks to you."

"I don't know what to say, other than—"

Dylan stepped back inside. "I have to head out. About tomorrow night. Jenny and Autumn are flying to New York in the morning to visit Savannah. Thought you two might want to come over. Beer and steaks are on me."

Adam jerked his gaze to Dylan. "Savannah okay?"

"Far as I know. They just got it in their heads to go see her."

Until a few days ago Autumn would have told me her plans. Everything was so mixed up inside me that I didn't know what I was feeling. Angry? Hurt? Sad? All of those things?

"Gotta go," Dylan said. "We on for tomorrow night?"

"Sure," Adam and I said together.

After Dylan left, Adam touched my arm. "Stand by a sec. Let me get my crew started on the living room floors."

The kitchen had a large window over the sink with an amazing view of the valley below, but I wasn't seeing it. I'd heard it said that being in love turned colors brighter, made your heart feel like it was going to burst with happiness. It wasn't true. Colors were duller, and it felt like something had its claws dug deep into my heart. It hurt.

I hadn't even realized I was in love with her until she was gone. Why was that? Shouldn't I have known something like that, and would it have made a difference if I'd told her how I felt?

Adam returned, dragging a beat-up wooden stool behind him. "Sit. Get off that foot."

"Thanks." I gratefully sat, stretching my leg out in front of me, resting it on my heel. The medical boot I had to wear wasn't so bad. It was the crutches I hated.

"You need a game plan," Adam said.

"For what?"

"Autumn. I told you a few days ago that she was running scared."

"I still don't understand how you know that."

He leaned back against the counter and crossed his arms. "If you'd think about it, you would, too. What's she afraid of?"

"Being hurt again."

"The minute she realized you could hurt her, she panicked."

Hope tugged at my heart. "What makes you so sure that's the problem?"

"Christ, Connor, stop being so dense. Because she figuratively did run. That's not Autumn. If you were still just a fling to her, she'd still be around, or if she'd decided the fling was over, she would have told you to your face. If you don't know that, then you don't know her."

He was right, and I really was being dense.

"Give me your phone." Puzzled, I handed it to him. He typed something, then handed it back to me. "Send it."

I read the text to Autumn.

Lost: Heart belonging to Connor Hunter. Last seen in the vicinity of Autumn Archer. If found, please treat with care.

"I don't know if that's a good idea." Yet, I wanted her to know that she'd hurt me.

He sighed. "Listen. Can you honestly say that Autumn's it for you? I'm talking about a lifetime here."

I thought about it for all of three seconds. "Yeah, I can totally see a lifetime with her." I looked at my brother in amazement. "I never thought I'd say that about any woman."

"Then send the text. Give her something to think about."

"Maybe I'll send it later." I needed to think about it first. A text like that might have the opposite effect than I wanted, like sending her running away even faster if Adam was wrong and she wasn't in love with me.

CHAPTER FORTY-THREE

~ *Autumn* ~

"STOP STARING AT YOUR PHONE and call him, Autumn."

Poor Jenn. I was spending the night at her house since we had to leave for the Asheville airport early in the morning to catch our flight to New York. We'd closed ourselves up in her guest room, leaving Dylan to fend for himself, even though she was leaving for two days. He'd been cool about it, though.

"I will after we see Savannah." Connor had been so cold and angry with me this morning. I couldn't blame him. Between the flowers and note and what I'd said before he drove off, I'd as much as told him to get lost. I'd messed up with him so badly, and I didn't know how to fix it.

We sat cross-legged on the bed, a pizza between us, and we each had a glass of wine. Jenn picked up a second slice, taking a bite off the cheesy end. I was more interested in my wine.

"Not all men are like Brian or your father."

"I know Dylan's not. Can I have him?"

"No, you cannot have my husband." She pointed at the box. "Eat. You're going to be on a plane in the morning, and you don't want to be hungover."

I picked up a slice, nibbling on the crust. "When did you know you were in love with Dylan?"

"I kind of knew it before I left for Greece, but I refused to admit it. It really sank in when I stood on the beach in a country on the other side of the world from him and missed him so hard that it hurt to breathe." She looked at me with understanding in her eyes. "It hurts to breathe, doesn't it?"

Tears stung my eyes. "So much."

"Oh, hon, call him."

I shook my head. "Not now, okay?" And then the tears I couldn't hold back streamed down my face. "I . . . I just can't."

She pushed the pizza box aside, took my empty glass of wine from me, setting both our glasses on the end table, and then wrapped her arms around me while I cried my heart out.

"He's not a forever man," I said minutes later when I could speak again. "We agreed from the beginning that we were in it for the fun. I thought I meant that at the time."

"Things change, Autumn. He might have changed right along with you."

I snorted. "Where women are concerned, Connor has the attention span of a goldfish. Can you even count how many women you've seen him with?"

"And who has he stayed with the longest?" When I didn't answer, she said, "He's rarely seen the same woman more than two or three times, but he's different around you." She put her hand on my arm. "You and Connor have always had a special connection. Remember in fifth grade when he gave Billy Adams a bloody nose for trying to kiss you?"

I grinned. "And I was mad at Conner because I wanted to be the one to bloody Billy's nose."

"And what did Connor do?"

Tears filled my eyes again. "He apologized for not letting me throw the punch, then said I could bloody his nose if it would make me feel better."

"A boy doesn't offer something like that unless the girl is special to him. Savannah once said that she half expected you and Connor to end up together, and honestly, the more I think about it, the more I can see it. You two have been in love with each other since you were in pigtails.

You've both just been too blind to see it."

"I never wore pigtails," I grumbled. Was she right, though? I mean, I loved Adam right along with Jenn, Natalie, and Savannah. But Connor had always been a little more special. I'd just never put it into words before, forcing me to admit it.

"You're the one hiding. If you'd stuck around, Connor might have surprised you." She glanced at the clock. "We need to get some sleep." She pushed off the bed. "I'll wake you up in the morning." At the door she paused. "You really should talk to him before you accept that it's over between you."

Alone, I opened the screen on my phone, bringing up his name. After staring at it for a long time, I put it away. I wasn't ready to have it confirmed that Connor and I were honest-to-God over.

𝒞

The taxi pulled up in front of Savannah's apartment, and Jenn paid the driver. We'd checked into our hotel, dropped off our bags, and now we were about to surprise Savannah.

"We probably should've told her we were coming," Jenn said as we took the elevator up to Savannah's apartment.

"Why, so she could tell us not to?"

"Yeah, there is that."

"What if she's not home?" I was starting to feel a little uncomfortable about ambushing Savannah.

"We camp out at her front door."

"That'll work. Well, unless Jackson calls the cops. He's not going to be happy to see us."

Jenn made a noise that sounded a lot like a snarl. "Ask me if I care. We were her friends long before he ever came into the picture."

We arrived at Savannah's door, looked at each other a moment, then I fisted my hand and rapped my knuckles on the wood. I couldn't hear anything from inside the apartment, no TV or radio.

"She's probably out on a shoot," Jenn said.

"So, we're going to stand out here in the hall like stalkers and wait for her to come home? What if she's on location somewhere? We should have told her we were coming."

The door opened, and there stood Savannah, looking at us with wide eyes. "Autumn, Jenn? What are you doing here?"

"We came to see our friend who never calls us anymore," I said.

Jenn threw up her hands. "Surprise!"

"I . . ." Savannah leaned past us and peered down the hall toward the elevator, then pulled us inside and closed the door. "I don't know what to say." She held out her arms as tears pooled in her eyes.

We fell into a group hug, the three of us sniffling and laughing, so happy to see each other. I pulled my head back and scrutinized Savannah. She was still too thin, but her face was devoid of makeup and she had her hair in a ponytail. She looked like a young Savannah, the way she had in high school. Her eyes, though, were sad.

I darted a glance around her apartment, my decorator's eye cringing at the ultramodern decor. This place was a man's idea of a hot bachelor pad. A black leather sofa and two black Euro chairs perched on a bloodred rug thrown over a glossy white marble floor. Chrome and glass end tables and a matching coffee table, along with abstract paintings in red, black, and white made me want to weep in despair that Savannah had to live here.

There was no warmth in this apartment, and I didn't have to ask to know that Savannah had not been allowed any input into this cold place. Her favorite decor had always been a mix of shabby chic and vintage. She loved things that were warm and special to her, and I didn't see one single item in this room that could be considered even close to being special to her.

"It's so good to see you both, but you can't stay here," she said, her words trembling with emotion. "Jackson will be home soon."

Jenn scowled. "And you're not allowed to visit with your friends?"

Her gaze lowered to the floor. "You don't understand."

I put my fingers under her chin, forcing her to look at me. "Then explain it so we do. We flew seven hundred miles to see you, and we mean to spend time with you."

She glanced over to my left, and I followed her gaze to see a clock on the wall. "You have to go. I'll tell Jackson the photographer called from today's shoot and said I need to come back in the morning. Where are you staying? I'll be there by nine."

"It's not right that you have to lie to see your friends, hon," Jenn softly said.

I wasn't feeling so generous. "Swear to God, Savannah, if you don't show up in the morning, we'll come camp out on your doorstep. Screw Jackson and his sick idea that you can't spend time with us." I said that not at all softly. I was pissed.

Savannah Graham had been controlled all her life, first by her mother and now obviously by her manager or boyfriend or whatever the hell he was. I wanted to shake some sense into her, tell her to learn how to stand on her own two feet.

"I'll be there. I promise," she whispered. "Right now, please go."

We went, but it took every bit of my willpower not to drag her with us out of that oppressive apartment.

☾

"I mean it, Jenn. If she doesn't show up, I don't care what kind of trouble it causes her, we're going right back to her apartment and refusing to leave until she tells us what's going on in her life."

Jenn lifted the silver cover to one of the plates. "Everything's getting cold."

We'd ordered a girl feast. French toast, bacon, both banana nut and apple cinnamon muffins, strawberries, blackberries, and—Savannah's favorite fruit—pineapples. Also on the cart was her favorite breakfast drink, chocolate milk. For Jenn and me, there was a pot of coffee that we'd already started on while waiting for Savannah.

She was ten minutes late.

Jenn glanced at her watch. "She's not coming."

"She promised," I said, although even as I said it, it sounded stupid since she wasn't here. "So what do we do now? Spend today and tomorrow sightseeing until it's time for our flight home? Or do we mount a rescue? She's not happy, Jenn. You had to see that."

"I did."

Her voice sounded so sad that it brought tears to my eyes. "Do you remember when we swore that we'd be friends forever and that we'd always be there for each other? I think we were fifteen at the time. We promised that no matter what happened, if one of us was in trouble, we could count on each other to save us." I'd been pacing the length of the room, but I stopped in front of Jenn. "She's in trouble."

"I know, but she has to want us to help her."

That brought me up short. "Because if we kidnap her and take her home, the first chance she gets, she'll just come back to this place that is killing her?"

"Probably."

I hated the defeat I heard in Jenn's voice, but I was feeling it, too. We couldn't help Savannah unless she wanted us to. Before I could decide if I cared and kidnapped her anyway, we heard a knock on the door.

"She's here," I whispered as if Savannah could hear me from the other side of a hotel door.

"Don't scare her away with your caped hero I-have-to-save-my-friend heroics," Jenn said as she walked to the door of the suite we'd splurged on.

I couldn't guarantee that wasn't exactly what I'd do, so I kept my mouth shut. Not an easy thing to do when I'd always been the one who'd done and said anything that was on my mind.

Savannah came into the room, so obviously reluctant that I wondered if she felt like she was walking into an angry lion's cage. My anger drained away, my only concern that she felt comfortable being with us. Yeah, I was raging mad, and so was Jenn, but if we didn't hide our worry for her, she'd bolt like a scared rabbit.

"Thank God you're here," I said. "I'm starving, but Jenn wouldn't let me eat until you appeared." I turned to Jenn, waving my hand at Savannah. "There she is. Can I stuff my face now?" From the corner of my eye, I saw Savannah's shoulders relax.

"How long do you have?" Jenn asked.

"Two hours tops." Savannah eyed the cart, then went to the chair farthest from the food.

Two hours wasn't good enough, but better than nothing. "I'm fixing you a plate." And she was going to eat if I had to force-feed her. Her mother had watched her calorie intake like a hawk when Savannah was growing up, and I guessed that Jackson did the same. The sad thing about that was that Savannah liked to eat. As teens Jenn and I had snuck her food. Whether it was sandwiches and goodies from Mary or even a Georgia peach dripping with juice, she would devour them like someone starved.

Because I didn't want to overwhelm her with a plate piled high with food, I cut a slice of French toast and a banana nut muffin in half, and then added some fruit. I took the plate and the glass of chocolate milk, setting it down on the table next to her chair. Not saying a word, I returned to the cart and made myself a plate. Jenn did the same, and the two of us sat on the small sofa.

"So what should we see while we're in New York?" I asked. Savannah was no doubt expecting us to jump right in, giving her the third degree, and relief at my harmless question crossed her face.

"I want to go to Ground Zero and see the museum and memorial," Jenn said.

"You should. It's very moving." Savannah picked up a slice of pineapple and nibbled on it.

"I want to go to the New York Design Center." I glanced at Jenn. "It's this huge building that's full of furniture showrooms."

"Why am I not surprised," Jenn said. She and Savannah looked at each other and then laughed.

Savannah tore off a tiny piece of French toast and popped it into her mouth. "Remember how as soon as she could drive, she would watch for open houses and then drag us to see them?"

If we kept ignoring that she was eating, she'd finish off that plate. "Hey, y'all could've said no." That made them laugh again, and just like that, we slid back into how we used to be.

Jenn rolled her eyes. "Saying no to you, Autumn, is like standing in front of a steamroller you have no hope of stopping."

For an hour we reminisced, laughed, and ate. I don't think Savannah even realized what she was doing when she walked over to the cart and picked up the second half of the banana nut muffin. Jenn apparently noticed, too, because she looked at me and smiled.

"Your mother must be happy about your success," I said. Mrs. Graham wouldn't be happy to see what Savannah was eating, but I wasn't going to mention that.

Savannah's gaze dropped to the floor. "She died last year."

I exchanged a shocked glance with Jenn. "And you're just now telling us?"

"What was the point? None of you liked her, and I can't

say I blame you."

"So we could have come to the funeral," Jenn said. "So we could have been there for you."

"Damn it, Savannah," I said. "That's the kind of thing you tell your best friends."

She shrugged. "It wasn't like she and I were close. Besides, Jackson handled the arrangements, and it was so over-the-top that it was embarrassing."

What she wasn't saying was that Jackson wouldn't have wanted us there. "Savannah, exactly what's going on with you?"

"How's Adam?" She wrinkled her nose. "Ah, I mean, how are Adam and Connor?"

Yeah, right. That wasn't what she meant at all, and she was going to avoid answering me. "Same as always." I took a deep breath, knowing I was going to ask an unwanted question. "Are you happy, Savannah?"

She plastered her fake smile on. "Why wouldn't I be? All my dreams have come true." She held up her wrist, looking at her watch. "I have to go."

Jenn grabbed her hand. "We're worried about you. Remember the promise we once made that we'd always be there for each other? It still holds true."

Tears gathered in her eyes. "I know. But I'm okay, and I really have to go."

She wasn't okay. "Swear you'll call us if you need us or when you're ready to tell us what the hell is going on in your life."

"Autumn," Jenn said, warning me that I was pushing too hard.

I shut up, but it wasn't easy. After a tight hug for both Jenn and me and telling us how much she loved us, she was gone. She might as well have been a ghost.

"Did you notice how bitter she sounded when she said all her dreams had come true?"

Jenn nodded, and the worry in her eyes reflected what I

knew was in mine. "Yeah."

"At least we got to see her, but I'm more concerned for her than ever."

"Yeah, me, too." Jenn sighed. "But I don't know what to do about it if she won't let us in."

Neither did I, and I didn't like feeling helpless.

CHAPTER FORTY-FOUR

~ *Connor* ~

"NO WAY AM I LETTING anyone wax my chest." I pointed the neck of my beer bottle at Dylan. "And stop laughing. You, too," I said to Adam. "And don't try to claim that either one of you are going to do it."

Dylan laughed harder. "Full disclosure. Mary's not getting near my chest."

The thick Angus steaks and the oversize baked potatoes with all the fixings Dylan had fed us had been great. Our stomachs full, we were chilling on the back deck of the log home Adam and I had built—well, Adam had built it, but I'd found the perfect piece of land—for Dylan and Jenn. The view looking down over the valley was spectacular. The lights of the town of Blue Ridge Valley glittered below us.

"Amen to that. She's not getting near mine either," Adam said. "Although, I still think it would be fun to hear Connor scream when he got his hair torn off his chest."

The mere thought sent a shudder through me. I pushed up from the lounge chair and glared at my twin. "The hell, bro? I put my tiny little hands over your ears when we were still in Mom's womb every time our dad put his mouth on Mom's stomach and sang to us. Remember how much that hurt your ears? Where's the loyalty, man?"

Adam smirked back at me. "I also remember you kicking me every chance you got."

"You do not remember anything of the sort."

"I absolutely do. By the time we popped out, I was black-and-blue all over."

"And even after all these years, you're still crying about it."

Dylan's gaze swung between us as if he were watching a tennis match, his eyes filled with amusement. "You two are hilarious. Makes me wish—" His phone played "I Just Called to Say I Love You."

I grinned. "Dude, seriously?" And although I was razzing him, my heart beat faster knowing it was Jenn and that Autumn was with her.

The smile on his face at hearing the song was that of a man in love. He put the phone to his ear. "Hey, Red."

Adam's attention was as focused on Dylan's conversation as mine, and I knew he was listening for Savannah's name. I clamped my teeth together to keep from asking how Autumn was—or better yet, demanding to talk to her.

"If she doesn't want your help, Jenny, there's nothing you and Autumn can do at this point."

I glanced at Adam, who was frozen in place, his gaze on the phone Dylan had pressed to his ear. I hated that after all this time, he was still in love with Savannah, still hurting. It was an unwelcome reminder that being in love sucked.

"How was the rest of your day?" Dylan said into the phone.

"Beer?" I asked Adam.

He blinked as if coming out of a trance. "Yeah, sure."

I went inside and got three beers from the fridge. By the time I returned, Dylan was off the phone.

"How's their trip going?" I asked, handing him a beer, then giving one to Adam.

"Good and bad. The good, they had a great time doing some sightseeing. The bad, they only got to see Savannah for an hour, and they're more worried about her than ever."

"Why's that?"

"She wouldn't open up to them, but they both think she's extremely unhappy."

Adam had remained silent, but I could tell that every bone in his body wanted to get in his car and go get her. I knew the feeling. I wanted to do the same thing—get Autumn, bring her to my house, and never let her go.

We were a pair, Adam and me, falling in love with women who were determined to break our hearts. Whoever said *lucky in love* didn't have a clue. Never again. For me, anyway. I hoped Adam felt the same.

"When are they coming home?"

"They have a flight out in the morning." Dylan studied me for a moment, then said, "Any idea why Autumn was crying last night?"

I sat up and pointed at myself. "Me? How would I know?"

Adam gave me one of his you're-too-stupid-to-live looks. "You didn't send that text, did you?"

I shook my head. I'd lost count of how many times I'd put my finger on send but had chickened out, still afraid that telling her how I felt would backfire.

"You're an ass," Adam said.

"Thanks, bro. Love you, too." Why was she crying, though?

All three of our phones buzzed with an incoming text. That usually meant a call had gone out for the search and rescue team, and we each grabbed our cells. It was from Mary, however.

Heroes of Blue Ridge Valley calendar meeting tomorrow Town Hall at 2:00

The three of us groaned in unison.

"If Mary's doughnuts weren't the best thing this side of the Mississippi, I'd run her out of town for this," Dylan said.

"We would've helped," Adam and I said at the same time.

C

Later that night, the urge to go down to the river came

on strong. I slipped on a lightweight jacket and grabbed a flashlight. When I reached the water's edge, I aimed the light on the other side, and sure enough, there was Adam. We'd each put benches down here, and Adam was sitting on his. I rested my crutches on my bench, sat, then turned off the flashlight. There was enough moonlight to see Adam's outline.

"Hey, brother," I said. He didn't answer, and I settled in to wait. When he was ready, he'd talk. I spread my arms along the back of the bench and looked up at the midnight sky, remembering the night I'd wished on a falling star. All I'd wanted was to kiss Autumn. Now I wanted a lifetime with her.

Would she ever be able to learn to trust me? She had no reason to. I had a history of avoiding relationships, of which she was fully aware. Add to that the fact I hadn't told her I was falling in love with her, and it wasn't a surprise that she'd panicked if she was falling for me, too. As far as she knew, I was still on board with our having some fun together and nothing more.

I knew in my heart that I would never cheat on her. For one, I understood what that would do to her, and I would never hurt my best friend like that. And although I'd sworn never to fall in love, I had, and it was with the most amazing woman I knew. But what to do about it?

"I don't want you to make the same mistake as me."

"He speaks." I leaned forward, resting my elbows on my knees. "And what mistake is that?" The river wasn't wide at our place to talk, and in the quiet of the night, our voices carried without having to raise them.

"I didn't fight for Savannah when I should have."

"Exactly what did happen between you two?"

Adam stood and walked to the water's edge. "It doesn't matter anymore. The time for Savannah and me has passed. But it doesn't have to be like that for you. Autumn loves you, Connor, and she could be the best thing that happened to you. Don't let that slip through your fingers."

He picked up some rocks and began skipping them across the water. "And don't use me as your excuse. That's not fair to you or Autumn, and frankly, it pisses me off."

"Stop reading my mind, bro."

He chuckled. "I'll always be able to read your mind."

"Works both ways," I grumbled.

"My point is, you have a chance to be happy. I mean, really happy. Or you can go through life having meaningless relationships." He threw another stone across the top of the water. "Like me."

After tossing that out there, he turned and walked away, and I felt his heavy retreating footsteps in my heart. But it was that very pain that told me I didn't want to be like him. I didn't want a life of regrets.

It wasn't something that I'd ever thought before, but sitting here in the dark, hurting for my brother, I believed that Adam and I were destined to only love one woman in our lifetime.

☾

Mary stood in front of us, glittery gold hair sparkling under the neon lights of Town Hall and looking a lot like Tinker Bell in a shimmering green dress and matching boots, smirking as her gaze roamed over us.

My eyes hurt looking at her, and I wished I'd brought my sunglasses in with me. I glanced nervously at the door that had been locked behind us, the one that Sarah Griffin, captain of our police department, and Kim Payton, junior detective, stood guard over, smirks matching Mary's on both their faces.

I was afraid. Very, very afraid.

"Not a one of you made an appointment with Renee, so she's here today to give you a chest that women all the way to Atlanta are going to drool over."

Thirteen men stared in horror at Mary, and then, as

one, our gazes swung to Renee from Hair for All Seasons. Damn if she wasn't smirking, too. Standing alongside her were three stylists I recognized from her salon, their expressions mimicking Renee's.

"I'm outta here," Gene Lanier, Dylan's lead detective, said, heading for the door.

Kim crossed her arms over her chest, blocking his exit. "You might be my boss when we're on duty, but in this I get to tell you what to do. Sit. Down."

"What she said," Sarah said.

Gene turned to Dylan. "You're the chief of police. I demand you fire both of these traitors right now."

Sarah and Kim snorted.

Dylan grinned at his detective. "Give it up, Gene. The ladies have outmaneuvered us." He leaned back in his chair and winked at Mary. "Doesn't mean we aren't going to get our payback," he said in a stage whisper, then shifted his gaze to Sarah and Kim, an evil smile on his face. "Carry on, ladies, at your own peril."

They both grinned. "Whatever you get up to, Chief, will be worth hearing all thirteen of you guys scream when all your chest hair is ripped off," Kim said, sounding too cheerful.

Us guys sucked in a painful breath, and Renee hadn't even touched us yet. "We can make a break for it, since we outnumber them," I muttered. "They can find some other twins for June."

"I'm on board with that plan," Adam said from my left side.

On my right Dylan chuckled. "Pretty sure they'll shoot us if we tried."

"Shirts off, boys," Renee said, way too much glee in her voice.

A ton of grumbling accompanied the removal of our shirts. Once our chests were bared, every single one of us darted glances at each other to identify who had the most chest hair, and who was going to scream the loudest. I winced at seeing the thick pelt on Roger Cummings, one of our firefighters.

Then I narrowed my gaze on Dylan's chest. "Dude, you've been waxed already."

He gave me a smug grin. "Had Jenny do it before she left for New York. I had a suspicion Mary would pull something like this, and I wasn't about to sit here and scream like a girl in front of half the town."

Adam leaned around me. "Could have warned us, Chief."

"And miss the fun of hearing the Hunter brothers cry like babies?"

"Bastard," Adam and I said together, which, by his laughter, Dylan found hilarious.

Mary, Renee, and the other stylist spread out, and forty minutes later, everyone except Dylan had been stripped of every hair on his chest. Roger Cummings won the award for loudest screams—still ringing in my ears—with several of us coming in a close second.

"I'll risk getting shot before I'll ever do this again," I said, aiming my words at Sarah and Kim, who had thoroughly enjoyed themselves at our expense. Although Adam and I weren't all that hairy, it still hurt like a son of a bitch.

Mary clapped her hands to get our attention. "You boys are eye candy. The minute the finished calendar goes up on Facebook, we're going to be bombarded with orders." She beamed. "The photographer will begin with Mr. January at nine tomorrow morning. Sarah and Kim will give you an appointment card for your time as you leave. Do not be late for your turn. Also, I expect every single one of you to attend the June Bug Dance Saturday night. The theme is heroes, which means costumes. Any questions?"

Not a one of us had a question. We just wanted our shirts back on and to get out of here. Finally we were dismissed. As I walked out, I slipped my hand under my T-shirt and rubbed my smooth chest. Would Autumn like it? Not that

I'd ever get a chance to find out if I didn't get off my butt and come up with a plan to win her back.

CHAPTER FORTY-FIVE

~ *Autumn* ~

I'D CALLED LUCAS AS SOON as I arrived home, asking when he'd be back in Asheville. Turned out he'd returned to Asheville to meet with his contractor one more time. Lucas hadn't closed on the land yet, and I meant to have a say in whether or not that happened. He'd given me a choice of driving to his Asheville home or waiting until the next day to talk to him when he was in the valley. Since I wanted to get what I had to say over with, I'd elected to see him this afternoon.

On our flight home Jenn had asked me one question. "What makes you happy, Autumn?"

"Connor," I'd whispered.

She'd smiled. "Thought so. I ran to the other side of the world from Dylan before admitting to myself that I loved him. Don't do that with Connor, okay?"

I had no intention of going to Greece or any other country, but I was going to Asheville on Connor's behalf. When I pulled up outside Lucas's home, instead of the butler greeting me, it was Lucas himself.

"Hello, Autumn. I wasn't expecting to hear from you so soon, but I'm delighted." He tucked my arm around his and led me up the steps. "It's a lovely day, and I thought we could enjoy a glass of iced tea or lemonade out on the veranda."

I pulled to a stop. "Lucas, this isn't a social call."

"No?" He glanced down at me and smiled. "I thought you probably had some questions about our project. But whatever it is, we can still enjoy refreshments."

He escorted me through the house, then out to a lovely covered porch, where a table was set with pitchers of iced tea and lemonade and assorted cookies. Lucas pulled out a chair, and after I was seated, he sat across from me.

"What's your pleasure?"

"I'm fine, really." I just wanted to plead my case and then go home. Although I didn't have high hopes I'd be successful, I had to try.

He poured an iced tea for himself, studied me for a moment, and then filled my glass. "You don't have to drink it, but Mother would skin me alive if she got word that I enjoyed a glass of tea in front of a lady and didn't offer her any." He glanced behind him with a sneaky look on his face. "Charles—that's our butler—is her spy, and he tattles on me every chance he gets."

He smiled and winked, letting me know he was teasing. It was impossible not to like the man. "Heavens, can't have that." I took a sip of the tea, getting another smile from him.

"So, Autumn, what is this 'not a social call' about?"

I'd practiced what I was going to say, but couldn't remember a single word I'd planned. "I want you not to buy the Humphrey property," I blurted.

Lucas leaned back in his chair and steepled his hands, resting his chin on his index fingers. "Because?"

He seemed to have taken that in stride, but maybe because as a senator, he was used to hiding his reactions to absurd statements. "Because Connor and Adam wanted that property. They made an offer, but your offer was higher."

"That's business, Autumn," he said, not unkindly.

"I know, but see, they really, really wanted it, and they're local boys, you know?"

"That's all very nice but not a good enough reason."

He was right, and the only chance I had in getting him to agree was being honest with him. Encouraged that he was still listening instead of showing me the door, I lowered my gaze and wrapped my hands around my glass of tea. "Okay. This is something I should be telling Connor and not you, but . . ." I lifted my eyes to his. "I'm in love with him, but I screwed up really bad."

"And how did you mess up?" He reached over and pried my fingers off the glass. "You squeeze that any harder and you're going to break it and cut your hands."

I dropped my hands onto my lap, clasping them together. This was so awkward. Lucas was a nice guy, and I shouldn't be dumping my problems on him. I was sure he had much more important issues to deal with than my broken heart. But he sat there, patiently waiting for me to explain myself, as if he had all the time in the world.

"I panicked," I said. "When Connor fell down the mountain and ended up in the hospital, I realized that I cared for him, and that wasn't supposed to happen."

"Cared for him or loved him?"

"That I was in love with him," I whispered. Lucas lifted a brow, signaling for me to continue. "So I stopped seeing him, but I didn't tell him or explain. I just avoided him."

"What are you afraid of, Autumn?"

"Turning into my mother." But I was so not going there with him. "Listen, I wasn't expecting you to agree, but I had to try. For Connor." I stood. "I've taken up enough of your time. Thanks for seeing me." I picked up my purse, then remembered that I needed to tell him that I wouldn't be working with him on his mystery dinner theater. As much as I would have loved that job, it would be a betrayal to Connor.

He studied me for a moment. "My family owes you and Connor a debt that we'll never be able to repay, and I don't know what you said to her, but Taren is smiling again. Because of those things, I'll withdraw my offer on the property on three conditions," he said before I could resign from his project.

Taken by surprise, I plopped my butt back into the chair.

"Really?" His smile should have melted my heart, but apparently I only melted for Connor's smiles.

"Don't get excited until you hear my conditions."

"Okay, I'm not excited." I totally was.

He held up a finger. "One, you help me find another suitable property for my dinner theater in Blue Ridge Valley."

When I opened my mouth to agree, he shook his head. "Don't comment until I'm done." He lifted a second finger. "Two, you stay on as my interior designer." Another finger joined the first two. "And three, you talk Connor and Adam into finding me a site with beautiful views where they can build me one of their log homes."

Stunned, I stared at him. Had I really gotten him to agree to let Connor and Adam have Humphrey's property? Every single one of those things was doable.

When I continued to stare at him, he said, "During the few times I've spent in your town, I've grown to love it. I'd like a place where I could get away now and then where no one would bother me."

"Mary might bother you. I can see her talking you into accepting the position of Blue Ridge Valley's Hot Guy and then plastering your picture all over her Facebook page."

He laughed deep and long. "She's one of the many reasons why I've fallen in love with your town, Autumn. Also I was lucky enough to get a jar of Hamburger Harry's lemonade with cherries and mint moonshine. I would live there just for the opportunity to get more of that."

"You do know he's making moonshine illegally?"

"Are you worried about your state's senator getting arrested?"

"A little." The more I was around Lucas, the more I liked him. He'd be a totally cool friend, so I hoped that was what would happen between us.

"I like you, Autumn, and I'll admit that I'm jealous of Connor. So, what's your answer?"

"How soon do you want your log home built?"

"Good answer," he said, then lifted his palm.

I high-fived him. Elated with how the afternoon had progressed, I told him I'd let him know when I found some properties for him to look at. The trick now would be convincing Connor to help me find Lucas some land. Maybe I should talk to Adam first, get him on board.

He walked me to the door. "Everything will be okay, Autumn. You and Connor will figure things out."

"There is no me and Connor."

He just smiled. "Forgive me if I don't take bets on that."

☾

As I drove by Mary's Bread Company, I made an impulsive decision to stop and get something decadent. A poor-little-me slice of her chocolate fudge cake. When I walked inside, I came to a dead stop at seeing the back of Connor. I guess I was so wrapped up in my misery that I hadn't realized the Jeep I'd parked next to was his. Deciding to make a hasty retreat, I took a step back.

"You leaving already, Autumn?" Mary said.

"Um… no." If I walked out now, it would cause all kinds of speculation, and God forbid Mary getting involved in my troubles.

Connor's back stiffened, but he didn't turn around. "The guys will appreciate this, Mary, but it's the least you can do after that trick you pulled yesterday."

Mary laughed. "It was the only way to get you boys all pretty."

He let out a snort as he picked up the large box sitting on the counter, and then he turned and headed for the door.

"Hi." I forced my mouth to smile as he passed. He nodded, barely glancing at me, and kept going. It was as if we were mere acquaintances now, and that made me sad. Sadder than I already was.

"Uh-oh," Mary said as the door closed behind Connor. "Trouble in paradise?"

I pasted on a blank face. "Have no idea what you mean. So what trick did you pull on the guys?"

She beamed. "Tricked them into getting their chests waxed. Couldn't have hairy chests for our Heroes of Blue Ridge Valley Calendar, now could we?"

"Of course not." Connor was manscaped? "I'll take a slice of that chocolate cake." And I wouldn't get to see his chest? "On second thought, I'll take the whole thing."

CHAPTER FORTY-SIX

~ Connor ~

"LET'S SEE SOME SEXY SMILES," said the photographer Mary had hired to shoot the photos for the calendar.

"I thought our smiles were naturally sexy," Adam muttered.

"Guess not."

Wearing only hiking boots and camo pants, our chests and backs slicked up with some kind of oil, we were hanging from ropes halfway down the outside wall of the firehouse. Apparently the photographer was going to Photoshop us scaling the side of a mountain. The truth? I'd rather be scaling the side of a mountain right now over hanging here without my shirt on while half the town hooted and hollered. And was that Mary wolf whistling? I glanced toward the direction the whistles were coming from. Nope. It was Granny, Hamburger's ma.

"Pull hard on those ropes as you climb so your muscles expand and flex," the photographer instructed. "And look at me over your shoulders." He snapped his fingers. "You both look like you're sucking on sour lemons. Where are those sexy smiles?"

"Just shoot me now," I said as I smiled through gritted teeth.

"And leave me alone to do this? Not happening, bro."

Careful not to put too much weight on my injured ankle, I pushed my good foot against the wall, flexed my arms to show off my muscles, looked over my shoulder, and bared my teeth in what I hoped was a smile sexy enough to satisfy the photographer. My doctor had released me from the crutches, which had made me enormously happy. I still had to wear the medical boot, but for the photo shoot I'd wrapped my ankle and eased my foot into my hiking boot, leaving it unlaced.

Another twenty minutes of torture as the photographer took pictures of us in ridiculous positions and we were finally done. Thank you, God.

"Loving me some eye candy," Granny hollered, giving Adam and me a toothless grin.

I couldn't get my shirt on fast enough. And how did Granny even know the words *eye candy*? It seemed that the only town resident missing was Autumn. Even Jenn was here and had done her share of hooting. Dylan was up next, and Adam decided to stick around. I just wanted to be gone.

Seeing Autumn at Mary's when I'd stopped to pick up the box of pastries to bring to the shoot had left me in a foul mood. To keep from causing a scene in front of Mary, I'd walked out. If I'd even looked at Autumn, I would have done something stupid, like kiss her until she admitted we meant something to each other. Then minutes later a video of me attacking her would pop up on Mary's *Happenings in the Valley* Facebook page.

Autumn and I needed to have a long talk but not in front of witnesses. Not knowing where else to go, I went home. I used to love my log home, but Autumn had ruined that. Too often the past few days I'd wandered through the rooms, seeing all the places she had sat or ate or watched a movie with me. I especially hated my bed, where I could still catch her scent on the pillow. Or maybe that was just my imagination. I didn't know anything anymore.

✺

I was sitting on my back deck, a beer bottle dangling from my fingers, watching the sun set, and considering how to tell Autumn I was in love with her. I should have talked to her when she'd walked into Mary's, but I'd panicked. It wasn't a good feeling to realize that I really was the idiot my brother claimed.

Adam had called earlier, asking if I wanted to meet him at Fusions for a beer, but I'd blown him off. Apparently when you were in love and the woman didn't love you back, you preferred to wallow in your misery. Who knew?

My phone buzzed again, reminding me I had a new e-mail. I set my beer on the table and picked up my cell. After reading the e-mail twice to make sure my eyes weren't deceiving me, I called Adam.

"We got the land," I said when he answered.

"What land?"

"Humphrey's land. Apparently Blanton withdrew his offer."

"Seriously?"

I nodded, then realized that he couldn't see me. "Yeah, weird, right?" Blanton had the money to outbid us, so I knew that wasn't an issue. It made no sense. "Maybe his plans fell through. Who cares? All that matters is the property is ours."

After hanging up with Adam, I stared at my phone, wanting to call Autumn and tell her. No matter what was wrong between us, I was sure she'd be happy to hear our news. Or maybe not. She was now out of a job.

The June Bug Dance was tomorrow night, and she would be there. Come hell or high water, we were going to settle this thing between us, even if I had to kidnap her and take her somewhere private so we could talk.

☾

My date to the dance was Adam. "Am I really the best you could scrounge up for tonight?" I asked him as we walked up to City Hall.

"Pathetic, isn't it?"

I put my hand on my brother's shoulder and squeezed it. "We both are." But if nothing else, we had each other, and that was the one thing, the only thing we could always count on.

We were fashionably late, both of us not wanting to be here. At least I had the excuse of my ankle to not dance. The party was in full swing, the dance floor crowded with couples. This year's theme was, unsurprisingly, heroes and heroines. Everyone was supposed to dress as their favorite hero or heroine, and I saw several Supermen, Batmen, Wonder Women, and so on. Some, like Adam and me, wore their regular clothing.

"You've got to be kidding me," Adam said.

I followed his line of sight, groaning when my gaze landed on twelve huge posters on one of the walls. I scanned each poster, stopping when I came to the one of Adam and me hanging from the side of the firehouse. They weren't the finished product that would go in the calendars but ones probably taken by someone's cell phone and then enlarged. Our calendar months were scrawled across the tops of each one in black magic marker.

"Mary did this."

Adam nodded. "No doubt. And speak of the little devil."

Even though I wasn't happy with Mary at the moment, it was impossible to maintain my scowl at seeing the tiniest Ms. Marvel in the universe aiming for us. Beauregard trotted alongside her as if he wore a cape and eye mask every day.

"Where in the world did she find a dog cape and mask?" Adam said.

I didn't care about the answer to that. If Beau was here, then so was Autumn, and I did care about that. Not that it would matter, but there was this yearning inside to find her and get her to admit she loved me. I really was pathetic.

"Why aren't you boys in costume?" Mary said when she reached us. She swiped at the bangs of the long-haired red wig she wore.

"Ah . . ." Adam looked at me.

"We are. We're the Superhero Twins." I smirked at Adam.

"He's the girl twin." My gaze settled on one of the posters. "Why did Dylan get to keep his shirt on?" Granted it was unbuttoned and open, but still.

"Because I threatened to arrest Mary and throw away the key if she made me take it off," Dylan said next to me.

"Hey. Didn't see you there. Doesn't seem fair you got to keep your shirt on." I looked pointedly at Mary. It was hard not to laugh, though. She was seriously funny in her little costume. The wig was too big for her small head and kept falling forward, covering her eyes.

"Well, he does have a jail cell and you two don't," Mary said, lifting her bangs and holding them up.

"I'll deputize myself the next time you tell me I have to take off my shirt for pictures." I leaned down, putting my face closer to hers. "Then I'll have a cell to threaten you with."

She tittered.

"Where's Jenn?" I asked Dylan. Usually wherever she was, he was, too. But maybe she was with Autumn.

He sighed and pointed. "Over there admiring my poster."

I glanced across the room and laughed. Jenn was standing in front of Dylan's picture, studying it as if she were admiring a painting in an art gallery. "She'll probably take it home with her tonight and hang it in your bedroom."

"God forbid," he muttered.

But where was Autumn? She definitely wasn't over there admiring my poster, which was surprisingly disappointing. I stepped away, scanning the room.

Ms. Marvel tugged on my sleeve. "I need you to go down to the basement and get the cake."

"And the cake is down there because…?"

She rolled her eyes. "So no one ate it before it's time."

"I think you've confused cake with wine." At her blank

stare I rolled my eyes right back at her. "Don't drink the wine before it's time. Get it? It was a joke, Ms. Marvel. Granted, a poor one. Where do you want me to bring the cake to?"

"The kitchen. You'll need the basement key." She handed me an oversize key dangling from a shoestring tied together at the ends.

"Must be a cake of the ages if you had to lock it up."

"You have no idea," she said.

As I headed for the hallway, I had the unnerving feeling that people were watching me. Glancing around, it seemed that as soon as my gaze met someone's, theirs shifted away. I looked over my shoulder to see Mary, Adam, Dylan, and Jenn in a huddle, and were they sneaking peeks at me? I subtly reached down to make sure the zipper on my jeans was closed. It was, so that wasn't the cause of the weird attention. Hamburger Harry and Granny sat in chairs next to the entry to the hall. Hamburger winked and Granny cackled as I passed. What was up with these people?

At the door to the basement I slipped the key into the lock, then hooked the opened lock on the hasp. The lights were already on, I guess from when Mary had brought the cake down. I'd reached the bottom of the stairs when I heard the door close behind me. A breeze must have blown it shut.

City Hall's basement was used for storage, and I made my way past filing cabinets, broken office chairs, and stacks of boxes. In the middle of the room, on a card table, was Mary's cake. I frowned when I reached it. A large slice was missing. Mary was going to kill someone, probably me.

A trail of crumbs caught my eye, and I followed them as they led me across the floor, around the back of a framed whiteboard on wheels, and to a tattered couch where I found a sleeping Goldilocks.

"Autumn," I whispered, the breath leaving my lungs. I knew I'd missed her, but until seeing her now, I hadn't really understood how deep that hole in my heart ran. Dried tears stained her cheeks. How long had she been down here?

Now I understood why Mary had Autumn's dog. I glanced at the door at the top of the stairs. A quick jog up confirmed my suspicion. We were locked in, and based on all the sneaky looks earlier, every damn resident of Blue Ridge Valley was in on it. Which meant that banging on the door would fall on deaf ears. At first I was furious, especially at Mary. Then it hit me that this was my chance to make things right with Autumn.

I returned to my girl. At least I hoped that would be the outcome of Mary's little trick. A wheeled stool sat off to the side, and I rolled it over, then sat. My gaze hungrily roamed over her. She wasn't wearing a costume either. Instead she had on a jean jacket over a white camisole, a short jean skirt, and blue cowgirl boots. Totally sexy.

"Hey, beautiful." I brushed my fingers over her cheeks. Still asleep, she smiled. And damn if that soft curve of her lips didn't make my heart turn over. Did she know it was me, even asleep? And did that make her happy?

"Autumn, honey, wake up."

Her eyelids fluttered, and then blue eyes looked up at me. "Connor?"

"No, I'm Adam," I said, teasing her.

"Good. I'd rather talk to Adam anyway."

Although I knew very well that she could tell us apart, her words hurt. "So what would you say to Adam?"

She pushed up, slid to the end of the sofa, curled her legs under her, and crossed her arms over her chest. "I'd tell him I shouldn't have fallen in love with his brother."

CHAPTER FORTY-SEVEN

~ Autumn ~

I'D SHOCKED HIM. GOOD. I probably shouldn't have said that, but I hadn't been able to hold in the words. Plus, pretending I was talking to Adam made them easier to say. And I wanted Connor to know that I was hurting, even though it wasn't his fault I'd fallen in love with him. Not really. That was all on me.

"Stop staring at me like I have two heads," I grumbled. "I know that's not what you wanted to hear, and don't worry, I'm not going to turn into some kind of crazy stalker woman, you know, calling you at all hours, spying on you, beating up your girlfriends, or—"

"Autumn, shut up."

I snapped my mouth closed.

In the blink of an eye I was somehow draped across his lap, both of us sitting on an ancient, musty-smelling couch. He spread his fingers over my cheek and turned my face, forcing me to look at him.

"Make no mistake. This is Connor holding you."

"I know." I would always know him.

He stroked his thumb over my cheek. "Why were you crying? Because you got locked in and were afraid?"

"No."

"Tell me why."

I didn't want to, yet the two of us alone down here in this basement room, me sitting on his lap, and seeing so much tenderness in his eyes, the words spilled out.

"I was sad." He didn't say anything, just stared at me and waited. "So I cried." Apparently that wasn't good enough because he stayed silent. I couldn't do this, rip my heart open for him only to have him smile and say he was ready to move on and we'd still be friends or whatever. I pushed away, scooting to the opposite side of the couch.

"Why did you cry, Autumn?" was his only response.

"Because I wasn't supposed to fall in love with you," I yelled. "But that wasn't why," I said in a softer voice. "I cried because you don't love me back." We were still locked up in this room, or I'd make my grand exit. As that gesture was denied me, I'd just go eat the rest of Mary's sheet cake since there wasn't a bottle of wine down here to drown my sorrows in. I should have known she was up to something when she sent me to the basement to get the cake.

"I'm sorry I sent you flowers and a lame message. That wasn't well done of me, but telling me to have a nice life was just sucky of you."

"It was, and I'm sorry for that. I was angry that you were blowing me off, and that was my knee-jerk reaction. But I have another one I want you to read."

"I didn't get a second one from you."

"Because I never sent it. I should have." He reached into his back jeans pocket, brought out his phone, scrolled through it, and then handed it to me. "Read it."

I took it from him with a trembling hand, and I wouldn't have thought my heart could beat any faster, but it did. He wouldn't be making me read an asshat text, not my friend Connor.

Lost: Heart belonging to Connor Hunter. Last seen in the vicinity of Autumn Archer. If found, please treat with care.

I read it a second time to make sure my eyes weren't deceiving me, that and because it was the most beautiful text anyone had ever sent me. Well, he hadn't actually sent it, but he'd wanted to. Tears pooled in my eyes, but they weren't the sad ones of earlier.

"Connor," I breathed.

"Beautiful," he said. "Come here. I really need you in my arms."

And that was where I really, really needed to be. I climbed onto his lap, straddling him, still holding his phone. When he reached to take it from me, I held it away. "No, I want to read it while you make love to me."

He laughed. "You're weird."

I laughed back, my heart filled to the brim with happiness. "You said that back in fourth grade when I traded you my PB&J sandwich for your tofu one."

"I'd forgotten about that." He leaned his head back on the couch and grinned at me. "Adam and I called Mom's year of going vegan the worst year of our life. You didn't really want a tofu sandwich, did you?"

"Not even, but you were hungry."

"I think that was probably when I fell in love with you, but love wasn't in my vocabulary at that age."

"Is it now?" He'd as much as said he was in love with me in his text, but he still hadn't said the words.

"My beautiful, beautiful girl, yes, I'm head over heels in love with you."

My heart would have exploded if it could figure out how to do that. But I had to make sure he understood the one thing I couldn't live with.

"You've never been serious about any woman before. If you don't—"

He put his finger over my lips. "I know. If I don't mean that you're the only woman I'll ever want for the rest of my life, I should hack my way out of that locked door at the top of the stairs and disappear right now. Do you notice me not doing that?"

I nodded.

"That's because I love you. I'll never cheat on you, Autumn. That's my promise to you. I never thought I'd fall in love, never thought I'd want to. And then you came along and everything changed."

"But I've been here since we were in first grade together."

"Okay then, since you flashed your pretty pink hoo-ha. That was the day everything changed."

I narrowed my eyes. "Seriously, Connor? Did you really just call my vagina a hoo-ha?"

"Love canal. Cooch. Honey pot?" He grinned. "Any of those work?"

"Oh God, stop it." I put my hands over my ears but couldn't stifle my laughter. "And exactly when did that happen?"

"You don't remember?"

"Vaguely. But I have other things on my mind right now." I tugged on his shirt. "Take it off." Now that I had his words of love, I wanted his body.

"What if Mary decides we've had enough time together to admit we love each other and free us?"

"I don't care. I want you right now." I dropped his phone next to us, then pulled on his shirt again. "Off."

"I like how you think." He ripped off his shirt, tossing it over my shoulder.

There was that manscaped chest I thought I'd never get to see. I flattened my palms over his smooth skin. "Sexy."

"Enjoy it while you can because I'm never doing that again." He leaned his head back on the couch and watched through hooded eyes as I explored him.

"I want you naked, beautiful, but since there's no predicting what Mary might do, I'll settle for sneaking my hands under this sexy little skirt, and then when I think you're ready, I'll bury myself so deep inside you and give you so much pleasure that you'll never want any other man but me."

"Big talker," I teased. I wanted everything he'd just offered me, a billion times over.

"Oh, ye of little faith."

As promised, his hands dipped under my skirt and he spread his fingers over my thighs. He stilled and looked straight into my eyes. "I missed you, Autumn. When I thought you were done with me, I was shocked at how miserable I was. I wasn't expecting that."

"I realized I was falling in love with you, and I got scared. So I—"

He put his finger on my lips again. "I know, and I understand."

And that was the thing. He did understand me. He always had. Even though he'd never had a serious relationship before, I trusted that he would never do the one thing I couldn't forgive. Connor would never hurt me like that.

"Just don't ever run from me again. Next time I'll come after you."

"I won't as long as you never cheat on me. That's all I ask."

"Always ask more from me than that, beautiful."

I loved that he said that. I trailed my fingers over his smooth chest. "Okay then, how about that pleasure you promised me."

He gave me a wicked smile. "Thought you'd never ask."

CHAPTER FORTY-EIGHT

~ Connor ~

FOR A MAN WHO SWORE he'd never fall in love, I was all in now that it had happened. It still amazed me that it was with Autumn, a woman I'd known most of my life. There was something comforting in that. We'd been friends forever, and I liked her as much as I loved her.

I tried to peer down at her, but she had her face buried against my neck and had been quiet for a few minutes. "Are you asleep?"

"I'm just trying to catch my breath."

"Ah, wore you out, did I?" She nodded against my neck, making me smile. I thought for a minute about what I wanted to say and then decided to go for it. "Remember telling me you were thinking about selling your house?"

"Yeah." She lifted her head. "Why?"

"I want you to move in with me." Since I planned to have her in my bed or hers every night, I saw no reason for us to have two houses.

A brilliant smile lit her face. "Okay, but only after you sell mine. That will give us a little time to get used to being together."

Ha! She had no idea how badly I wanted to see her living in my home. If that was the obstacle, I'd get her place sold in a week or less. "It's a deal." First thing in the morning I'd list it, and I already had a couple in mind who were looking for something like Autumn's house.

I smiled as I lifted her off me. "As much as I love having you in my arms, I'm guessing we'll be freed any minute now."

We straightened our clothing, and I followed her over to the table. As she stood, staring at the cake, I moved up behind her and wrapped my arms around her. "Did you eat Mary's cake or is there a giant mouse down here?"

She giggled. "She's going to be mad, but she knows I have a bad habit of eating cake when I'm sad."

"So it's her fault?"

"Absolutely. She should have known better than to lock me in with it."

"That's my girl."

She turned in my arms. "I love you, Connor. I thought I'd never get to tell you that."

"I love you back like crazy, and I didn't think I'd get to say that either. I also thought I'd never see the day when I'd want to thank Mary for her meddling."

"That's a problem, isn't it? If we thank her, we're only encouraging her, but yeah, on this one Mary rocks." She glanced away. "Um, I need to ask you a favor."

Why was she nervous? She could ask me anything. "What's that?"

"Okay, well, ah . . ."

"Autumn?"

"I need you to find property suitable for a large building and also some property for a log home and then Adam needs to build it," she said in a rush of words.

"Okay, we can do that. Who's it for?"

She lifted her eyes to mine. "That's the part you're not going to like. It's for Lucas."

I almost said no, not happening, but her eyes were pleading with me and the word died on my lips. "Why isn't he asking me instead of you doing it for him?" The surge of jealousy died as fast as it had arrived. Autumn wouldn't tell me she loved me if she had feelings for Blanton.

"Because those were his conditions for giving up Humphrey's property. Well, that and that I still agree to do the interior design."

"You'll be working for him?" I didn't like that at all.

She sighed. "I knew that was what you'd have the most problem with." She slipped her hands into mine. "I love you, Connor. You and you only. Lucas is a nice guy, but I feel nothing for him, not even the slightest twinge. If I didn't agree, he wouldn't have given up the property. And honestly, I'm excited about the project."

Autumn's problem had been about trust, and that worked both ways. If I couldn't trust her, then we had nothing.

"Not even one little twinge?" I smiled to show her I was teasing.

"Not one teeny-tiny one."

"Okay, but how did all this come about?"

"Because I asked him to give up the property."

"You did that for me?" Damn, I loved this woman.

"Well, yeah. For you and Adam, but mostly for you."

She still had her hands in mine, and I pulled her against me. "Anyone ever tell you how amazing you are?"

"Not that I recall."

"Then I'm telling you now that you are, and I'll remind you again every single day." I wondered if we had a little more time to play around some more.

"Y'all decent down there?"

Guess not. At hearing Adam's voice, I cradled Autumn's face and kissed her. "I love you, beautiful girl. You ready to go up?"

"They're going to know what we were doing down here."

"Yeah, they are. And I'm right proud of the fact that they'll know you're mine."

"That's a very chauvinist thing to say, but I'm good with it as long as I can say you're mine."

"I will die belonging to you, Autumn." At that smile on her face for my words, I vowed to make this woman happy for the rest of our lives.

"Yo, Connor, put your clothes on. I'm coming down."

Red spread across Autumn's cheeks. "Is there a secret tunnel we can sneak out of?"

Delighted with her, I laughed. "Not that I know of." It wasn't easy to embarrass Autumn, and it was totally adorable when it happened.

Adam came around the corner, his gaze alighting on the cake. "Uh-oh," he said, then looked straight at Autumn, whose cheeks went beyond red to flaming.

"Connor ate it," she yelled.

Adam and I both snorted. My brother met my eyes, and I could see that he was happy for me. There weren't any candles to blow out on Mary's cake and make a wish over, but I still made a wish that he would one day find an amazing woman to love him. That he'd end up as happy as me.

"Sure, I'll take the blame, but Mary's not stupid," I said, then grabbed Autumn's hand. "Let's go face your firing squad."

"Mary really is going to kill her," Adam said a bit too cheerfully as he lifted the cake.

I had to drag Autumn up the stairs, but I didn't blame her for doing her best to go in the opposite direction. I'd be deathly afraid of Mary's revenge at seeing her cake defiled, too.

"You both are asses," Autumn said right before we walked into the City Hall main room where every single person here tonight had divided themselves like the parting of the Red Sea, making a path for us to walk through. Mary stood at the end, hands on hips, looking like an avenging angel. Still wearing his cape, Beauregard sat obediently beside her.

"They do the hootchy-kootchy down there?" Granny hollered.

I turned my face to Granny and winked.

"They did!" she shouted, then cackled.

Beside me, Autumn pressed her face against my arm and

groaned.

Hamburger Harry stuck a mason jar of moonshine into my hand. "Fer tha honeymoon."

I grabbed it. No way was I turning down a jar of his 'shine, honeymoon or not. Adam stepped around us and carried the cake to Mary, holding it out to her like an offering.

"I'm a dead woman," Autumn muttered.

I couldn't stop my laughter. There was probably no better place to fall in love than this crazy town. I tucked her under my arm and led her to her fate.

Mary's flavor of the month stood beside her, clicking pictures on his phone. Before morning they'd be splashed all over the valley's Facebook page.

We stopped in front of Ms. Marvel, and I said, "I ate that missing corner of your cake." Yes, I'd sacrifice myself for my girl.

Mary let out a deep laugh. "Nice try, but we know better. Never put a cake near Autumn when she's sad." Mary glanced at Autumn. "You good now?"

Autumn blushed again. "Very."

"Great. And just so you know, that was a red herring cake. I woulda never locked you in a room with the one meant for our heroes and guests here tonight. Now go dance with your honey." She raised her hand, waving it in the air, and the band began to play.

At hearing the opening bars of "When a Man Loves a Woman," I smiled at Mary, who gave me a satisfied nod. I handed my jar of moonshine to Adam.

"That's mine. No sneaking any." Then I took Autumn's hand and led her to the dance floor. For Autumn I could ignore a little pain in my ankle. I'd danced with her before at high school dances, two friends just having fun. But we'd never slow danced together. I slipped my arm around her back and pulled her close. "Hello, beautiful," I whispered into her ear.

"Hello, handsome," she whispered back. She slid her hands to the back of my neck and rested her face on my chest.

How had I not recognized this woman as my soul mate the first time I saw her? Well, maybe not in first grade, but long before now. It seemed like we'd wasted too much time getting to where we were tonight. But that just meant we had a lot to make up for, and we were going to have fun doing that, starting right now.

"How soon can we blow this joint?" Autumn said.

I laughed. My girl was on the same page as me. At hearing a whine, we both looked down to see Beau grinning up at us.

"Ready to go home, Beau?" He barked twice. I reached down and picked up the leash trailing behind him. "Lead the way then."

Autumn grabbed my hand. "Wait." She pulled me to the kitchen, coming to a stop at a large chocolate sheet cake. Decorating the top were thirteen shirtless male figures, representing those of us in Mary's calendar, I supposed.

"Which one is you?" Autumn said. She studied the figures, then grabbed the knife next to the cake. "This one." She cut a large square out of the cake with one bare-chested man on it, then looked up at me with Autumn mischief in her blue eyes. "I'm going to eat you."

I grinned at her. "I'm so on board with that." This woman was going to be the death of me, but I would go out with laughter on my lips.

☾

Sign up for Sandra's newsletter here:
https://bit.ly/2FVUPKS

WHAT'S NEXT FOR SANDRA?

STILL SAVANNAH

Book 3 in the Blue Ridge Valley Series

Coming in October!

❧

HE WAS HER FIRST LOVE, the boy who broke her heart. When her life falls apart she turns to the man he is today. She is a wounded soul, and he is just the man who can help her heal, but only if he dares to risk his heart again.

Known simply as Savannah, a beautiful face on the covers of glamorous magazines, Savannah Graham has the perfect life… or so it seems to the world. Behind closed doors her reality is far from perfect. When a person she should be able to trust threatens her, she returns home to Blue Ridge Valley, the only place she feels safe. The valley is also where *he* lives, her first and only love.

Adam Hunter stepped out of Savannah Graham's life nine years ago so she could follow her dream. She was his first love, and there is still an ache in his heart for what he lost every time he sees her face on the cover of a magazine. Now she's home, needing protection, and he can't refuse. When the danger is over, she will return to her glamorous life. So she's not the only thing he as to protect, he also needs to safeguard his heart.

ACKNOWLEDGMENTS

I've said this in a previous acknowledgment, and it still holds true. It takes a village…

Where do I even start? With romance readers, I think. Without lovers of romance books, I wouldn't be writing this because there wouldn't be a book. Damn, I love y'all for so many reasons. For reading mine and other authors' books, for telling your friends about a book you love, for leaving reviews on those books.

I'm so lucky to have a whole list of readers who want to know why I can't write faster, and who do tell their friends they just have to read about Logan and Dani, or Nate and Taylor, or Dylan and Jenny. I know all your names, and it's a lengthy list, which is the only reason I'm not naming you all here. Just know that I love you!

To the members of my Facebook group, Sandra's Book Salon, OMG, you guys are the best… I mean the very best, most fun people ever! I seriously love each and every one of you. You make me laugh and sometimes you make me cry, but you always make me happy to be a part of such an amazing group.

From my very first book published, I've thanked my friend and critique partner Jenny Holiday, who is an amazing storyteller. Jenny and I live in two different countries, me in the US and Jenny in Canada, but we've never let a little thing like eight hundred or so miles between us amount to a big deal. Jenny, I think we're twins separated at birth.

I want to talk about editors. They are just about my favorite people in the book world. Without my editors my books would suck (not kidding). Oh, there would the bones of a good story, but my editors rein me in, tell me where I need to go deeper, and make suggestions for new scenes to better your understanding of the story. Melody Guy and Ella Sheridan, you both are rock stars!

To my family, my love for you knows no bounds. I know you don't understand how I can spend days inside my head, but you still let me be weird and you still love me. I love you back, so much!

ABOUT SANDRA...

BESTSELLING, AWARD-WINNING AUTHOR SANDRA OWENS lives in the beautiful Blue Ridge Mountains of North Carolina. Her family and friends often question her sanity but have ceased being surprised by what she might get up to next. She's jumped out of a plane, flown in an aerobatic plane while the pilot performed death-defying stunts, gotten into laser gun fights in Air Combat, and ridden a Harley motorcycle for years. She regrets nothing.

Sandra is a Romance Writers of America Honor Roll member and a 2013 Golden Heart Finalist for her contemporary romance *Crazy for Her*. In addition to her contemporary romantic suspense novels, she writes Regency stories.

Sign up to Sandra's newsletter to get the latest news, cover reveals, and other fun stuff:
https://bit.ly/2FVUPKS
Join Sandra's Facebook Reader Group:
https://bit.ly/2K5gIcM
Follow Sandra on Bookbub:
www.bookbub.com/authors/sandra-owens

CONNECT WITH SANDRA:
Facebook: *https://bit.ly/2ruKKPl*
Twitter: *https://twitter.com/SandyOwens1*
Goodreads: *https://bit.ly/1LihK43*

Follow Sandra on her Amazon author page:
https://amzn.to/2I4uu2Y

84327187R00170

Made in the USA
Middletown, DE
18 August 2018